Destiny Redeemed

DESTINY REDEEMED

Sentenced to spend the rest of his three remaining lifetimes in Nil, Amon Kalins is freed with the help of his Sidhe servant, Gethen, but now he must accept his life is never to be his again as the Council won't rest until he's safely back imprisoned within Nil's cold walls.

Broken and nearly dead from his time in prison, Amon is saved by an Aeveren healer named Althea Forester. As a healer, Thea has served her people for forty-five lifetimes, never having a destined one and always knowing each lifetime would ultimately end with her alone. But destiny hasn't forgotten her.

Drawn to the seductive Amon, Thea quickly becomes a pawn the Council uses to trap him. Taken prisoner by the sadistic leader of the rebel group, the Soren, Thea must survive the vicious world of the people hell-bent on taking her destined one away forever, and Amon must risk everything dear to him to free her from those who would sacrifice her to claim the bigger prize and return him to Nil.

DESTINY REDEEMED

(DESTINED ONES #2)

K.M. SCOTT

WRITING AS GABRIELLE BISSET

CHAPTER ONE

THE USUALLY QUIET MAIN STREET of Cochecton, New York hummed with the excited squeals of miniature devils, witches, and ghosts along with a variety of cartoon and movie characters. Stopping at each house with the hope for more treats than tricks, children scurried here and there as parents dutifully followed behind. The small town's downtown was lit up as bright as day, but behind a building two streets over, there were no costumed children or candy but a scheduled meeting of people who had finally ended their wait. It would happen tonight.

A solitary man walked nervously through the hoard of masked children and doting parents, looking for the first opportunity to move into the shadows. To be caught now would mean not only Nil for him but the end of him afterward. They'd never let him live another life if he failed this night.

A quick left off Main Street into the natural darkness of night forced him to adjust his eyes and for a moment he ceased his hasty march to his destination. His vision focused, he began his journey again, careful as always to make sure no one was following him. He listened for footsteps, the crackling sound of a shoe crushing the swirling dried leaves he'd just passed, but heard nothing. He was alone in the dark alley.

Up ahead he saw the flicker of lights and checked his watch. 7:56. The crisp October breeze hit him and forced him to stuff his hands into his pockets as he walked, and he picked up his pace.

What a difference a year makes, he thought to himself. One year earlier, he'd celebrated Samhain with a few dark Sidhe who had deliciously reinforced his love of their kind and brought in the New Year believing things were going to get better for him. How wrong he'd been! Not two weeks later one foolish mistake—of the many he'd made in his lifetimes—had brought the wrath of the Council into his life and made him enough enemies in the circles he traveled in to make him persona non grata in many of his favorite places. It certainly had been one hell of a year.

That would all change tonight. Tonight, he'd perform the most important magick of all his lifetimes. And when he succeeded, he'd get his life back. No more being shunned. No more being without the protection of the Soren. No more living in constant fear of the Council. Tonight would be the beginning of better times for him.

The meeting place was an old abandoned tailor shop accessed only by the alley he was now on. He hadn't chosen it and had no idea what to expect. He'd simply been given orders to be there at eight o'clock with the implied threat in the man's voice that if he didn't, he'd never find acceptance in the Soren again. Since he'd prayed for any chance to fix what he'd done, no threat was necessary. He would've moved heaven and Earth to get back what he'd had before. Instead he'd move Nil.

As he walked down the side of the building, he looked up to see the quarter moon above peaking through ominous dark clouds and then glanced down at his watch. 7:59.

Showtime.

He turned right around the corner of the building and saw just one person.

Was he early?

"Where's everyone else?"

The man he spoke to stood stiffly, looking back at him as sternly as he always had. Dressed in all black underneath a black overcoat, only his deep green eyes disrupted his funereal appearance.

"There is no one else. It's just us."

"Why? Has everything been called off?" he asked, his voice verging on frantic at the thought that his one chance at salvation had been ripped away at the last moment. Before the other man could answer, he continued, his hands punctuating his words.

"What happened? Why would they do this to us?"

"Markku," Gethen said icily, "nothing has happened. There was no need for more people to be involved, so I told them so. The plan remains the same."

"No need for more people? We're breaking the big man out of Nil, and you don't think we need anyone else? Have you lost your fucking mind, old man?"

GETHEN WATCHED AS MARKKU PACED back and forth past him in the small area they stood in, his progression halted by walls of discarded pallets on three sides of them. As was often the case when he was around the excitable Markku, Gethen felt heartburn stab at him just below his sternum. He was sure the man was something far more than just a magickian by the way he made both him and his master feel ill whenever he was around.

Sure he needed Markku to calm down, if not to help his heartburn then to complete the Herculean task they had ahead of them, Gethen put his arm out on one of Markku's passes by him and stopped him.

"Enough. We need to get going. Collect yourself now because if this doesn't work because you couldn't focus…"

Markku didn't let him finish the statement. Gethen knew no matter how much he found him irritating, the magickian understood how much was riding on what he did or didn't do tonight.

Putting his hand up to stop him, Markku interrupted. "Yeah, yeah. I know."

Gethen watched the man shake out his arms and then his legs as if he were getting ready to perform some feat of physical strength. Already disgusted in the short time he'd spent with him, he leveled his gaze on him as he gyrated like a man having a seizure and in a voice that he hoped signaled his irritation asked, "Are you done? May we leave now?"

"No problem, Gethen. Lead the way. Home, James."

Not appreciating his allusion to him being a chauffer, Gethen squinted his eyes into angry slits and mumbled, "Just follow me and get ready."

Gethen led Markku to a clearing on the mountaintop outside of town. As he stood waiting for the man, the chill of the wind cut at him, intensifying the feeling of dread that had resided in him for almost a year.

For every day his master had been imprisoned in Nil, he'd worked to find a way to bring him back. Each day the foreboding feeling that told him that Amon was suffering grew worse and ate at him, magnified by his failure to solve the puzzle of how to free him from his hell. But now, finally, he'd do what he must to return him to his life.

Markku set out his supplies and looked up at Gethen, who watched him closely. "I don't understand what you need me for if you can travel between worlds."

"Only I can travel between them. Amon is Aeveren, so he's why you're here. The spell is to protect him, not me."

Nervously, Markku fingered his knife. "What do you mean?"

Gethen glared down at him angrily. "What I mean is that you need to protect him or he could be harmed and then I may never get him out. So get moving and finish whatever you have to do to ensure he won't be injured when I bring him back."

Markku began to chant and the wind grew stronger, whipping over them. Gethen prepared himself for the journey to Nil, focusing on his master's soul for direction. He'd never been to Nil before, but he knew all he had to do was find Amon and take him out of there.

Looking up at Gethen, Markku nodded. "It's finished. He should be safe to bring back."

He better be.

Closing his eyes, Gethen became mist and the wind took him away as Markku looked on in stunned silence. Moments later, he rematerialized in Amon's cell and as his eyes refocused, he saw the horror he'd feared all those months.

Falling to his knees, he knelt next to his master and watched in fear and sadness for a sign of his breathing to ensure he was still alive. He wanted to reach out to touch him, to give any comfort to the one he loyally served, but hesitated out of fear of causing him further pain, his hand frozen in midair over a bruised and broken Amon.

His eyes catalogued the pain Amon had suffered in his time in Nil, from the scarred wounds on his back, to the cuts and bruises on his face, chest, and arms. In sadness, Gethen realized he barely recognized the soul that sat slumped over on the floor next to him, a man he'd known and served for lifetimes.

Swallowing hard, he pushed his emotions down to deal with the task at hand. He leaned in close to Amon's ear and whispered quietly, "Master?"

TINY TRAILS OF MOISTURE TRICKLED down the wall to the grey

cement floor. The prisoner in cell 801 felt one touch his shoulder as it was stopped on its journey, and he shivered at the feel of it as it touched his tender skin. The dampness of his cell, the chill, reflected what the place had done to him. Underground, in the bowels of the Earth, he did little more than exist in this place, like a creature unwelcome in the light of the sun and home only in the cold darkness of Nil. Beneath him, the cold floor made the painful areas on his legs ache, and a dull throbbing throughout his body reminded him of the countless punishments in his time there.

The nighttime noises of Nil stabbed at him, and as they had every night for the past year, they become the terrifying soundtrack to the worst part of Amon's time in Nil. The screams of the weak reverberated through his body, a reminder of the horrors he'd endured on so many nights there. Not that he needed to be reminded. The pain that ran over every square inch of his skin, tactile terrors chasing after one another in a constant game of sadistic tag, never let him forget what he'd suffered through and what lie ahead in his future.

His mind drifted back to the night just after he'd arrived when the guards not only looked the other way to allow the other inmates to perform their initiation ritual on him but also told them who he'd been before being sent to Nil, as if they'd needed any encouragement for their bloodlust. Nothing in forty-seven lifetimes had been as terrifying as the hungry look in the eyes of the men who pushed him down face first on the cold, damp concrete floor while the one with the knife loomed over him. He hadn't seen his eyes, but he'd heard his hollow laugh right before the sound of the vicious click of the blade coming out of its home made him stiffen in sheer terror.

How many nights since then had he lay on the hard floor listening to the screams of the most recent victim of the initiation into Nil? How many times had he heard the click of the knife and the tortured moments of silence just before the first cut?

Amon ran his fingertips over the scars on his right shoulder, evidence of his welcome to this place. If that had been all they'd done, he could know he'd survived and not be laid out on the floor of his cell praying for death to at least escape this lifetime, his mind unable to imagine the three future lifetimes ahead of him in this Hell.

He'd changed in his time in Nil. Naturally lean, he now rippled with muscle, a result of the only activity he was allowed other than work. The prisoners were encouraged to be bigger and stronger to survive, but years and lifetimes of experience and rage easily overwhelmed his newer, muscular body. In time, he'd rise to the higher ranks of the prisoners, but for now, just a year into his sentence, Amon remained at the very bottom, vulnerable to attack at any time.

And the attacks came often. Mostly at night, after hours of backbreaking labor when he'd give anything for just a few moments of rest and peace. Fists that pummeled his ribs and tore his muscles, trying to break him.

As he struggled to sit up, he had no idea what had been damaged that night. His right leg may have been broken. He didn't know. All he felt was blinding pain just below his knee.

Blood slowly trickled into his mouth from beneath his left eye, and he tasted the familiar tang of it on his tongue. The eye continued to swell so that now he only saw clearly with the right one.

The only thought that stayed in his mind was the one he had each night when he was finally alone.

God, let me pass out and never wake again.

"MASTER? PLEASE ANSWER," A VOICE said plaintively.

Amon heard a voice he was sure couldn't be near and cursed his mind for playing tricks on him. Struggling to open his left eye, he slowly lifted his head toward the sound of his servant's voice. To his left Gethen stared in fear at him.

Barely able to speak, Amon hoarsely whispered, "Gethen? Are you here?"

"I'm here, master," he answered, his voice full of emotion.

Amon's eyes filled with tears at the knowledge that he wasn't alone. He couldn't remember feeling more joy at the sight of another ever in all his lifetimes.

Gethen gently ran his hand over his head, and Amon saw by the sadness on his face that he remembered how he'd looked before being sent to this place. With his hands on the sides of Amon's face, he wiped away the blood that ran from the gash under his eye with his thumb, staying away from the swelling that had closed the eye completely.

Amon savored the warmth of Gethen's skin on his and leaned his cheek into his right palm, thankful for a touch of kindness after so long. If he died now, at least the last moments of this lifetime had been spent with one who cared for him. Closing his eyes, he began to slip into unconsciousness, happy to have Gethen with him once again at the end of a lifetime.

"Master, please don't leave me! I'm here to take you home!"

Amon struggled to remain alert, his eyelids fluttering as he tried to focus.

Home?

"Master…Amon, put your arms around me so we can leave."

He moved to crouch between Amon's legs as he tried to lift his arms but failed. "I can't do this if you aren't touching me." Gingerly, he took his hands and placed one hand and then the other around his waist.

"I need you to stand up. Can you do that?"

Slowly shaking his head, Amon's gaze traveled to his right leg. Gethen reached out and gently ran his palm over the pant leg, causing Amon to wince and softly cry out in pain.

"Okay. Just hold on to me and don't let go."

Amon kept his hands around his servant's waist and rested his head on his chest. He felt Gethen's hand lightly stroke the back of his head, and the rhythmic sound of his heartbeat in his ear lulled him.

"Stay with me, Amon. I'm going to get you out of here."

His eyes closed, he heard his servant whisper, "Please, let this work."

The sound of a guard's footsteps coming down the hallway

made Amon stiffen, and he lifted his head off Gethen's chest, knowing that if they caught his servant, they'd kill him.

"Gethen, go! I can't let them find you here."

He began to release his hands from around his waist, but Gethen grabbed them and held them fast to him. "Don't let go! The only way I leave here is with you!"

Fully conscious and working on adrenaline, Amon wrapped his arms tightly around Gethen. If they killed him, he still had three more lifetimes he'd willingly give up, but Gethen wasn't Aeveren and his death would be final. He had to make sure he escaped.

The noise drew closer, and slowly Gethen began to change to mist as he reminded Amon to hold on to him, no matter what. As they left Nil, Amon breathed a sigh of relief and felt himself begin to slip away.

MOMENTS LATER, GETHEN REAPPEARED SAFELY on the mountaintop, but he looked down in horror at the body of the man in his arms. Amon, unconscious, slid out of his grasp to the ground below him. Gethen fell to the ground next to him, devastated what he'd feared had happened. Because he was Aeveren, the journey between worlds had been too much for Amon.

"Markku! Give me your coat!"

"What happened?" he asked frantically. "I swear I did everything right, Gethen."

Gethen draped the coat over Amon's shirtless body.

"Coming from Nil to this world was too much for him. We need to get him to the house. And when we get there, I need you to do another spell to make sure no one can find him there."

Markku nodded and helped Gethen to his feet.

"Can you carry him? I'm too weak," Gethen said as he looked down sadly at Amon.

Bending down, Markku lifted Amon and quickly began to make his way to the house. As he walked, Amon opened his eyes and mumbled Gethen's name before fading out again.

"Don't worry, big guy. The old man got back A-OK."

As Markku approached Amon's house, Gethen stopped him and took his master's body into his arms. Turning to Markku, he nodded in the direction of the town. "After you do whatever you need to do so he'll be hid, I need you to find a healer."

"I don't know where any are, though."

Gethen glared over the still body in his arms, forcing Markku to step back.

"Okay. I get it. Find one!"

Gethen left Markku outside performing his spell and took Amon to his bedroom on the second floor. Carefully, he removed Markku's coat and laid Amon on the bed. He remained unconscious, and in the light of the room, Gethen once again studied the effects of Nil evident on his body. The former beauty of his master was absent, replaced with muscle, scars, and fresh injuries.

Weakened by the rescue himself and now nauseous from

the evidence of the violence he saw Amon had suffered, he stumbled back into a chair beside the bed and rested comfortably for the first time in almost a year, hoping that his weakness was merely overexertion and not something more.

Hours later, he awoke to find Amon still unconscious and no sign of Markku. His immediate reaction was to threaten the missing man, but Gethen stopped himself. Markku had successfully protected Amon on the trip back from Nil; he wasn't still unconscious because of any failure of Markku's. Gethen knew the journey from one world to the other might hurt him, but there was no true safeguard against that. Amon was Aeveren, unlike him, and they didn't move between worlds easily.

Markku would return with the healer soon. Literally, his future happiness depended on it. Still exhausted, Gethen settled back into the chair and with heavy eyes watched his master sleep. He'd done it. He'd saved Amon as he'd done for him so many years ago.

But would Amon ever be the same after what had happened to him in Nil?

CHAPTER TWO

T HEA FORESTER SAT ON THE edge of the bed glaring as her boyfriend of six months ignored her in favor of the latest sport he'd decided was more interesting than the beautiful woman next to him. Reclined against a stack of pillows pushed up against the wooden headboard of her bed, he stared in rapt attention at the football game on television.

It hadn't always been like this. When she'd begun dating Cole, it had been exciting. Thea knew once again in another lifetime that she hadn't been given a destined one, but Cole swept her off her feet, enchanting her with his passion and experiences, even though he'd only lived a mere two lifetimes. And although their lovemaking had never gotten above the average level, Cole's concern for her happiness had impressed her.

Those days were long gone now, and Thea wondered if this was all her forty-fifth lifetime had to offer. Although she'd told herself she couldn't stand one more day of the relationship, she'd made a deal with herself to try one more time to reawaken the romance that had existed between them just six months earlier.

As Cole sat transfixed by the spectacle in front of him, Thea trailed kisses across his stomach and down to the top of his pants. Hearing a sigh, she looked up to see Cole smiling.

Good. Progress.

She undid his pants and unzipped them slowly to find him already hard.

Very good.

Cole liked to talk during sex, so she was pleased to hear him begin to speak as she began to suck gently on him, even if she wasn't pleased by what he said. It always reminded her of how young an Aeveren he truly was, despite being three years older than she in this lifetime.

"You like my big cock in your mouth, baby? Yeah, suck harder."

Don't listen, Thea. Nobody's perfect. It's just an idiosyncrasy. Nothing you can't deal with.

She did as he ordered and felt his hand begin to push the back of her head. Grasping the base of his cock, she continued to bob up and down on him.

Sure he was close to coming, she glanced up at his face and suddenly stopped her motion. Instead of watching her or having his head thrown back in ecstasy and his eyes closed, he was watching the football game! Furious, Thea sat up and faced him. No amount of convincing herself could change the fact that whatever they'd had together obviously wasn't working anymore.

"Cole, I think it's time we talked."

Grabbing the remote, she clicked off the television and watched as a surprised look came over his face.

"What the …? Now what's wrong, baby? I loved what you were doing. Why'd you stop?"

"This isn't working. I'm sorry."

Cole's expression changed to reflect the hurt and anger he felt. "So now you're going to break up with me because I wasn't totally focused on you giving me a blowjob?"

Disgusted, she stood up off the bed and walked to the bedroom door. "I'm sorry. I just want something different than this."

Cole zipped up his pants and rolled off the bed to stand and face her. When he spoke, Thea knew how much she'd hurt him.

"You want something that doesn't exist anymore, baby. That's the problem with you ancient Aeveren. You want something that hasn't existed since the Middle Ages. That chivalrous knight-in-shining-armor shit doesn't happen anymore. And you'd better get used to that since you're not getting a destined one."

"Get out! Now!" she ordered as she ushered him toward the front door.

"Relax, baby. I'm just saying what you know is the truth."

As Thea opened the door, Cole stopped in front of her, grinning. "I'll wait for you to call me this time. But don't keep me waiting too long."

"Goodbye, Cole," she said as she fought back the tears.

Alone, Thea let herself have a good cry at the pain of what

he'd said. Yes, she was old-fashioned, but was that a bad thing? She was in her forty-fifth lifetime and had seen hundreds of years—over a thousand, she thought with a sigh—of men who respected and protected their females. For many of her lifetimes, she had that too. Was it any surprise that this is what she was used to?

But it wasn't just that the men she seemed to meet now weren't old fashioned like her. It was what Cole had said about a destined one that really hurt.

And you'd better get used to that since you're not getting a destined one.

Thea regretted ever telling him she was a healer. She usually didn't tell men about her gift because then they often found out that healers rarely were given destined ones. It made her feel less special than other Aeveren females, even though she knew that was foolishness. Her gift helped people.

That was little comfort as she watched nearly everyone she knew in every lifetime find true love with a destined one. She knew it may be a hopeless wish, but she couldn't help wishing once again on the star she spied out her window for a destined one to love her and for her to love.

And if it isn't too much to ask, please can he be old-fashioned like me?

Thea heard a knock at her door and sighed in disgust. Cole was nothing if not predictable. After every fight they'd ever had, he'd returned to convince her how much he loved her, and it seemed he was true to form this night too.

This time was different, though. Thea knew she'd have to

deal with him, but she wouldn't let him convince her to stay with him again.

I'd rather be alone.

Feeling empowered by her decision, she flung open the door to tell him exactly why she didn't want to be with him anymore, and God help him the first time he called her baby. But instead of seeing Cole standing on her front porch, she looked out to see a greasy man with no coat staring back at her.

"Althea Forester?"

"Yes. Who are you?"

"I need you to come with me."

Before she could slam the door and call 911, he grabbed her and took her into the house, holding her arms tightly. Seconds later, she'd been taken from her home—kidnapped by a strange man.

"ARE YOU OKAY, MY FRIEND?" Amon hoarsely whispered to Gethen who sat watching him.

The sound of his voice made the servant's face light up. Leaning forward in his chair, he smiled warmly.

"Yes, I'm fine. I was never the concern. I can travel between worlds with ease, remember?" Reaching out to touch Amon's arm, Gethen continued. "How are you feeling?"

Amon considered the question and struggled to put how he felt into words. The gratitude he felt toward the soul sitting next to him threatened to overwhelm him. He knew Gethen spoke the truth about his ability to travel between worlds, but the risk he'd taken in rescuing him from Nil was so profound that even as he lay there he found it difficult to believe he'd risked so much for him. Physically, his wounds made him ache all over, but emotionally, he felt so full from the love his servant had shown him he struggled to keep his emotions in check.

He looked into the deep green eyes that watched him carefully. "We're even, Gethen. Your debt is paid to me. If anything, I owe you."

Gethen shook his head and closed his eyes as tears began to well up in them. "Nothing I could ever do would be repayment enough for saving my life and giving me the one I've had with you."

Amon shook his head and smiled.

"No, master," he said sadly. "For all you've done for me, I could do nothing less than rescue you from that…" Gethen's voice caught and he cleared his throat. "I'm so sorry it took me so long," he said quietly, looking down at his hands resting on the bed.

"Don't do this to yourself, Gethen. You've given me the greatest gift of my forty-seven lifetimes."

Amon closed his eyes and prepared to say what he knew he should've said lifetimes ago. Opening his eyes, he met Gethen's gaze and smiled. "I should've done this so long ago, but I was selfish. You're free, my friend."

Amon watched a look of sadness cross his friend's face. Gethen had been away from his people as his servant for so many years. Almost as if he read the uncertainty in his mind, Amon smiled and said, "But I hope you'll stay now as my friend instead of my servant."

When he was rewarded with Gethen's smile, he knew he'd understood his friend's concern and was pleased he'd allayed his fears. Hoping to change the conversation to something far less maudlin, Amon asked, "Did I see Markku earlier?"

"Yes. He was necessary to cast a protection spell for your safety on the trip back," Gethen answered, his voice a mixture of appreciation and irritation. "I sent him to find a healer."

Amon closed his eyes as the pain in his right leg came raging back. Grunting through it, he said, "It's the least he could do since he was one of the reasons I was sent there."

Gethen's look of confusion told Amon that Markku had been less than candid with him. As the pain in his leg settled in to a dull ache, he continued, "You thought it was just Varek? No, but I'm not done with him either."

Callia flashed through his mind and the realization that he was alone, except for Gethen, bit at his heart. Loneliness seeped back into him, and he shut his eyes in sadness.

Callia was a source of regret and loss for him, even a year after seeing her for the last time just before he'd been taken from her to Nil. The betrayal in her eyes still stayed in his memory, and it made him wince. He'd truly loved her—maybe still loved her—but as he lay there now, he knew for certain she'd only cared for him because she hadn't known about her destined one and no matter of manipulating time would ever have changed that.

And what of his own destined one, Sevine? He thought of her refusal to even remain with him and wondered what her existence had become after turning him away as her destined one. So much he'd done wrong in his lifetimes.

And Victoria. Her death after what he'd done had tormented him during his time in Nil, when he'd had nothing else to think of other than the actions of forty-seven lifetimes and the torture that awaited him for three more. Her death, more than anything else, was the true indictment of him as a selfish, cruel man.

Pushing these memories from his mind, Amon reopened his eyes to look at Gethen. He remembered the moment they'd met and felt vindicated by at least this one action. Perhaps he wasn't a complete monster.

His freedom from Nil presented him with many opportunities, however, and he had no intention of sitting around regretting his past. A new world awaited him, and he planned to grab it with both hands.

"What do you plan to do with Markku, Amon?"

"Markku's the least of my concerns. In fact, I plan on keeping him around for a while."

Gethen's face clearly showed his displeasure at the prospect of spending more time with the magickian, and Amon smiled at the thought.

"I'll make sure he's kept busy away from you, my friend. I know how you feel about him."

"If you could just keep him silent, I'd praise the gods."

Nodding in agreement, Amon explained, "I know, but

we're going to need his talents if we want to enjoy any of the things life has in store for us. The Council isn't going to let me stay free if they can help it. I'm too big a prize for them not to try their damnedest to return me to that hellhole. And he's going to prove very useful in my plans for Varek."

As Amon spoke, the pain from his leg spiked and he grimaced. Gethen's expression became clouded with worry, but as the pain subsided, Amon waved away his worry.

"Gethen, I know what you're thinking, but don't worry. I'll be fine. I just need a few days to heal. Did you have Markku make sure we couldn't be found?"

"Yes. But your leg is going to need more than a few days, Amon."

"That's what the healer's for. Don't worry. Everything will be back to the way it was in no time."

They sat quietly for a while, but as Amon rested, he saw the look of concern that had settled onto his friend's face. "Gethen, what's on your mind?"

"Amon, I've served you these seven lifetimes, attending to your estates, your money, everything you've commanded of me. I've watched as…I wonder if now isn't the time to change the past?"

"Change the past?" Amon asked as he raised both eyebrows in disbelief.

"Yes, in a way. I've served you faithfully as your servant, a willing slave in return for your saving me all those years ago. But now that you've freed me, I hope I may speak freely."

Amon sat up in his bed intrigued by his friend's words and

bothered by the use of "slave" to describe him.

"Gethen, you were always more than a servant. If you have something to say, then speak what's on your mind. You're my friend and have been for longer than you believe."

Swallowing hard, Gethen hesitated and then began slowly. "You've been alone for lifetimes, Amon. Perhaps it's time to consider why."

"I haven't been alone, as you yourself can attest to. Think back to where you found me this lifetime. I wouldn't call how you found me that day alone."

Before Gethen had a chance to explain, Amon continued. "And the lifetime before that? I don't think alone would be the proper description for that either."

"You're intentionally misunderstanding me," Gethen answered in exasperation. "Having French farm girls service you and manipulating time to abduct another man's destined one don't count as proof you aren't alone."

Amon's flashed an annoyed look at him, letting his eyes change to almost black to signal to Gethen that he'd gone too far.

"I'm sorry. I'm out of line," he said quietly as he lowered his head.

Amon breathed deeply and considered what his friend had said. While his words had stung, they hadn't been untrue. Slowly, his eyes changed back to their original blue as he accepted Gethen's point.

"So what do you suggest, my friend?"

"Perhaps it's time to seek out your destined one?"

"Sevine?" Amon answered in disbelief.

"She is the woman you're supposed to be with. Your destined one. Even as a Sidhe, I know that means something."

Amon thought back to the last time he saw his destined one—the day she formally refused to continue to act as the woman destiny had chosen for him. He remembered the cold look in her eyes as she told him the man he'd become was enough to make her turn her back on seventeen lifetimes. And he remembered her threat to use a witch's spell to bind his powers.

"My destined one wants nothing to do with me, Gethen."

"And why is that?"

"What are you getting at, Gethen? Speak your mind."

Gathering his courage, the Sidhe answered, "You're alone, unwanted by your destined one, because of your actions. Perhaps this new chapter after Nil offers you a chance to repair your past."

"To regain the love of Sevine?"

"Yes."

"That's lost to me forever. All I have is the future now."

Amon closed his eyes and tried to remember a time when he'd simply been happy with a woman. Even though he'd tried with Callia and had truly loved her, the knowledge that she was another man's had haunted every day of their time together. He had to go back lifetimes before that—even before his destined one had forsaken him—back to the last lifetime his destined one and he had truly loved one another as Basir and Neylan.

As he remembered his time as a humble Turkish trader, Amon thought back to the day he married his destined one in that lifetime so long ago.

Dishes of food sat scattered along the tables as the wedding guests began to say their goodbyes and wish them well. He felt Neylan's hand slip away from his as she walked around the tables to clear away the guests' dishes. Walking up behind her, he took them from her hands as he nuzzled her neck.

"Leave them for the servants. We have better things to do now."

Neylan turned in his arms to face him and smiled. "Basir, you've known me as a woman before. I'm afraid I'm the same woman I was yesterday."

"No, today you became my wife. Now you are different."

"And am I different from the destined one you've had for thirteen lifetimes?"

He took her hands in his and squeezed them. "Neylan, you are forever Sevine who rescued me from loneliness and solitude all those lifetimes ago. No matter whatever occurs, you are the woman destined for me."

She wrapped her arms around his strong body and held him close to her, as he comforted her with the fact that once again she was safe with the one meant for her. As the last of the wedding guests left, the couple stood in the cool grass outside their new home together, more in love than either of them could ever remember feeling.

Basir looked at the house they were to spend the rest of their life in—in truth, little more than a shack—and wished he could give Neylan more than the meager life of a trader. He'd had more to offer her in past lifetimes and feared her memories of those homes and belongings.

"I may not have much now, but I promise to work hard to give you everything you deserve."

"Please don't worry, Basir. I have everything I need in you. I don't need anything else to be happy. Just you."

He dipped his head to kiss her and smelled the warm spiciness familiar to her. Her lips met his, and he tasted the remnants of wine on her tongue when she teased the inside of his mouth. He felt dizzy from the feelings she created in him.

Unable to contain his desire for her after waiting hours for wedding guests to leave, he took her hand and led her to the bedroom inside the house they'd now share. In the moonlight that streamed in through the shutters, she looked like an angel sent just for him.

Gently, he undressed her, removing the simple dress she'd worn to become his wife just hours earlier in front of friends and family. As she stood naked in front of him, he couldn't help but stare as his eyes drank in the beauty of her.

"I love you with all my heart, Neylan."

"And I love you, Basir," she said sweetly as she helped him remove his leggings and tunic. Beneath them awaited a body she'd adored before their marriage, but the thought of her mouth and hands exploring him now excited him even more.

He watched as her hands traveled thought the black hair on his chest that narrowed to a thin, dark trail down to even darker hair nestled around his erect cock. The feel of her fingers as she took him into her hand aroused him even more, and he moaned softly.

Before he gave in to the feel of her hand surrounding him, he led her to the bed and laid her down. Feathering kisses over her breasts and softly rounded stomach, he let his desire lead him to the dark triangle between her legs. With his fingers, he gently opened her and traced a single finger down her seam to the waiting wetness below. The soft moans he heard above him told him she enjoyed his attention as much as he loved giving it.

He fought back the urge to take her, instead touching her softly with his tongue and tasting just a sample of the sweetness that would soon be his. Slowly, he caressed her soft skin with his tongue, licking from her swollen nub to her wet entrance that begged him to taste her.

Each flick of his tongue excited her more than the last until the moans he heard from above told him she was close. With one last gentle suck on her excited clitoris, he felt her go over the edge and eagerly inserted two fingers into her to prolong her pleasure.

When the final spasms of her release trailed off, he slid up her body to kiss her and show her his appreciation for what she'd just given him. As she rolled him over onto his back, he waited for her to give him that same release.

"Neylan," he whispered and thought how true her name's meaning—fulfilled wish—was. She was everything he could ask for in a destined one, a gift he treasured.

He felt her mouth begin to tentatively suck on the swollen head of his cock, creating sensations that nearly took his breath *away. Lifetimes together had made her touch perfect. She knew every spot that excited him.*

Over and over again, her lips slid down his shaft and then back to the tip as her tongue danced over each sensitive area. When he was unable to hold back any longer, he exploded into her mouth as she took all he offered.

Amon shook his head to dispel the memories from his mind. But they remained, and thoughts of his destined one's sweet surrender later that night haunted him instead of soothing him for those times, when he happily lived a modest life as a trader in western Turkey with a woman who loved him with her very being, were long gone. Lifetimes of actions Basir could never conceive of, much less commit, had sealed Amon's solitary fate.

And didn't he deserve it? He'd acted selfishly when the choices of kindness and generosity were readily available. He'd hurt his fellow Aeveren without a second thought, often with no concern even when he'd seen the terrible effects of his actions.

Could he ever regain the love of his destined one? Gethen's suggestion had planted the seed in his mind, but Amon forced himself to admit that choice had been taken away from him and rightfully so.

No, he'd spend the remainder of his lifetimes without the love of his destined one. But he didn't seek to change the past as Gethen did. He'd made his choices, and he'd live with them.

For now, he needed to focus on getting healthy enough to travel. When he could, the world and time would both be his oysters. There would be no place or period unavailable to him once he was well and his powers were restored.

His time in Nil had shown him the value of not only freedom but his powers. Now he'd use both to their full extent, with no regrets. Until fate showed him a reason to think of the past, it would stay right where it belonged.

In the past.

Amon turned toward Gethen and grinned. "Thank you for caring about me, friend, but I've thought about it and decided the future is where my focus should be."

"I understand," Gethen said somberly, "but just as I must deal with my past, you too must face yours someday."

"Well, I'll let you deal with that, but don't let your need to repent get in the way of our future. The world is waiting, my friend. There are good times to be had."

Gethen cocked his head and quietly disagreed. "The past can't be that easily dismissed, Amon, no matter how much we wish it could."

CHAPTER THREE

F ROM THE FLOOR BELOW A terrible pounding noise broke the silence, and Gethen jumped from his chair to find out the source of the racket. As he left the room, he shot Amon a reassuring look to tell him he would handle things.

Approaching the front door, he saw Markku and another person struggling with one another. Gethen opened the door to see Markku forcing his hand over a young woman's mouth and her flailing her arms in fear.

"I got one, old man!" Markku exclaimed as he pushed past Gethen dragging the woman with him. "How's the big guy?" he asked as he swiveled his head from side to side looking for Amon while he worked to keep control over his captive.

Gethen opened his mouth to chastise Markku but was rendered dumbstruck when the magickian lost control of the female after she bit him and lunged away from him.

"Get over here, you bitch! Fucking bite me?"

The woman spun around to grab onto Gethen, and he quickly took control of her to calm her down.

"Save me, please!"

Gethen took her by the arm and guided her to the stairs to Amon's room. Halfway up, he turned to Markku and sternly instructed him to make sure the spell that kept others from finding Amon was secure.

"But I want to see him," he whined. Then in a far more threatening voice aimed at the woman, he growled, "And I want to show her what happens when you cross me."

Gethen's mood darkened as he remembered what Amon had said about who'd sent him to Nil. Anger rose quickly in him and he barked sharply, "Stay where you are until I tell you otherwise!"

By the time he'd made it to the second floor, the female had stopped fighting him and was pleading to be released in a voice so frightened that it normally would have affected him. But Amon needed to be healed.

"I won't hurt you or let Markku hurt you, but I need you to heal someone. If you refuse, however, you can be assured I will harm you. Do you understand?"

The woman nodded, her eyes wide with terror.

Gethen guided her into Amon's room and placed her next to the bed, positioning himself in the doorway to ensure she couldn't escape.

"Master," Gethen began and then stopped himself. "Amon, this is the healer Markku found to help you."

Turning to the woman, he motioned toward Amon. "Help him."

AMON LOOKED UP AT THE terrified woman standing in front of him and pity for her washed over him. As she stood frozen, he spoke to her, hoping to calm her fears.

"What's your name?"

The woman stood as silent as a statue, her gaze fixed on the floor.

"Tell him your name," Gethen said in a low, menacing voice.

Amon grimaced at his friend's threatening tone and repeated his question. When she didn't answer again, he added, "Please don't be frightened. Gethen won't hurt you. He's just worried about me. I promise you're in no danger in my home."

Slowly, she lifted her eyes to his right leg. Without a word, she moved to the opposite side of the bed and focused intently on the injury.

Amon watched in apprehension as she stared at the main source of his pain. She seemed to forget anyone but the two of them were in the room. When she moved to touch his leg, he flinched and groaned, "No," but she seemed oblivious to his refusal.

Gently, she touched just below his knee, and Amon waited for the searing pain to return with a vengeance. Eyes closed, holding his breath, he waited, but only relief came. His pain ebbed away, and when he was convinced it wouldn't be back at least while she touched him, he allowed himself to exhale fully and slowly opened his eyes.

The left eye was still swollen, but through his right eye he studied the creature that had just taken his pain away. For the first time since she'd entered the room, he noticed how placid her expression was. Long blond hair softly framed her face, falling in tendrils toward her waist, and pale blue eyes looked to his leg, as if she were willing him better.

Amon's study of her was broken only by Gethen's shifting positions against the door frame as he nervously watched her do as he'd commanded. The noise interrupted her focus, and she looked up into Amon's face. He winced expecting the pain to return, and she slowly moved to touch his face near his swollen eye.

"Thea," he heard her whisper as she gingerly placed her right hand over his left eye.

Involuntarily, he relaxed and closed both eyes as a sense of calm flowed over him. He wasn't sure how long he lay there with her soft touch on him, but he felt the loss instantly when she moved away.

He opened his eyes in time to see her sway back toward the wall. He reached out to grab her, but in his weakened condition, he knew he'd only be able to support her for just seconds before she fell to the floor.

"Gethen!"

The man raced around the bed to catch her as she slipped from Amon's hold. As he held her limp body in his arms, he looked to Amon with a confused look for guidance as to what to do with yet another injured person.

"Place her next to me here," he said pointing to the unoccupied half of the king size bed he lay in.

As Gethen did as he requested, he asked, "What happened?"

"Aeveren healers can become overwhelmed if the person they're healing is severely injured. Considering the amount of pain I had before she touched me and how little I have now in both my leg and my eye, it's not surprising she found it to be too much."

Amon inched up into a sitting position and looked down at Thea as she lay motionless next to him. He regretted Markku having to take her against her will and having to hold her there, but the effect of just her brief healing touch was wonderful.

Looking up at Gethen, he whispered, "I'm tired, friend. Dim the lights and let me rest for a while."

"Do you think that's wise? She may wake up and hurt you."

"Gethen, she's a healer."

"Amon, she bit Markku downstairs."

Smiling, Amon joked, "That's Markku. She wouldn't be the first person to want to harm him, and certainly not the first woman. And she had the right to fight back. She's not here of her own free will."

Gethen continued, undeterred. "I'm just worried she may try to leave."

"Then you can remain outside the door, if you'd like. But I'm sure downstairs would be fine and far more comfortable. There's only one door to the outside, and it's on the first floor."

Gethen accepted Amon's argument and dimmed the ceiling light until the room glowed a pale amber color. He closed the door with one last glance back at him, and Amon listened as he made his way down the stairs.

Sleep began to come over him and he welcomed it like an old friend absent from his life for what seemed like years. For the first time in almost twelve months, he was in a bed and his body didn't ache so much it would keep him up all night. And for the first time in all those months, he wasn't alone.

He inhaled deeply and let the air out of his lungs slowly, savoring the safety he felt.

Turning to look at the woman next to him, he watched as she lay silently still except for her breathing. Her hands seemed so small until his gaze traveled the length of her body and he saw all of Thea was small. She'd seemed so much larger as she stood over him, but the person he saw beside him now was petite. As he noticed this, sleep took over and his eyelids drooped closed.

THEA'S EYES FLEW OPEN, AND she awoke confused and frightened. She couldn't remember where she was, and she had no idea who the man next to her in bed was. She looked around the room for any clues to show her how she'd ended up there, but nothing appeared to her. All she knew was that the room she was in was expensively furnished but where she was remained a mystery.

An even bigger mystery was who the man was. She

carefully turned to look at him, moving as little as possible as to not wake him. He was light haired, as far as she could tell by the little hair he had with it cut so close to his head. Her eyes traveled over his face and body, noticing the painful cuts and bruises along with scars from past injuries. He seemed to sleep peacefully, however, and she concluded this was partly her doing, no doubt. But how had she gotten to where she was? Had the man next to her brought her here?

Before she had the chance to recollect exactly what had happened, Amon began to stir. Thea watched as his tight stomach flexed and his large chest began to heave, as if he were experiencing a nightmare. His hands balled into tight fists at his sides, causing her to fearfully inch toward the edge of the bed away from him.

Amon awoke with a start and grimaced in what looked like agony. His hand shot out to grip his leg, and he let out a low cry of pain. She watched as he held his breath, waiting for it to subside so he could finally breathe again. Thea's sympathy for him grew as she watched him suffer. It was in her nature to help those in pain, but she feared what he might do if she simply reached over to help. As his suffering increased and he writhed in pain, she swallowed her fear and gently leaned over his body. Carefully, she laid her hand over his on his leg and began to feel relief come over him. His pain was excruciating and as she took it from his body, she thought in sadness how much pain he must feel if it nearly made her cry to simply help him.

Thea kept her hand over his until she heard him begin to

breathe normally again. Exhausted from healing him, she moved to lie back in her original position on her side of the bed, but he stopped her, grabbing her arm.

"Please don't go."

The anguish and sadness in his voice struck at her heart, and she let him hold her next to him. She looked up to see his face, but his eyes had shut and he'd fallen back to sleep.

Tired, she reluctantly laid her head on the only available place—his stomach—as she draped her arm over his body. Within moments, she was fast asleep on the stranger next to her in a strange place but more peaceful than she'd ever been.

HOURS LATER, AMON SLOWLY OPENED his eyes and felt the presence of another person on top of him. Looking down his body, he saw pale blond waves spread out over his abdomen and thighs. Slowly it returned to him why Thea would be so close to him. She'd helped him when he'd awoken in pain and must have passed out again because of it.

As he stared at the scene just above his lap, he thought how erotic it looked to have a beautiful woman's head so close to his cock. After feeling no kindness or closeness in his entire time in Nil, he enjoyed the warm feeling of her next to his body. Her soft breath drifted across his skin near his navel and for the first time in months, he felt himself begin to grow hard.

Gently, he stroked a lock of hair away from her face and followed it down her back. It felt silky against his fingers, and with each stroke he grew more excited. He needed to see the face of the angel who stirred feelings in him he'd thought might be dead forever. Moving her hair back, he saw a beautiful pair of pouty pink lips and long, dark lashes resting on her pale ivory skin.

His cock arched up against her arm that remained across his body. Even if much of him was bruised and battered, he wanted her. Closing his eyes, he let the thought of her kissing him with those lips on his mouth, down his neck, over his chest and abdomen, and finally on his cock take him away.

Amon's breathing became heavier, waking Thea. As she blinked the sleep out of her eyes, her face registered the embarrassment from her head resting on his lower abdomen. His erection pushed on the underside of her arm, and she sat up abruptly.

"Oh!" she said in a surprised voice.

Amon smiled at the sight of her awake. "Good morning," he lazily drawled, still enjoying the fantasy he'd created about her.

"Where am I?" she asked as she looked around the room.

Watching her through heavily lidded eyes, he answered, "My house."

"Who are you?"

"Amon."

"Amon who?"

"Kalins."

Thea recoiled from him with a look of horror, crying out as she skittered across the bed away from him.

CHAPTER FOUR

———

T HE CHAMBERS OF THE COUNCIL of Nil had never been in such turmoil. Council members, typically stoic, buzzed around in an uncharacteristic panic, along with pages, sorcerers, and a variety of assistants. By the looks on the Council members' faces, something had happened that had terrified them.

Ryu Jansen stood watching the scene in front of him, mildly curious as to what had occurred to send this generally staid group into such an uproar. As he scanned the chamber, he saw fear more than anything else. Not knowing if what had transpired had anything to do with why he'd been recalled by the Council after being released from his position almost a year before, he waited and watched.

"Bring in the guards who were on duty when Kalins escaped!" the head councilman bellowed.

Underlings scurried out of the room, official papers in hand, to speedily retrieve the men who'd most likely be standing in front of the Council a few hours later to answer the charge of dereliction of duty. Minutes later, Ryu stepped aside as the four men responsible for allowing the escape of one of the most powerful Aeveren to ever live were led in. They stood somberly for what awaited them, their heads hung.

The escape of a prisoner was a rare event, having only occurred a handful of times in all Aeveren history. Like Amon Kalins, the others had been the most powerful of the race, but it hadn't been their powers that had enabled their escape from Nil. Those were stripped from each prisoner, no matter how great or insignificant, along with the opportunity to have a destined one, upon conviction and sentencing to the Aeveren prison. No, Amon Kalins and the others had escaped because powerful Aeveren had powerful friends, and if those friends were Sidhe or any of the other kinds of beings who could evade Aeveren preventative measures, no amount of guarding could keep them in. In truth, everyone in the Council chambers had known from the moment they threw Amon Kalins into Nil that his incarceration may just be temporary.

Every eye focused on the four guards, large monsters in the shape of men who otherwise terrified prisoners with merely their stares. Now they cowered in front of men half their size but with infinitely more power. Each guard stood silently staring at the chamber's glossy black marble floor.

The first words the head councilman spoke set the tone of the proceedings. "Gentlemen, how did you let the most important prisoner in all of Nil escape? Whose incompetence is to blame?"

Ryu knew every person in the chamber believed this question to be unfair. That someone as powerful as Amon

Kalins had been freed from his time in Nil wasn't a surprise. That he'd served a year of his sentence was the only surprise. But someone would have to be sacrificed to continue the judicial facade the Council required.

The four guards said little useful in reply to the question. Each one had shared some pleasure in making the last year of Amon's life as painful as possible and the previous night had been no exception. All any of them could truly know was that when they finally left him for the night, he was in no shape to go anywhere without help.

"Gentlemen, look at us," the head councilman ordered, his tone less angry than officious. "We need to know everything about Mr. Kalins' time under your control. For example, may we assume he was treated to the customary welcome by the other prisoners?"

The guards looked up toward those in the upper level of the chamber and nodded solemnly.

"And was he treated to any other courtesies by the other prisoners…or you gentlemen?"

Ryu knew the reputation of the guards, but he also knew what they'd done to the prisoner would bring no reprimand. None of the guards answered the question, but finally the largest guard, an enormous bald man, said, "Kalins wasn't liked by the other prisoners because of who he was."

"So it would be fair to say that he would have some distinguishable marks from his time with you?"

Again, the same guard answered. "It would."

"And what of his last night with you?"

The guard next to him answered this time. "Wherever he is, he can only see out of one eye and hobble around, if he can move at all, since his leg's most likely broken." His tone indicated with a sadistic sense of pride that he'd been the one who delivered the majority of Amon Kalins' last beating in Nil.

The more sensitive members of the Council gasped, but the head councilman noted with pleasure that the man they sought wasn't as strong as he needed to be to evade recapture. He finished a note he wrote on the file and waived his hand thoughtlessly to indicate he was finished questioning the guards.

"We'll see you back here later, gentlemen," he stated cryptically without raising his eyes from the file.

Ryu watched the four guards file out of the chamber room and didn't envy their fate. His past dealings with the Council had shown him that they knew little of the concept of leniency. That he stood in front of them again might convince some that this was untrue, but he knew better. If they were willing to reinstate him, they wanted his particular skills to deal with their lost prisoner.

The head of the Council stared down at him and pointed to the spot left vacant by the guards. As he took his place, Ryu's memories of the last time he stood in front of the Council flashed through his mind.

"Welcome back to Nil, Mr. Jansen."

At six feet tall, Ryu stood proudly facing the Council but as he nodded, he heard the oppressive sound of the words pushing down on him. Welcome back to Nil.

When he'd left, it had been against his wishes but with no regret. He'd known when he'd failed to capture his assignment that he'd be reprimanded, but he'd never conceived of them dismissing him. He wouldn't have done things any differently given the choice again, though. He'd done what he'd thought was right, and they'd sacked him.

"I'll skip the pleasantries and get to why we brought you here. As you heard from the interview with those guards, we've had an escape." After a long pause, the councilman said, "Amon Kalins."

Ryu waited for him to explain more about Kalins but heard nothing. Was he supposed to know who this Kalins was, other than what rumors he'd heard before and what he'd heard here? Shrugging his shoulders, he let the Council know that the man who had them all atwitter was no one to him.

"Don't be so cavalier, Mr. Jansen. This is your opportunity to come back home."

Ryu blanched at the idea that Nil would ever be anything like a home. But he knew what the head councilman meant. Finding this Kalins would return his life to him. With forced humility, he accepted that the Council could make things much better for him if he did as they wanted. His exile from his job as a bounty hunter hadn't been easy. Unlike in the movies when a character makes a choice that goes against the powers that be and has to live with the consequences, he hadn't retired to the country to sanctimoniously reflect on just how right he'd been. The last year had been hell, and he'd do just about anything to regain even part of the life he'd once had.

He focused his eyes on the Council above. "What do I need to know?"

The councilman grinned in satisfaction. "Amon Kalins is a powerful Aeveren. An ancient. He had the power to travel through time, and may have had other, lesser powers. He was stripped of these powers, of course, when he was here, but we must now assume he has regained them or will shortly. He's responsible for the deaths of any number of Aeveren. We have no doubt he will murder again, if he feels it serves his purposes."

Happy to hear a break in the laundry list of negatives for his new assignment, Ryu hoped to hear something that would aid him.

"Those are the bad things, Mr. Jansen. Let's call them challenges. Now for the good. He's injured, and because we sent an edict to the healers forbidding them to help him, he's in bad shape."

A small murmuring sound among a few of the Council members followed the head Council member's discussion of the points in Ryu's favor. He'd hoped for more than the aftereffects of the sadistic behavior of the guards. "Any chance he'd go to a human for help?" Ryu knew that just because he had no problem with humans didn't mean Kalins didn't.

"We would know if he did. Our sorcerers have no sign of him, which means his friends from the Soren are probably involved. He's been known to have a magickian of theirs with him on occasion."

Crazy motherfuckers.

It had been years since he'd had an assignment that involved that group. Human haters every one of them, they sought to dominate and enslave them.

"How'd he get out?"

Ryu knew instantly that he'd overstepped his bounds by asking, but the anger quickly melted away from the head councilman's face and he answered, "He has a Sidhe who's his slave. It's likely he helped him."

A tempuster. Those maniacal bastards from the Soren. And a Sidhe. At least this job will be interesting.

"Anything else I should know?"

"Kalins has three lifetimes left. I want them spent in Nil."

From behind him, Ryu heard footsteps and turned to see a council page with a box for him.

"Mr. Jansen, the tools you're being given will help you catch Amon Kalins. But know this: you're being recalled because he's the most powerful prisoner we had in Nil, and we need you to be the man you used to be. Ruthless. We want him alive, but we don't care what shape he's in. Complete this job and you'll have your pick of local councils. Fail and you'll return to what you've been for the past year."

Before he could answer, the council members and their entourage left the chamber. Ryu looked down in curiosity at the container he'd been given. Opening it, he found what he'd need—a talisman to travel through time and a knife he knew by the acrid smell rising from the box was coated with Anjer, a poison deadly to the Sidhe. As he looked at Kalins' prisoner photo, he hummed.

This one will be a challenge.

THEA COULDN'T BELIEVE THE NAME she'd just heard. "Oh no...Amon Kalins?" Full of fear, she quickly backed away further from Amon. Fully awake, the knowledge of what she'd done terrified her.

"Don't be afraid. I won't hurt you. And thank you for helping me during the night."

"No, this can't be. None of this happened."

"Thea, relax. Nothing happened between us. All you did was heal me," Amon said calmly.

"Oh, my God! You know my name?"

Amon looked at her, obviously confused at her reaction to what was natural behavior for healers. "It's okay. You didn't do anything wrong."

Putting her head in her hands, she sobbed, "Yes, I did. Something very wrong."

Gethen came in and seeing Thea crying, looked at Amon curiously. "What happened?"

Shaking his head, he said, "I don't know. She says she did something wrong."

Both men stood waiting for Thea to explain. Before she could clear up what was becoming a very confusing situation, Markku appeared in the doorway, much to Gethen's displeasure.

"I told you to stay downstairs."

"Hey, Amon! You look much better. Must be her," he said. "Wish I could say the same." As he spoke, he lifted his bandaged hand to show him his injury from where she'd bit him earlier.

Markku's voice sent terror through her, and she began to back around the side of the bed in fear. Seeing her move from him, he threatened, "Not so brave now, huh? Don't worry. I'll pay you back for this, healer."

The last word came out in a hiss and Thea backed up into the dresser, knocking over the glass bottles that sat on its top. As they crashed to the floor, Amon shot Markku a nasty look and roared, "Enough!"

Thea froze in fear and saw Markku and Gethen stand quietly, obviously used to Amon's temper.

"Gethen, please get him downstairs."

Then turning to Markku, Amon warned, "Don't threaten her again."

"Sure, but I came up here to tell you something. They've sent out a bounty hunter to take you back."

Gethen's face grew ashen, and he turned in fear to Amon.

Smiling, Amon shook his head. "Not to worry, Gethen. I'm getting stronger by the minute, thanks to Thea here, and as soon as my powers return, we can go anywhere and anytime we want and the Council will never catch me."

Gethen seemed to be calmed for the moment, and Amon turned to Markku. "I want you to find out everything you can about this bounty hunter and let Gethen know when you do."

"Sure, Amon," Markku replied obsequiously as Gethen

pushed him out of the room. Alone again with her, Amon turned his face toward her, as she stood still cowering near the dresser.

Thea watched the man in front of her with fear, but there was something else too, something she'd never experienced before as a healer. She didn't just feel sympathetic for him, didn't want to merely make his pain go away. She felt drawn to him, and not only on a physical level. She could understand that after resting her head on his hard body. He was more masculine than anyone she'd ever met. Even after what had obviously been repeated beatings, he seemed stronger than any man could be. So her physical attraction she understood.

But there was something else. After only a few hours near him, she realized with sadness that she'd miss him when he released her. But why? She knew little about him, and what she knew wasn't good. He was Amon Kalins, the escaped prisoner from Nil. She'd been warned, as all other Aeveren healers had, not to help him in any way. She hadn't had a choice, though. His wretched man had kidnapped her from her home and when she saw him suffering before her, nature had taken over. Healing him had never been a choice but a need.

"Thea, don't be afraid. I told you I wouldn't let any harm come to you, and I won't. You're safe as long as you're with me."

The tone of his deep voice was softer now, but it didn't make her feel any better. She remained fearful, her fingers tightly gripping the drawer handle behind her.

"You're Amon Kalins..." she squeaked out as her voice

failed her. The hard surface of the dresser pressed against her back when she attempted to take another step back away from him.

"Yes."

"The escaped prisoner from Nil."

"Yes."

Thea's body relaxed almost against her will. Each affirmation should have made her fear for her safety all the more, but it didn't. Something in his voice soothed her.

"And you're a tempuster?" This the Council hadn't mentioned in its edict to healers.

"Yes."

In all her lifetimes, she'd never met any Aeveren with the power of time travel. Amon Kalins must be a very powerful man, she realized.

"Is it my ability that frightens you?" he asked in a voice she was sure was intended to put her at ease.

Thea thought about this for a moment and answered in a small voice, "No."

His being a tempuster was probably the least frightening aspect of him. The truth was she was most frightened of how much she already liked him. She shouldn't. She knew this. But something about him called to her.

"Then my being a prisoner from Nil?"

Thea drew in a deep breath and let it out slowly. "I'm not supposed to help you."

"Why? You're a healer. It's your gift. Why would you be banned from healing someone who needs your help?"

Thea was ashamed to admit that she'd never considered this question, not when she was ordered not to heal him nor all the other times those who dictated her power ordered her not to help another in need. How many times had she followed edicts and watched half-breeds or full blooded Aeveren suffer needlessly for breaking one of the many rules of their world?

The thought of her blind heartlessness made her shoulders droop and the regret she suddenly felt overwhelmed her. Sadly, she explained, "The Council ordered all healers to not help you. Under no circumstances were any of us to heal you." As she spoke the words of the edict, she felt guilty not because she had helped him, but because for the first time in her forty-five lifetimes she'd truly lived up to her nature.

"But you did. Not that we gave you a chance to follow your orders."

"Now I don't know what will happen to me. When they find out what I did..."

Thea's voice trailed off as she thought of how the Council would punish her for healing Amon. As she winced at the thought of her reprimand, Amon clenched his fists at his side. Thea saw the anger in his expression and wasn't sure how to react. She was reasonably sure his anger wasn't because of her, but something in him had changed.

"Are you in pain?"

Amon relaxed his hands. "No."

Slowly, his face returned to the handsome, albeit bruised, expression he seemed to usually have. Thea stepped forward toward him and carefully placed her hands on both sides of his face. She didn't know why as he'd said he wasn't in pain, but something in her pushed her toward his bruised face.

The swollen left eye had returned to normal, and she felt the gaze of his ocean blue eyes on her as she coaxed the pain out of his features. Gradually, the slash under his eye closed until all that was left was a faint pink line. The light purple bruises that marked near his jaw and above his eyes, remnants from a prior assault than the one on his last night in Nil, faded under her light touch as the pads of her fingertips softly glided over his skin.

Amon sat stunned by her unsolicited help. As she focused on healing him, she saw him study her, his breathing turning to shallow pants and sensed his desire when she saw him lick his lips. As a healer, she wasn't gifted with the ability to read minds, but her power came with the complementary ability of being able to read others' reactions better than other Aeveren.

That something inside her that had pushed her toward him now told her to kiss him, and she leaned in and gently pressed her lips to one of the pale black and purple marks on his forehead. When she finally pulled away, she saw his eyes were closed and his face was calmer than at any time since she'd met him the night before.

Her mind raced. Should she apologize for kissing him, even if it was just on his skin? She'd never wanted to do anything like that ever before with anyone else she'd been charged to heal. But nothing about being near this man was like anything she'd ever experienced before.

Unsure of how to act, she found it difficult to know what to do next, and words began to tumble out of her mouth. "I'm sorry...I didn't mean...I don't know why..."

Amon opened his eyes as Thea felt the color rising in her cheeks. She may have been saying she was sorry and claiming she didn't know why she'd kissed him, but she was still positioned right next to his face.

"No need to apologize. In fact, there's no need to stop."

A sound of surprise escaped her lips and her eyes grew wide at the idea that there was more to come. Her heart pounded in her chest as his deep blue eyes stared into hers. Would he kiss her now? All at once, she realized she wanted so much to feel his lips on hers.

CHAPTER FIVE

A MON WATCHED AS THE PALE green flecks in Thea's blue eyes seemed to dance. He hadn't noticed how beautiful her eyes were before—how incredibly breathtaking she was, overall. Her face was so close, her pink lips just inches from his...

He certainly didn't mind her touching him anywhere since her touch was naturally pleasing to start with and only became more so because he wanted her. And he didn't mind the feel of her soft lips on his skin, either. In fact, he had a number of other places he'd like her to visit with those lips.

As he looked into her eyes now, he saw not only beauty but desire and insecurity. What a wonderfully interesting woman this healer was!

Slowly, Amon saw the insecurity disappear from Thea's eyes, leaving only desire for what he offered. Need filled his cock, making it impossible to leave their little interlude unfinished. Months of loneliness had made him respond to her touch far more than he ordinarily would have, he reasoned. This was nothing more than the simple need to sexually be with another.

But he'd seen the look on her face before, when Sevine had come to him and found he was her destined one. That was impossible with Thea, though. He still had a destined one, regardless of how she'd manipulated him with magick to escape him. He couldn't be another's destined one as long as his still hadn't finished her fifty lifetimes.

He knew it wasn't right for him to lead Thea on if she wanted more than he could give, but she was so close and she'd felt so good next to him earlier. All those painful nights in Nil had left him with an emptiness he yearned to fill, and he wanted Thea to heal that too.

Leaning in to her, he caressed her soft lips with his before increasing the intensity of his kiss. Afraid she would back away, he cradled her face in his hands as he slipped his tongue into her warm mouth.

She returned his kiss with a passion that signaled she wanted him. When she moaned into his mouth, Amon knew he didn't want this to end with a kiss. As she began to feast on his mouth, he guided her onto his lap, setting her up against the base of his rigid cock. Realizing her position, she pulled away, frightened, but with his hand on her lower back, he trapped her against him.

"Please let me go," she begged.

"Why?"

"I can't do this."

Amon's mind listed the reasons why she possibly couldn't, crossing off all but one. "Do you have a destined one?" he asked, searching her eyes.

Thea dropped her eyes to look at his chest and stopped trying to get away from him. Quietly, she answered his question. "No, I don't have a destined one. I've never had one in forty-five lifetimes."

"Never?"

Amon couldn't imagine what mistake of nature had been made to ensure the sweet creature that sat on his lap remained ultimately alone for so long. He'd been a heartless fuck for many of his forty-seven lifetimes, and he'd had three destined ones.

Thea said nothing but continued to avoid his gaze.

"Why?"

As soon as he said it, he hated himself. She most likely wouldn't know why every life promised her she'd be alone.

"I'm a healer. It's uncommon for us to be blessed with destined ones. Our calling is more important than our individual happiness."

Every word she said dripped duty and loneliness between them. Amon looked up to see her eyes filled with tears, and his heart broke for her. He'd often thought of how unfair his life had seemed in the past year, but he knew he'd done more than enough to deserve his sentence in Nil. Thea had done nothing to deserve her fate.

He wiped the tear that had dropped onto her cheek with his finger and lifted her chin to make her meet his gaze. He couldn't just sleep with her now. The look on her face showed him that she mistakenly believed she'd finally found a destined one in him.

"I'm sorry, Thea."

Thea began to cry, her tears flowing down her face from his rejection. God, he felt like a fuck!

"Let me go," she said sadly as she pulled away from him.

Amon knew he should just release his hold on her, convinced her emotions were bound to begin affecting him at any moment. But he couldn't. He was responsible for much of her sadness and needed to do something to fix what he'd done.

Putting his arms around her, he pulled her upper body to his, holding her tighter as she resisted more. As she sobbed into the side of his neck, her body softly heaved against his. Wanting more than anything to make her feel better, he stroked her long blond hair while her crying flooded his ears.

Amon braced himself for his reaction. He'd always fed off the emotions of others and used them to his own benefit, careful to minimize his exposure to sadness. He vividly remembered Callia's effect on him and dreaded a replay of that with Thea as he was sure his body couldn't take much more abuse, but with relief he remembered that his destined one's curse on him only worked if he was in love with the woman. Safe in his belief that while he'd grown to care for her in the short time he'd known her he wasn't in love with Thea, Amon held her until her crying stopped and she was still in his arms.

Lifting her head, she wiped her tears from her face. "Why don't you want me as your destined one?"

A lump formed in his throat at the sound of the sadness in her voice. There was nothing he'd like more in this world than to have Thea for his. But that couldn't be.

"It's not a choice, Thea. It's just not possible."

"Why?"

He looked into the beautiful eyes of the one who'd already given him so much kindness and hated what he had to say.

"Thea, I already have a destined one."

Amon saw the shock register on her face. She had been so kind to him, and he hated having to say those words, more than she could ever know. Obviously embarrassed, she dropped her eyes and climbed off him, saying nothing.

She stood on the floor on the opposite side of the bed and straightened herself. "I...I want to sleep somewhere else. If you're going to hold me here against my will, I'd at least like to be alone."

Amon felt the sting of her sadness and regretted telling her, no matter how much she needed to know. But the selfish part of him didn't want to be without her.

"I need you here to help me heal."

He knew he was being insensitive. He didn't care. He didn't want her to leave.

"I can heal you just as well sleeping in another room," she said angrily.

Amon wanted to refuse her again, but the hurt coming from her crushed any desire to keep her in his room. Concentrating, he silently reached out to Gethen. As he waited for him, Amon watched Thea with sadness, wishing more than ever their world wasn't like it was.

When Gethen appeared in the doorway, his face was lit up

with happiness.

"Why so happy?" he asked him, eager for something to break the tension.

"You're getting your powers back."

Amon realized he was right. "Yeah." Shifting his gaze toward Thea, he said, "Thea wants to stay in another bedroom. Can you get one ready for her?"

Gethen nodded and turned to walk across the hall. "It will take just a few minutes."

"That's okay. I can help," she said quickly following him.

As Amon watched the door close, his heart felt like something was squeezing it in his chest. He hadn't meant to hurt her. The idea of having a kind heart like hers wanting him was almost more than he could ever wish for, but that didn't change the fact that nature had already given him the gift of a destined one. That she refused to be with him didn't matter. As long as she existed and hadn't moved on, he'd have to accept that another destined one wasn't something he could have.

No matter how much he wanted her.

GETHEN MADE QUICK WORK OF readying the other bedroom and when he left, Thea was happy to be alone. Kicking her shoes off, she lay on the bed. As she fought back the tears, the reality of her situation came clearly into focus.

I have no idea where I am. I'm being held hostage at an escaped prisoner's home, an escaped prisoner the Council expressly forbade me to help.

Then, as the tears began to fall, she thought about what was probably the most frightening part of everything that had happened.

My destined one doesn't want me.

"No, no…" she mumbled to herself as she wiped her eyes. "No, I'm mistaken. If I were ever to be given a destined one, it would be just like everyone has always said it would be. He'd want me even if he didn't want to."

Lifetimes of helping others had been punctuated by many brief dalliances, but the end result had always been the same— each lifetime she could only look forward in sadness to the next in which she'd be ultimately alone. And now that she truly believed she'd been released from her lonely prison, the man she knew was her destined one didn't want her, and worse yet, pitied her.

But didn't he have to want her? Isn't that how destined ones worked? Thea had listened with eager ears any time someone had spoken about the topic, desperate to know, even vicariously, the thrill of having someone meant just for her. She'd never heard anything about choice. In fact, it had always seemed to her that the defining feature of destined ones was the distinct lack of choice. She'd heard many an Aeveren bemoan nature's choice of a mate for them, convinced that a mistake had been made, so how did she feel the draw of a destined one if he didn't or wouldn't feel it?

Thea thought about the scent of his skin, a manly smell that appealed to her. Everything about him seemed to call her to him. Was she mistaken? It was true she had no real knowledge about what it would feel like to finally have a destined one. Maybe this was just another facet of being a healer—another way to torture her for being born with her gift.

Unsure of so much, she sat up on the bed to examine her new room. Very similar to the one she'd just left, it had dark wood floors, but the walls were a deep burgundy color and her king size bed was a four poster.

Very comfortable for a prison.

Looking around, she saw a window covered with heavy burgundy and gold draperies. Curious to see if there was a trellis or anything she could use to help her escape, she padded across the dark red carpet and then the floor to the window. When she pulled back the fabric, she was surprised to see daylight. She'd been so disoriented after being snatched from her home in the dark that she hadn't been sure what time it was.

After realizing with disappointment that there was no safe way down from her second floor room, she scanned the countryside she could view from her window. She saw nothing in the nearby distance. Wherever she was, she was far away from anyone who could help her.

Thea stood staring into the rolling hills and valleys and thought about how different her life had been just one day earlier. She'd gotten home from work at the daycare center and had sat down to a meal alone before Cole had come over. Panicked, she now wondered if her boss would ever believe some madman had kidnapped her so she could help his friend—or was he his boss?—who had just escaped from Nil. Sadly, she concluded she probably wouldn't.

Turning back toward the bed, she wondered why fate had chosen her to be the healer for Amon Kalins. She didn't feel like anything special, as far as healers went. It was true she was more advanced in the reincarnation cycle than most, but healing fellow Aeveren wasn't something you applied for. When one received the power, thankfully, one was instructed on how to use it. But as much as she was loathe to admit it, Thea knew there was something in her that made her special. She'd been born with her power.

It hadn't been easy for her. She'd been born in her first lifetime in Italy during the rule of the ancient Etruscans. When her parents realized the gift she'd been given, their duty was to provide their daughter to Aeveren authorities so she could benefit all her kind. Separated from those who loved her, she was treated almost as a deity, but even being worshipped couldn't replace the love of her family.

With a smile, Thea admitted she'd been in far tougher situations in her forty-five lifetimes. Being a healer could be a dangerous job as she was relied on for life and when she was unable to heal another, those closest to the person were often unable to understand their loved one's time had come.

She had to find a way to escape. The longer she stayed at Amon's house, the more she wanted to be with him. Even now, she had to remind herself that she must have been mistaken when she'd thought he was her destined one because thoughts of him continually crept back into her mind.

If she couldn't escape through the window in her room, perhaps she could do so through a window in the bathroom. She couldn't just undress and waltz to the bathroom, though. She'd need Amon's friend's assistance. If she made it look like she simply wanted to refresh herself with a bath, she might have enough time to devise a way to escape, hopefully to a lower roof or a porch. She was no acrobat, but she'd do what she must to escape.

Thea opened the door and peered into the dim hallway. Amon's door was closed, and she spied the bathroom at the end of the hall at the front of the house. A spark of hope ignited in her when she remembered walking onto a covered porch the night before when she'd arrived. Now if she could get the props she needed to convince them she was actually going to take a bath, she'd be set.

"Hello?" she said quietly at first, hoping not to attract the attention of the one who'd threatened her earlier. When no one came, she repeated it a little louder and added, "Gethen?" At once, Amon's door opened and in seconds she stood facing Amon himself in her doorway.

The vision of him filled her eyes, and they grew wide in a mixture of fear and desire. As he stood before her, he was much taller and larger than he'd appeared in bed as she'd healed him. Eye level with his collarbone, she found herself letting her eyes roam over his naked torso. Never had she seen another man with such hardness to his body.

She remembered the exhilaration she'd felt at the first brush of his kiss and then when his hands had touched her face. A need she'd never known had slammed her heart into her chest and made the area between her legs run wet. For the first time in all her lifetimes, every part of her body had come alive when she was next to him.

Her eyes drifted lower, and she noticed scars on his abdomen and hips that showed just above the waist of his black pants. As she stared at what looked like a branding, she heard him speak and she looked up to see him looking down at her, one eyebrow curiously lifted.

"Do you want something?" he asked in a voice that sounded warm and seductive.

Control your hormones, Thea. You have a plan to put into action.

"I was looking for Gethen. I'd like to take a bath."

As she spoke, she forced herself to look up at his face and not focus on his powerful body that was oh-so-close.

Amon smiled. "I sent him on an errand. What do you need?"

"I'd like a towel, please."

"There are towels and everything you might need in the bathroom. If anything's missing, just let me know and I'll have Gethen get it."

Thea worried that what she planned was written all over her face. She also worried her desire for him was all too apparent as she stood looking into those beautiful blue eyes that seemed to swallow her now.

"Okay. Thanks," she said awkwardly as she squeezed past him and marched down the hallway to the room she prayed held the way out and back to her life before Amon Kalins.

CHAPTER SIX

A MON WATCHED HER WALK DOWN the long hall to the bathroom as his body registered his interest in her, even if his mind had decided something else. Each step she took caused her long hair to bounce slightly and move side to side. He absentmindedly put his hand between his legs to adjust his rapidly hardening cock, and as the bathroom door closed, he stood staring, lost in a fantasy his vacillating mind was conjuring up.

Shaking his head, he reminded himself of what he'd decided—to be a decent man for one of the few times in this life. But as he thought about her pretty ass walking away from him, he wished he could be the Amon who'd be all over her clean body five minutes after she finished her bath. Or better yet, in the bath with her. He'd considered trying to enter her mind to get a sense of what she was thinking, still not sure all his powers had returned, but he thought it better not to because the facts were that he couldn't have her and it wasn't fair to simply use her.

Even if they'd both enjoy it immensely.

Frustrated, he walked back to his room, noticing that his leg didn't hurt much at all anymore.

THEA WASTED NO TIME IN her investigation of a potential escape route through the bathroom. As soon as she'd turned on the water, she quickly explored the area outside the window. Her heart leaped with excitement when she saw just what she'd hoped for—the bathroom was close enough to the porch roof that with a little careful maneuvering, she could lower herself down and then scale a trellis that enclosed the end of the porch. It was perfect!

Except for one thing. She'd forgotten her shoes in the bedroom. Cursing her stupidity, she raced through ways to get to the bedroom, grab her shoes, and get back to the bathroom without being seen by Amon, or worse, the animal that had dragged her there.

The running water might obscure the sound of her returning to her bedroom. It was worth a chance. She had to get free.

The water was about halfway up the sides of the marble tub, so she figured she had only a few minutes to race to the bedroom and back. Carefully, she opened the door and peaked out. There was no one in sight.

Thea tiptoed toward the room, making sure to be as quiet as possible. About five feet from the room, she stepped on a noisy floorboard she hadn't noticed on her first trip down the hallway and froze. Her heart felt like it was going to leap out of her chest, and she feared the sound of it would alert Amon to her presence it was so loud. Seconds ticked by and no one came out of his room. Believing herself to be in the clear, she scampered to her room and grabbed her shoes.

"Do you wear shoes in the bathtub?"

Thea spun around, shoes in hand, to see Amon standing in the doorway. Oh, God! He'd caught her! What could she say? Quickly, she thought of an excuse for why she was standing fully dressed and with shoes when she'd made such a big deal of having a bath.

"No, that would be silly," she said with a nervous laugh. "I…" she began as she looked down at the shoes in her hands. "My feet get cold after a bath, so I like to have something to cover them. I usually wear slippers, but since I don't have them, I thought I'd use my shoes."

Thea avoided meeting Amon's gaze, sure she'd see disbelief in it. Her eyes flitted nervously around the room. Anywhere but on him.

Amon took two strides and suddenly was standing a foot away from her. Smiling, he reached down and took the shoes from her hands. As he carefully placed them on the floor, Thea knew her plan had failed completely.

Straightened to his full height, Amon picked her up in his arms in one fluid motion. Pressed to his naked chest, she felt suddenly lightheaded. Staring into her eyes, just inches away from her face, Amon explained in a voice that nearly made her melt, "Not to worry. I'll carry you to the bath and then carry you back so your feet don't have to touch the cold floor."

Carrying her to the bathroom, he continued, "And I'll have Gethen get you slippers so tomorrow you don't have to worry." Then with a sly smile, he said, "Not that I mind taking you in my arms for this or any other reason."

Thea felt like her body was on fire. Cold feet? Not a tiny inch of her felt anything but scalding hot! He set her on her feet on the bathroom rug next to the tub and bent down to turn off the water. She watched as his intricately scarred back faced her, and she cringed at the thought of how much pain he must have endured to have a back full of what looked like scars from knife wounds. She wished she could touch him, wished she could heal that part of him.

Amon turned to her, and she looked up to face him. "Is there anything else I can do to make you more comfortable?"

She shook her head and silently wished he would leave her to her misery. She was stuck there, at least for a little longer until she could find a way to stage another escape attempt. But that was only half her torment. Her captor was a gorgeous, incredibly built man who had already rejected her but now seemed to be teasing her into wanting him more. The idea of being caught between the devil and the deep blue sea crept into her mind, and she was unsure which Amon would be.

"I'll listen for the sound of the door opening so I can carry you back to your room," he said in a voice so sexy she had to avert his stare.

"You don't have to do that," she said sheepishly as she stood looking down at her feet.

"Of course I do, Thea. Your feet get cold after a bath.

Remember?"

As he walked past her, she again saw the painful looking reminder of his time in Nil and felt sad at the thought that he'd been tortured. No matter what he was doing to her, he didn't deserve that.

I'll fix that after my bath.

Thea stripped and got into the tub to sink down in the hot water. It felt so wonderfully soothing as it eased the tension in her muscles, and she let her head gently fall back against the edge of the tub. Relaxed, what she'd just thought occurred to her.

What am I thinking? I can't worry about him. I have to find a way out of here.

Feeling like she was back in her right mind, she relaxed once again and looked around the room. It had escaped her attention that there was a fireplace on the far side of the room. She closed her eyes and imagined how amazing it would feel to relax in a bath near a roaring fire. Once again, she immediately chastised herself for forgetting what her primary goal should be.

Unable to enjoy her bath, she climbed out and began to dry off. A knock at the door startled her, and she scrambled to knot the towel around her before she answered it. Opening the door just a crack, she peered out to see Amon standing there, still shirtless.

"Yes?" she asked, her words sounding something far closer to, "What do you want?"

In his lazy, comfortable tone that only made her edgier, he

drawled, "I thought you might need something to wear. I don't have any pants that would fit you, but maybe one of my shirts will."

Thea looked down to see a white dress shirt in his left hand. Thankful but still startled, she grabbed the shirt and closed the door. Through it, as she stripped out of her towel and slipped into her bra and his shirt, she heard him say, "I'll be out here waiting to take you back to your room."

She opened the door dressed in her jeans and his dress shirt that came to the middle of her thighs. As he swept her up into his arms, Thea meekly protested that she could walk. Inside, she loved any touch of his body to hers, but she fought the desire to mold to him, telling herself that he'd made it very clear that what she'd thought she felt for him was impossible.

If only her heart understood.

AMON WAS SURE THE SHIRT had never looked as good on him as it did on her. Long blond waves tumbled over the stiff collar and fell over her shoulders to her back. He thanked God she'd decided to put her pants back on, sure that if he'd seen her just in his shirt he wouldn't have been able to stop himself from taking her right then and there on the bathroom floor.

Walking slowly down the hall, he sensed her discomfort by how rigid she seemed next to him now. Soon, he began to feel his own discomfort because he'd overexerted himself so soon. He reached her bed but that was all he could do. Unable to stand anymore, he placed her on the bed as his body began to give out.

Propping him up, Thea scooted next to him to better support his body. "Amon, sit until you feel better," she said quietly near his ear.

She wrapped her arm around his back, and he gently leaned into her as his breathing grew labored.

"Tell me where it hurts."

In a strangled voice, he groaned, "My ribs."

Thea tenderly pressed her palms to the skin under his chest to take away his pain. Slowly, his breathing returned to normal as she continued to glide her hands over the muscular ridges of his torso.

She stopped, and he hung his head slightly. The pain was gone, but now he was left exhausted. She ran her hands softly over his back, over the raised scar pattern that ran from his shoulders to his waist, as he rejoiced in her touch.

Slowly, her fingertips caressed over each line that marked where someone had carved into his skin as he felt her hands erase the harm inflicted on him. With each gentle touch, she healed him, and the scars began to fade away. Amon leaned his head on hers and sighed deeply as he began to feel the skin on his back return to how it had been before that first night in Nil.

A myriad of sensations flowed through him. Her fingers danced across his skin, bringing it back to life, renewing him. Because of her, the scars that reminded him of that night every time his finger grazed his shoulder disappeared. The depth of her kindness touched his heart, and he began to feel his attraction to her was more than physical. Perhaps what she'd felt was real? But did he dare to believe that a person like him could ever have someone like her? And how could he while Sevine still existed?

As she lovingly stroked his skin back to health, he wished he would never have to leave her side, never be without her sweet touch. How many times had another caressed his body in ways that had delivered such exquisite pleasure and had been followed by moments of pure ecstasy, and how those times paled in comparison to the innocent, selfless touch of the angel who sat next to him, her head lightly resting on his shoulder?

God, he couldn't bear to lose her! He'd sensed she'd planned to attempt something when he'd carried her to the bath, and he'd considered letting her go. Letting her leave to return to the life she'd been forced to leave because of him. He'd convinced himself that's what the decent man he wanted to be would do.

But now the true man he was cried out to keep her with him for as long as he could. To hell with being a destined one! He wanted her next to him. Now. Forever. He wanted to wake up next to this beautiful creature each morning and fall asleep after loving her each night. He didn't care if he was selfish. He wanted someone this good in his life. He knew he didn't deserve her. He didn't care. He wanted her.

Thea's hand left his back and fell to the bed as Amon realized with relief that his pain was gone. He felt healed, but he looked down at the gentle soul next to him and saw the toll her compassion had taken on her, her blue eyes hidden behind their lids and her long, dark lashes resting on her pale cheeks.

Amon ran his finger across her cheek, sweeping away tendrils of pale blond hair from her face. He yearned to lean down and softly touch his lips to hers to show her how much he appreciated her kindness.

"Thea?" he whispered near the top of her head, feeling the silkiness of her hair against his lips.

She stirred and slowly opened her eyes. Looking up at him, she asked," Are your ribs better?"

She straightened up and placed her hands on his sides again to continue healing his painful injuries. Amon took her hands from his body and held them between his own hands. Looking into her eyes, he lowered his head to meet hers and stopped as his mouth brushed her cheek.

"I'm fine, Thea."

Inhaling, he smelled soap and her shampoo, something delicate like honeysuckle. "Why did you heal my back?" he asked quietly next to her ear.

"Because it's what I do. I'm a healer," she whispered softly.

Amon needed to see her face, but she'd turned away as she answered. He couldn't say what he so desperately wanted to say with her avoiding his gaze. Turning her face toward him, he saw her drop her gaze—anything to not look at him.

"Thea, why won't you look at me?"

She remained silent, staring down at the enormous shirt cuffs on her small wrists.

"Thea, look at me."

Turning to face him, she asked in a voice that betrayed how much his words earlier had hurt her, "Why? You've already been very clear. I'm mistaken. It's impossible. So I leave to go to another room, but you follow me, carrying me to and from the bathroom half naked. And now you want to look into my eyes and make me want you even more. Why? So you can tease me and then tell me again how I'm not who you want?"

Amon instantly felt pain race through his limbs. Wincing in agony, he balled his hands into fists and hoped the pain would leave before he passed out. The ache from Thea's emotions caught him by surprise. Because he'd convinced himself he wasn't falling in love with her, he hadn't expected to feel any effect from her emotions. But here the pain was, different from everything else his body was going through from his time in Nil. This was because he'd made her unhappy. And that meant he must be falling in love with her.

"Amon! What's wrong?"

"Nothing," he croaked out. Catching his breath, he remembered what Markku had said—what had worked with Callia—just make her happy.

Thea turned to him and began to frantically seek out the source of his pain, but he stopped her and took hold of her hands. She looked at his eyes staring longingly at hers and relaxed in his grip.

"There's nothing you can do. This isn't something you can heal."

"Amon, what do you mean?" she asked, her voice more

frightened than confused.

Within minutes, as he sat silently with her, the pain had gone and Amon could now say what he'd planned to say. "Thea, I told the truth when I said I already had a destined one. Her name is…well, I don't know what her name is now, but to me she was always who she was when we were first drawn to one another. Sevine. But we grew apart after almost twenty lifetimes, and I haven't seen her since the late 1700s."

"What do you mean 'grew apart'? Why aren't you together?"

Amon wrestled with how much he should tell her about his past. Should he tell her who he'd been for lifetimes—the heartless, selfish prick he'd been? Suddenly, everything he'd ever been came back to haunt him. He'd found someone to care about and now his past could chase her away. He knew the risk. If she couldn't accept his past, he'd lose her. But he knew he had to try to tell her.

"I've manipulated people, hurt people, used my powers to only my benefit."

"Hurt? What kind of hurt?"

Amon hung his head to avoid her wide eyes that seemed to beg for the truth. He had no choice. He had to hope she would see he was a different man now.

"I was responsible for the death of Sevine's human friend. I used my tempuster power to manipulate someone into falling in love with me when I knew she had a destined one she loved and who loved her."

Amon stopped for a moment and then said, "I was in Nil

because I belonged there."

Silently, he waited for her to respond, but for a long time she said nothing. Sure he finally understood what Gethen had tried to tell him earlier, he moved to leave.

Gently, Thea placed her hand on the back of his neck and began to trace the muscles to his shoulders. "Amon, in actuality, I'm not better. I may not have done what you did, but I've let them die."

"No…you don't understand."

"I was born with my powers, Amon. I've never been anything but a healer. But because I'm under the control of the Council, I've been forbidden from helping others they deem unworthy. So I've watched people die all out of blind obedience when I could have saved them. I'm ashamed to say that if Markku hadn't brought me here, I would have refused to help you."

Amon looked at the sadness in her face and knew she was wrong. She was so much better than he, but she was like him in one way. He heard the regret in her voice and understood. They were both blessed with immense power, but neither one had fulfilled the promise of greatness they possessed. Never before in all his lifetimes had he met one who seemed like such a kindred spirit.

He'd finally met someone like him, but it wasn't meant to be. Destiny had already made her choice.

CHAPTER SEVEN

R YU LET HIS WEIGHT FALL back onto the old couch, and he relaxed before dealing with his assignment. As the late afternoon sun streamed into his rooms, it illuminated just how little care he'd taken with his home for the past year. Dust stuck to the tacky circles on the coffee table and settled in the scratches and gouges of the furniture's legs.

On the table next to his beer lay the file on Amon Kalins. Ryu had skimmed it earlier, gleaning some basic information to add to that he'd gained from his meeting with the Council. Kalins was definitely a bigger fish than his usual fare, but he'd be caught for the same reason all his other assignments—but one—had been. Because he was good at his job. Great at his job was more like it. Because with only one exception in all his lifetimes since he'd been released from Nil, he'd never let anyone escape.

Why he'd let that one get by him was something he'd questioned every day for the past year. Never before had he even considered not fulfilling a task he'd been charged with. Until that day, he'd been a machine and a damned efficient one. His job was to catch Aeveren like him—those who'd chosen to break their laws—and deliver them to their punishment, just as he'd been by the bounty hunter who'd captured him.

But Ryu had taken pity on that man the year before. Something in his eyes, in his pleading, had touched him inside and for the first time, he'd chosen not to be who he'd been for four lifetimes. The man's crime was a petty one, he'd comforted himself. People shouldn't be punished for falling in love with humans. He'd never really agreed with mating with them, but then different strokes for different folks. He'd always hated collecting Aeveren women who'd broken this Aeveren edict since invariably they were forced to abandon children. That had never sat right with him. But he'd done his job for the Council of Texas, bringing in Aeveren to answer for their crimes, year after year.

Then he'd gotten that assignment on Halloween the year before and his life changed from one of contentment, if not happiness, to one of misery. All he had to do was bring him in and be done with him. The guy would've been sentenced to a few years in the easy part of Nil, for Christ's sake. He'd done his time for aggravated assault in the real Nil, not the fucking country club the people he caught went to, and he'd come out alive.

Why the hell didn't I just do my job?

Ryu grabbed the file from the table and flipped it open. No, Kalins wasn't just some guy who liked venturing out of his race. Page after page of crimes flowed past his eyes. Murder.

An association with the Soren, a group Ryu knew the Council desperately wanted to eliminate. Assorted lesser crimes of "abusing the trust" of fellow Aeveren.

None of this surprised him. Kalins had been born with his tempuster powers and continued to gain more. As he sat in his living room drinking the last of his beer, Ryu angrily wondered how the Council thought anyone given all that power could ever remain good. He knew he wouldn't be able to. Each time he'd temporarily been given the power needed to capture someone, it had been seductive to want to keep it. Who wouldn't want to take advantage of power, and Kalins had multiple powers.

As much as he may envy or sympathize with him, Ryu knew he had a job to do and completing this job would give him his life back. As he read down the list of places he was suspected of hiding in, he mumbled, "It's either you or me, Amon Kalins. And this time, it's got to be me who wins."

Two hours later he knew everything there was to know about his man. He checked his gear to ensure he had what he'd need. Smiling, Ryu ran his fingers over the talisman that would enable him to travel through time. He'd only been given that power once before, and the person he'd been after had only had his powers for one lifetime, so he'd been pretty easy to catch.

That poor fuck.

Kalins wouldn't be that easy, however. He'd had ample lifetimes to perfect his ability and unlike Ryu's other charge, he was sure to have people in many places and times to help him.

No, Kalins was going to be a challenge, but he knew if a prisoner from Nil with only the powers the Council had given him could capture him just a year earlier, then he certainly could now.

As he prepared to go, Ryu took one last look around. His eyes scanned the nondescript rooms that had been his prison for the last year, and he silently bid that life farewell. When he caught Kalins, he'd be able to return to the life he'd lost when a moment of kindness doomed him and pick up where he'd left off. Hiking the bag up over his shoulder, he closed the door behind him and left for the Council of New York.

THE CHAMBERS OF THE COUNCIL of New York stood in front of him, the beginning of his job to catch Kalins. Located next to all the other local councils, they housed the local council for the New York, New Jersey, and Pennsylvania area, and since his target had a home on the border of two of those states that he frequented more than his homes in the Carolinas and New Mexico, the Council of New York seemed to be the logical place to begin.

As opposed to the size and grandeur of the Council chambers in Nil, the far more meager chambers he currently waited to enter left him unmoved. While the Council members here sat above as they did in Nil, the New York chambers were brighter and far more bureaucratic looking, almost like that of a courtroom. Ryu reasoned this was because like all local councils, New York handled minor cases, such as petty crimes and relations with humans.

Sure isn't like I'm used to.

He waited as the line of people he stood in slowly shrank, forced to hear the beginnings and endings of each person's presentation when the guards opened and closed the chamber doors. Like an assembly line of misery, he and his fellow Aeveren waited for the doors to open to walk forward, Ryu one step closer to beginning his journey back to claim the life he'd left behind.

Over three hours later, he finally entered the chambers of the Council of New York ready to get this portion of his job over with. Frustrated, he stepped up to begin the proceedings only to find that it wasn't just the décor that seemed more bureaucratic. As he stood waiting, the words of the head councilman's assistant told him they weren't going to make this easy on him.

With a hearty chuckle, the head of the Council of New York turned to Ryu and asked, "What are your dealings with this council?"

"I'm here about an escaped prisoner from Nil—Amon Kalins."

The amusement on the councilman's face was obvious by his grin. "Escaped prisoner from Nil? Interesting."

As he spoke, he turned to look left and right down the long table at his fellow council members to share his delight among them.

Ryu felt a surge of anger as he watched the show of petty bureaucratic jealousy exhibited in front of him. He didn't have time for their bullshit.

"Yes, an escaped prisoner. He owns a home in this council's area," he said in a tone he hoped would indicate his distaste for their behavior.

Instead, he got more governmental obfuscation.

"We know nothing of any escaped prisoner, and we can assure you that while we have no experience with losing prisoners, we'd certainly know if one from Nil was in our area."

All Ryu wanted to do was turn around and leave as it was obvious that the Council of New York had no intention of helping him to apprehend his target. In a show of even further Aeveren red tape, they kept him answering questions on every minute detail of Amon Kalins' escape, obviously relishing the failure of the Council of Nil with each answer.

Finally, after they'd exhausted every line of inquiry into a case they had no interest in assisting with, Ryu was excused with no apology for their lack of helpfulness but with a halfhearted good luck with his assignment.

As he left, he hoped he wouldn't have to count on their help for anything in the future. And he knew one council he had no interest in working for once he got his life back.

AMON LAY IN BED SAVORING how good his body felt and wishing Thea was next to him. Even the pain he'd suffer if he upset her would be worth it if she were nearby. After she'd healed him earlier, he'd left her room as she'd fallen asleep, not wanting to but feeling wrong for wanting to remain with her.

He knew he shouldn't let himself want her, but he did.

She was just across the hall—so close, yet so far away. Grimacing, he gave in to his darker nature he'd been fighting and let his mind reach out to hers. He touched her thoughts softly, like a whisper, and waited to find out if he was on her mind.

Afraid to move and miss something, he sat with his head pressed against the headboard, silent except for the sound of his heart beating against his chest. Without realizing it, he held his breath in anticipation of what he'd find.

Long moments passed as he waited for her mind to fully open to his. He knew this was wrong. It was an invasion of a person who he wanted to trust him. But no matter how much guilt he felt for it, he didn't retreat from her mind. He needed to know if she felt love for him as he was growing to feel for her.

A soft caress touched his mind—the slightest thought of him. His heart began to beat wildly. He exhaled softly and panted as he began to sense her thoughts. They came in gentle waves that slowly rolled into his mind and joined with his. Her memory of kissing him in his bed. The feel of his hands pulling her to him as she sat on his lap wanting so much for him to be inside her.

Heat traveled over his skin and his cock swelled. Her memory of how he'd felt—the hardness of him pushed against her—excited him, even more than his recollection of the moment. Her memory showed him how affected she'd been, how much she'd wanted him. His memory only told him how it had felt for him.

He pushed his hand down the front of his pants and fisted his thick erection. His guilt melted away, and he wanted more. More of her thoughts. More of her feelings. More of her.

The memory of her touching him sparked in her head. She replayed healing him, but now her thoughts weren't focused on him as a patient but as a lover. Her fingers skimmed over his skin, and she noted with pleasure how he felt under them, how the friction between them and him excited her.

His breathing became shallow with the desire to make her thoughts reality. By now, even if he wanted to, he couldn't leave her mind. To know she wanted him so badly was like a drug. He needed more. As the thoughts in her mind danced into his, he fought the urge to leave his bed and go to hers. He wanted so much to make her his, but the tiny part of him that held on tenaciously to reality stopped him. He'd have to settle for knowing he'd had an effect on her.

He wanted her to think more of him. He knew he could make it happen. A gentle idea left in her mind of what he would do to her, how he'd come to her to make her body sing with his. But that was pure manipulation, and he wasn't that man anymore. At least he didn't want to be that man with Thea.

As he wrestled with giving her mind a tiny nudge, he felt her mind grow enflamed with her own idea of what it would be like between them.

She was fantasizing about him.

Amon sat still as a statue, his hand motionless as it gripped his now stiff cock. Closing his eyes, he let himself get carried away by the fantasy she was creating in her mind.

She kissed his mouth with a need that almost burned him up. In her mind, he responded with a need of his own she so desperately wanted to fill. She teased him, piquing his desire more, bringing out the male he'd always been and was now fighting.

Excitedly, Amon saw in her mind what kind of lover she wanted him to be. As the fantasy of him as a dominant lover capable of fulfilling her every desire played out in her mind, his hand stroked his length from base to tip. God, he wanted to give her what she wanted!

She fantasized about him taking control of her body, his hands pinning her to the bed as she looked up at him, her eyes urging him on to master her passion. As he held her captive, his mouth traveled to her breasts, softly planting kisses across her neck and shoulders along the way.

Amon heard her voice in her thoughts and his eyes rolled in ecstasy.

"Please...Amon...give me what I need."

Then he heard her answer—what she wanted him to say to her, and he sat riveted to the bed, her thoughts in total control of him.

He lifted his head from her nipple, his lips damp and shiny, and smiled up at her to answer her plea. "Don't worry, Thea. I know what you need," he purred. Without another word, he returned to her nipple to resume the sensual pulls that were driving her out of her mind with desire. She writhed under him, moaning and arching her back toward him to feel the rest of his body touch hers.

"Althea," he moaned. "You taste so good."

As he stayed in her mind, relishing her fantasy, Amon filed away her real name for future use as he continued to stroke his cock. Althea…

He kissed her stomach down to where her pants' button waited to grant him entry. Releasing her hands from his restraints, he slid his forefingers along the inside of the waist of her pants. His touch tickled her, and her body trembled in anticipation of where he'd go next.

She ran her hands over his head, feeling the soft, new growth of hair. From his forehead to the nape of his neck, her fingertips touched him almost reverently, as if he were someone dear to her. Her fingers trailed along the sides of his face and traced the shell of his ear delicately, exciting him by her care.

He looked up under half-closed lids and saw her watching the attention he paid to teasing her. The look in her eyes was one of submission. What he wanted was his for the taking.

As he slowly unbuttoned and unzipped her pants, tugging them off her hips in one slow, smooth motion, he whispered, "I know what my Althea needs."

Still alone in his bed, Amon grew more excited each time he heard the words she put into his mouth. He stretched his long, muscular legs down the bed to ease the tension her thoughts were creating in him, and his stomach muscles flexed as he continued to stroke himself toward sweet release.

With his finger, he traced a line up her damp seam through innocent, white panties. She was ready for him. So ready.

But he wanted her more than ready. He wanted her needy for him. Slowly, he slid his fingers under the dainty edge of her panties, close to where she so desperately wished he would touch. He stroked her soft, moist folds, exciting her more. She was so soft, so delicate under his fingers—so open for him.

Her hands pushed on his head to urge him to take her into his mouth, but he resisted with a groan. He wanted to taste her, but he wanted her to wait just a minute more. Her impatience excited him.

She moaned out his name wishing he'd give her the relief she needed. Spreading her legs wider, she nudged at his mouth to touch her through her panties.

Amon loved that she desired him like this. His nature was to be dominant, but he'd often had to suppress it, particularly with modern women. That Thea could be so strong and caring yet so eager to let him take control of their lovemaking was something that made him want her even more. How far would she let her fantasy take her?

He waited for her to continue, stroking his length with more urgency and wondering if she was touching herself across the hall.

With his thumbs, he opened her up to his eyes, which feasted on the sight of her—soft and pink. He inhaled her delicious fragrance and pressed his lips to her delicate skin, unwilling to wait any longer. Slowly at first, he let his tongue glide over her sex, hearing soft moans coming from above as his tongue created sensations that traveled straight to her core.

Amon felt himself getting close. He wanted to come as he listened to her fantasy of his mouth pleasuring her, but he wanted more, if there were to be more. Her fantasy was controlling more than just his thoughts now.

A gentle suck on her swollen nub sent her over the edge into a million pieces, and Amon fought to control his own orgasm, wanting to see if she'd continue. As she recovered in her fantasy, his silent wish was granted and she moved to give him pleasure.

She swirled her pink tongue over the tip of his cock and then slowly took only the head into her mouth, sucking tenderly as she looked up at him with wide blue eyes. Her hand gripped him and slid over his skin, her touch feeling so good.

He watched as her blond head and her sensuous waves moved down around his body and back up again. The soft touch of her hair draping over his thighs sent shivers up his back. She slid her left hand out from under her veil of hair and ran it over his abdomen, gently raking her nails across his skin.

"Thea," he moaned as he watched her slide her lips to the base of his cock. He fisted his hands in her hair and tugged it gently to direct her speed. She didn't fight or resist, allowing him to set the pace of her movements.

Amon needed release but fought his body's demand by willing himself to stay in her mind when she fantasized about climbing on top of him, ready to have what they'd begun earlier in his bedroom.

Thea whispered softly in his ear. "Amon, mine. My destined one."

God, how he wished that were true! He heard the sweetness in her sexy voice, heard the desire not only for him to physically be hers but to truly be with her. But he pushed that from his mind and concentrated on what he knew he could be for her, if he'd let himself...

Thea's fantasy and his desire merged into one, and he let his body go as his cock spilled over his stomach and hand. Better than any fantasy of his own, her thoughts had given him more pleasure than he'd had in a long time. Satisfied, he cleaned himself up and closed his eyes to relax.

Amon silently summoned Gethen, but found he was still away getting supplies and clothes for Thea. Thea...his time listening to her thoughts had been utterly enjoyable and more than ever he wanted her, but that part of him that still clung to the idea that he could be a decent man stopped him from stalking over to her room and making love to her like no one else had in all her lifetimes.

That part was also the part of him that held out for the tiniest glimmer of hope that he'd been freed from the cold loneliness his destined one had imposed upon him. Was it possible Sevine had moved on?

Reaching out to Markku, he sought to find out the answer. In seconds, he heard the heavy footsteps of the magickian as he plodded up the stairs toward his room.

Markku timidly poked his head through the crack in the door.

"You need something, big...uh, Amon?"

Nodding, Amon ordered, "Close the door and get in here.

I have a job for you."

Markku closed the door and began to listen with interest to the task he was charged with.

CHAPTER EIGHT

THEA STRETCHED HER BODY DREAMILY on the four poster bed, satisfied with her fantasy. Never before had she met anyone like Amon, and she was sure he was the one destined for her. However, she also knew she wouldn't simply stay trapped at his home wishing he'd realize the gift he'd been given.

She knew leaving would be dangerous, and he'd come find her. At least she hoped he would.

Thea listened as someone climbed the steps, and she froze in panic that the brute who'd kidnapped her was coming to her room. She analyzed the footsteps and knew they weren't Amon's or Gethen's. Neither man was so heavy on his feet. They had to be Markku's. Terrified, she sat up on the bed and waited, ready to defend herself but hopeful that Amon would save her.

Gradually, the sound passed her room and when she heard Amon's door open, she breathed a deep sigh of relief. Her muscles relaxed, and she unclenched her hands from the fists she'd unconsciously made. She was safe, for the moment.

Amon's door closed, and she listened again, terrified for the man's footsteps but heard none. Where had he gone? Thea's mind raced to the only logical conclusion: he was in Amon's room. Even more importantly, this meant no one was guarding the door downstairs because Gethen had been sent to run errands. Adrenaline pumped through her body. Now was her chance to escape!

Knowing she had only seconds, she grabbed her shoes from where Amon had placed them earlier and tiptoed to the bedroom door. She listened closely but heard no one in the hallway. Praying whatever Amon was doing behind his door would keep him distracted, she slowly turned the doorknob and opened the door just a crack. As she peered out into the hallway, she squeezed her shoes in her hand. She was ready this time!

Holding her breath, she stepped out into the hallway, fearful her next step might be on the squeaky floorboard but sure she had to take the chance. Each silent step to the stairs produced a rush of relief that coursed through her. She took the steps, careful to make no noise and felt such utter joy when she reached the main floor that she wanted to shout. Only a few more steps and she'd be free.

The fear that Gethen would find her just as she was so close to freedom that she could taste it came over her as she opened the front door, but a quick look around told her she'd done it. She'd escaped!

Thea barely had her shoes on before her feet were running down the road from Amon's house. The November chill hit her through his dress shirt, but nothing could take away from the feeling she was experiencing. Her brain gave her body one command over and over. Run! She had no idea where she was; she had no way home. She didn't even have money. But she was free.

MARKKU LOOKED AT AMON QUIZZICALLY. "Are we talking about the spell broad? The one who cursed you to have to be nice to any woman you're in love with?"

Amon hated talking to Markku. Just the sound of the greasy man's voice irritated him. He'd just spent ten minutes explaining exactly what he wanted him to do—a simple task really—and now he was forced to endure the usual inane series of questions that came with dealing with him.

"Yes," he said through gritted teeth.

Markku scrunched up his face as if he'd just tasted a lemon for the first time. "And you want me to find her?"

Amon wondered why anyone in the Soren kept this guy around. In utter frustration, he began to explain for the second time what he needed Markku to do.

"Yeah, yeah. I know what you want me to do. I just don't see why."

A flash of pure rage rose up in Amon, and he wanted to strangle the greasy man in front of him, but then he'd have no one to do what he needed. Reluctantly, he relaxed and worked to keep his tone calm.

"I already told you. I want to know if I still have a destined one. I've recently had a sense that I may not."

Markku seemed placated by this answer and a thoughtful look passed over his face. He leaned up against the door and appeared to consider what he'd just heard as if any of it were negotiable.

"Okay. I'm sure my guy in the Directorate can give us what we want, but I'm going to need some more information about her. And some cash. A lot of it because I have no doubt anyone checking into anyone even remotely connected to you now will be taking a huge risk."

"Fine. Have Gethen give you what you need. As for information, the last time I knew her she was Frederika Blake and lived in Hinwick in Bedfordshire, England in the late 1700s. She was my destined one for seventeen lifetimes at that point."

Amon thought for a moment of the description he'd just given. Seventeen lifetimes. When she'd come to him as Sevine all those lifetimes ago, they'd been so happy. Even now, as he thought about the memories they'd created, the children they'd brought into the world, a small smile crept onto his face.

But somewhere along the way that happiness had turned into something hurtful and ugly, and he knew it had happened because of him. She hadn't changed so much as grown tired of his ways. He'd been warned that his time with her would be a repeat of his lifetimes with his second destined one if he didn't change.

"Seventeen!" Markku exclaimed and then whistled. "God

bless you and save me from a fate like that."

Markku's insult brought Amon back to the present, and he sat up in his bed staring at the man and wondering in disgust why he hadn't left yet.

"Can I ask you something, Amon?"

Sure he didn't want to hear Markku's question but just as sure he was too tired to scare the hell out of him so he'd leave, Amon simply stared back at him and Markku took the lack of any verbal threat as approval to ask his question.

"Does this have anything to do with the girl?"

Amon shrank his eyes into slits, letting Markku know he'd gone too far, so he hastily added, "Because I just wanted to say I was sorry for threatening her. And if I hurt her when I was bringing her here. I don't know what she said, but I was just doing what Gethen told me to do so we didn't lose you."

As he spoke, he fingered the bandage on his hand and looked down at the floor, and Amon knew he was at least somewhat sincere in what he said. Markku was a toady and any number of other repellent things, but he wasn't truly a person who would harm a female intentionally.

That didn't mean he wanted to have a bonding session with the man, though, so Amon waved his hand and rolled over to avoid any more discussion with him. He was tired and wished to revisit Thea's thoughts if he couldn't see her.

Closing his eyes, he realized he was even too tired to do that and drifted off to sleep thinking how much he hoped Markku would come back with the right answer.

PAIN STABBED IN THEA'S SIDES, and she slowed down to catch her breath next to a group of bushes. She'd run her fastest for fifteen minutes, but she knew she wasn't safe yet. At any moment, they'd realize she was gone, if they hadn't already, and would track her down.

A twinge of sadness pinched at her when she thought of how Amon would feel when he found out she'd left. Their last conversation had been as kind as he'd been to her in her time there, and she knew he'd be hurt by her leaving. In truth, leaving hurt her too, but until he saw what they were meant to be, she couldn't wait, a hostage in his home.

What if he sent the same man to find her and bring her back? She believed Amon when he promised her she'd be safe as long as she was with him, and she knew that included keeping his henchman away from her.

But I'm not with him anymore.

Thea drew a deep breath and pushed away the sadness that had crept into her heart. She'd see Amon again. She just hoped he'd understand why she had to leave.

She made her way to the nearest town and found a coffee shop on the first main road. The Cuppa Coffee Shop was empty, except for a waitress and one female sitting at the counter, and Thea hurriedly walked to the back of the restaurant just in case Gethen was still nearby running his errands.

As she sat at the pale green Formica table, a heaviness settled inside her. He'd sent Gethen to get her slippers.

Stop it! You were being held against your will! Do not feel bad for saving yourself!

What she did feel especially bad about was not performing as a healer. She knew he'd recover fully as she'd healed him sufficiently already, but it would take longer than if she were there for him. For that, she was truly sorry.

"Honey, what can I get you?"

Thea looked up and saw a top heavy older woman with teased white hair like cotton candy and pink stained lips. The waitress had a pen and order tablet and was ready to hear Thea's choices from the combination paper menu and placemat placed on the table in front of her.

In reality, she didn't want anything, even though she hadn't eaten in hours. Amon had sent Gethen to her room with food every few hours, and she'd finally given in when he brought the last tray and enjoyed a turkey sandwich and potato chips. What she really needed from the woman in front of her was information and a telephone.

"Just a coffee, I guess. Can you tell me the name of this town?"

"Cochecton, honey. Are you lost?"

"No. Do you have a phone I can use?"

"There's a pay phone near the bathroom."

Thea ran her hands over her pants pockets hoping she'd left a spare dollar or two in them. Feeling something in the right one, she reached in to find a twenty-dollar bill. Thrilled, she looked up and smiled.

"Can I get change?"

"Sure, hon. Say, is that your boyfriend's shirt? He must be

a big, strappin' man," the waitress replied with a wink as she turned to get her coffee.

Thea ran her hands down the sleeves and fingered the cuffs as she thought about the waitress's word for Amon.

Boyfriend.

Returning with her coffee and change for the phone, the waitress smiled and went back to her discussion with the woman at the counter. Thea took a sip of lukewarm coffee that tasted like it had sat in the pot since the day before and pushed the cup and saucer away from her. Calling her sister was more important than a cup of coffee anyway.

"THEA! WHERE ARE YOU? I'VE been worried sick!"

As she listened to her sister's fear coming through the phone loud and clear, Thea wished she could explain all that had happened in the past few days, but she knew she didn't have the time. Every second she spent at the diner kept her in danger of being found.

"Kat, I'll explain everything, but I need you to come get me. How soon can you get to the town of Cochecton?"

"Where?"

Thea heard her sister tapping on her computer keyboard searching for directions.

"Google maps say you're seventy-five minutes away from me. I'm getting in my car right now." Kat paused and the phone grew quiet. "Thea, are you okay?"

"I'm fine, Kat. Just get to the Cuppa Coffee Shop in Cochecton as fast as you can. I'll be inside."

"Okay. Don't worry. I'll drive fast," her sister reassured her.

Thea hurried into the ladies' room and closed herself in one of the stalls. She knew Kat would make the trip in record time since she always drove fast. If Kat was behind the wheel, wherever you were going became a rollercoaster ride of thrills. For once, she was happy that her sister was a speed demon.

Fifty minutes later Thea heard the bells on the door to the coffee shop jingle. Peaking out of the ladies' room to see her sister standing near the counter, she motioned to Kat to come into the bathroom, hoping she'd noticed anyone outside.

"Thea," she said as she wrapped her arms around her. "What's going on?" Looking her sister over, she continued, "And whose shirt is that?"

"I'll tell you later. Right now, I need to know if you saw anyone outside."

Kat knitted her eyebrows. "Thea, were you kidnapped?"

"Kat!"

"All right. No, I didn't see anyone."

"Are you sure you didn't see a man with black hair and a scar down the side of his face or a greasy man about five foot eight?"

Thea watched as her sister shook her head. There was a chance she'd actually gotten away.

"Okay. Then let's get to your car and get out of here."

THEA CLOSED HER EYES NOT only to block out the usual fear she experienced in the passenger seat next to her sister but also to deter Kat from wanting to talk anymore about what she'd been through. Thea knew the vague explanation she'd offered wouldn't suffice forever, but she truly hoped her closed eyes would convince her sister to let her curiosity rest for a while.

As they rode over rural roads, Thea's mind vaguely registered the sounds of the tires against the pitted pavement and the whirring sound of the wind whipping by the car. She wanted to shut her mind off from thinking, especially about Amon, but she could think of nothing else. She pictured the look on his face when he found she was gone, unsure of whether she should cast him as hurt or angry. Was she just flattering herself by thinking he'd be more hurt than anything else? Before their time together in her room, she'd have said yes, but the way he'd touched her, the things he'd said made her think otherwise.

As she thought of Amon, the beginning notes of a song filtered out of the car's stereo. Thea smiled at how it reminded her of Amon, not because he'd been what the song called a "devil" to her but because of what she knew her sister would say if she told her how she felt about him. A much younger Aeveren in just her tenth lifetime, Kat had no idea of the people Thea had met in her many lifetimes. Not everyone was as wonderful as Kat. In fact, not everyone was even as wonderful as the three men who'd held her captive for the past two days, Thea thought as she remembered another time in her history when she'd been forced to heal someone.

"He must live! Heal him!" the Tsar's guard bellowed next to her head, so loud her ears began to ring.

"I cannot help him if you continue to berate me," she said looking up at him. "I'll do what I can, but yelling at me won't help him."

"What is your name, healer?" the guard asked as he adjusted his hold on his gun.

"Yevtsye Karevshenko, sir."

"And you are the local healer here?" he asked as his eyes scanned her small house in disgust.

"I am. There isn't another healer until you reach the border."

The guard seemed even more disgusted by this news and snorted before going outside to speak to the other guards.

Turning to the man who lay across her table, she gently ran her hands over his head. He'd been rendered unconscious after a mysterious attack had thrown him from his horse and her Aeveren neighbors, seeing the Russian Tsar Nicholas I was a fellow Aeveren, directed his guards to bring him to her.

For more than a half hour, he'd laid there unconscious while Yevtsye tried to revive him and dealt with his guard's intimidation and impatience. She'd examined him but found nothing physically wrong, except for his inability to wake.

Over and over, she touched his head hoping to sense some feeling of pain but felt nothing. She moved her hands to his torso, opening the top of his heavy military uniform coat. Carefully, she unbuttoned each shiny gold button until she was able to see his white uniform shirt underneath. As she moved to lift it, the guard returned and placed the end of the gun's barrel in her back.

"What are you doing?" he barked.

Terrified, she slowly lifted her hands and began to explain. "I cannot find anything wrong with his head. I want to check his chest and stomach." As she spoke, her voice wavered as the feel of the gun in her back began to hurt.

The guard retreated to the other side of the table and watched her movements carefully. Slowly, she lifted her patient's shirt to examine his skin for any evidence of illness or injury. Her hands moved over his rough skin sprinkled with thick black hair, and she noted each section of his body until she turned to the guard.

"There is no reason for him to not wake. I've checked him thoroughly, and I can find nothing."

Enraged, the guard lunged at her over the patient's legs, pushing her back against the wall. As she pleaded for mercy, he slapped her face repeatedly, causing her to cry out in pain. Finally, he pulled her by the hair back toward the Tsar and held her there.

"Heal him or die. It's that simple."

Tears rolled down over her cheeks and fell onto the man's chin and neck as she prayed for a miracle to save both the Tsar's life and hers. Nothing in her abilities as a healer seemed to help her revive him.

Beneath her, she saw the slight flutter of his eyelashes as he began to wake. Hoping to God he wasn't about to die, she gently stroked his face as she whispered to him.

"Tsar, please wake. Are you well?"

The patient's dark brown eyes opened slowly, and Yevtsye

thanked God for hearing her prayers. Gruffly, he asked the guard, "Ivan, where am I?"

"My lord, right outside the village where you were thrown from your horse."

Slowly, the Tsar raised himself to sit upright and looked at Yevtsye as if to study her. He turned to face his man and ordered, "Get the guard ready. I'm ready to travel."

Ivan bowed and left to alert his men of the plans, and the Tsar said, "Did he hurt you?"

Silently, she nodded and touched her hand to her still stinging cheek.

"I'm sorry, healer. Ivan isn't Aeveren. He has no respect for what you do."

"He threatened to kill me if I couldn't heal you, but I found no injuries or illness to heal."

Standing, he held his hand out to her and explained, "I have the shaking sickness my mother had. Nobody but my personal healer knows this, but I foolishly left him at home."

Bowing his head slightly, the Tsar apologized for inconveniencing her and left with his men without another word.

What she'd gone through at Amon's was nothing compared to having her life threatened by a Russian soldier. Thea thought about the time she'd spent at Amon's house, wishing she could tell Kat the wonderful news that finally she'd been given a destined one. Unfortunately, even he didn't believe that was true.

CHAPTER NINE

———— ✧ ————

OUTSIDE IN THE HALLWAY, AMON heard Gethen return.

"Miss?" Gethen called through the closed bedroom door across the hall.

Greeted by silence, Gethen repeated his question only louder. Behind him a door opened, and he turned to face Amon standing in the doorway.

"Gethen, what are you doing?" he snapped.

Stunned by Amon's tone, he quickly answered, "I was trying to give Thea her new clothes."

Amon knew he shouldn't be uncomfortable with his former servant's actions. No matter what Gethen was, he'd always been loyal and more a friend than an employee.

"I'm sorry. It must be the pain I'm in," Amon lied.

The two men stood awkwardly looking first at one another and then the hallway floor. After a few moments of tense silence, Amon was thankful Gethen began to speak again.

"Where is Markku?"

"I sent him on an errand for me. Here, let me take those clothes."

As Amon took the pile of clothes out of his arms, he was sure the other man saw the apprehension in his face. Eager to escape the situation his jealously had created, he moved toward Thea's door.

A feeling of guilt came over him and he turned to Gethen. "Thank you for doing this for me, Gethen. I can always count on you."

The man smiled, but Amon sensed his outburst had offended his friend and another rush of guilt passed through him. He knew full well there had been no one as true to him in his many lifetimes and treating him like a second class citizen who hadn't earned his trust time and again was insulting.

But Amon found himself jealous, nonetheless, something he hadn't felt in lifetimes.

As he gently tapped on the door to Thea's room, he anxiously waited to see her after what he'd seen in her mind earlier. He hoped against hope that Markku would return with the answer he wanted that would vindicate the feelings he'd begun to have for her.

"Thea?"

Behind him, Gethen whispered, "Maybe she's worn out from healing you. You did say it took a toll on her."

Amon didn't respond to the comment and knocked again, this time harder.

"Thea?"

Turning the antique doorknob, he opened the door just a crack and peered in. It only took a quick sweep of the room to see no one was there. He thrust open the door and let it bang off the wall. In a few strides he crossed the room, but it was no use.

She was gone.

Fearfully, Gethen stood in the doorway, while Amon fought to control his emotions. Not fully healed, he immediately felt exhausted from the anger and betrayal that raced through him. When he finally turned to face Gethen, he knew his eyes had changed to near black he was so angry.

"I want her found. Now!" he barked.

"I'll need Markku's help. I don't know where he found her, Amon," Gethen said plaintively.

"Then get him back here," Amon growled.

Gethen disappeared to contact Markku, and Amon sat down on Thea's bed. That's how he thought of it. Thea's. He looked down at the clothing in his lap. Thea's clothes.

How did I get so attached in such a short time?

Ten minutes later, Gethen roused him from daydreaming about Thea to announce Markku's arrival. His strength returned, Amon bounded past him into the hall, stopping dead as he collided with Markku.

"Come with me," he ordered and yanked the man by the arm into his room, slamming the door behind them.

Markku stood nervously with his back pinned to the door as Amon paced back and forth in front of the bed.

"What did you find out?" Amon seethed.

Markku breathed a sigh of relief. "Yeah, yeah. I had my man check into your lady. She's gone."

Amon stopped next to the bedpost and steadied himself

against it. "Gone?" His voice was barely more than a whisper.

"Yeah, something she did for a child—you know, a selfless act, and poof! She's moved on."

Amon stared at a point on the far wall and exhaled heavily. "When?"

"While you were in....the summer," Markku answered awkwardly.

Amon waved Markku out of the room and sat down on the bed. Now that he'd gotten the answer he'd wanted, he felt a sadness he hadn't expected. Sevine was gone. The destined one he'd spent lifetimes with, the woman who'd been his wife for almost half of his time on Earth was gone.

His shoulders sagged as he dropped his head and sighed his grief. Much of what he'd been to her had been negative, and after the initial anger at her dismissal of him as her destined one in their seventeenth lifetime together, Amon had missed her and mourned the end of them. Now he mourned his behavior once again.

A soft knock on the door fifteen minutes later brought him back to the present. "Amon, may I come in?"

Gethen's tone sounded worried, so Amon quickly opened the door. "Come in."

Seated on the bed again, Amon stared off in the distance. In a voice that sounded faraway, he quietly said, "Sevine's gone."

"I'm sorry, Amon."

In what seemed to be a new habit for them, the two men remained in silence for a long moment before Gethen spoke.

"Markku is going to take me to where he found Thea, and I'll bring her back."

Amon took a moment to process what he'd just heard and then thought he heard an edge in Gethen's voice—an edge that concerned him.

"I'm going. We'll leave immediately."

Gethen's expected protest came before Amon finished his statement, but Amon's hand in front of him stopped his speech.

"Get ready."

As Gethen turned to leave the room, Amon added, "And I'll handle bringing Thea back."

Turning to face him, Gethen fixed his gaze on Amon. "As you wish." The silent word master hung in the air as he turned back toward the door and walked out of the room.

As he sat alone, Amon had to admit to himself that jealousy wasn't the only emotion he was experiencing with Gethen regarding Thea. He also felt fear.

Lifetimes with Gethen had dulled his memory of the circumstances surrounding the man's entrance into his world, but Thea's arrival and the hope that she could be his destined one brought the events of his meeting Gethen into sharp focus for Amon. What had for a very long time meant almost nothing to him now seemed far more important because of his feelings for Thea. As the long forgotten memory of a much younger Gethen's actions came back to him, Amon's need to protect her pressed onto his heart.

The Irish countryside glowed under the silver touch of

moonlight and the warm July air hung heavily on Riordan as he slowly led his horse along the path. To his left, in the shadows, he heard the soft rustling of branches. On his guard in the darkness, he warily watched the wooded area for highwaymen lying in wait to descend upon a traveler like himself. Ready to snap the reins and escape at a moment's notice, his heart pounded in anticipation of the next sound. The horse sensed his apprehension and tensed under him as if to assure him that it understood his thoughts and knew how to react, if necessary.

The final leg of his journey home, this section of countryside was by far the most remote. Despite being armed, he preferred not to kill anyone that night. As he ambled closer to a bend in the path where wooded areas banked both sides of the road, he quietly took his gun in hand.

As he rode between the woods, to his right he heard the faint sound of a moan and then another. His hand tighter now on his weapon, he looked into the darkness of the trees and spied the small, yellow light of a fire. A sense of relief washed over him momentarily as he considered the unlikelihood of highwaymen announcing their presence with something as obvious as a fire.

While he reasoned the owners of the fire to instead be vagabonds, he heard moaning again growing louder as he continued. If someone were hurt, he should stop to aid them, but while he debated the safety of stopping for an injured stranger, a woman's scream pierced the night, sending a shock through his body. In a flash, he had his horse at full gallop toward the sound of the woman in danger.

Moments later, he found the source of not only the screams

but the moans. A woman lay on the forest floor in a clearing just off the path. Her long, black hair trailed over her shoulders and nearly hid the knife that stood buried in her chest, surrounded by a red stain that had begun to spread over her pale skin. Naked, her body showed signs of the activity she'd been engaged in at the time of her death.

As he climbed down from his horse, he noticed the aura that surrounded all Aeveren begin to fade from near her body. In seconds, she'd vanish as all Aeveren did upon their deaths, so he silently said a quick prayer of hope for her safe passage to her next life. Without a sound, she left that lifetime, and he stood staring down at the bloodstained ground in sadness.

The sound of footsteps behind him startled him out of his grief, and he spun around, gun aimed forward, to see a young man with black hair and a slash from the outside corner of one eye to his mouth. He stood bare-chested, the blood from his wound running down his chin.

"I didn't mean to kill her," he said in a sad voice.

Riordan studied the man in front of him for a moment and slowly lowered his weapon. The man before him wasn't Aeveren as he had no aura surrounding him. However, this stranger had killed an Aeveren, and for that Riordan knew he had a duty to his people to see that this murderer of his kind faced justice.

"She wouldn't accept me—my kind—but I loved her," the man said softly as he fell to the ground where the woman's body had lain. "My Aine…"

"You killed the woman you loved." As he spoke the words, Riordan felt them slice into him. He reached into his pocket for *a handkerchief and handed it to him.*

The man looked up at him sadly as he took the cloth and pressed it to his cheek. "She refused my love because I'm not one of you."

Stunned by the stranger's ability to know he was Aeveren, Riordan asked, "How do you know what I am?"

"You show the mark of all Aeveren, the aura."

"But you are not Aeveren, so how is it you see what only those of my kind can?"

"I am Sidhe. We can see what marks all peoples."

"Why wouldn't Aine accept you? We, Aeveren, have no quarrel with the Sidhe."

"I could never be her destined one."

Riordan watched as tears ran down the man's face and felt a pang of sympathy for him. No, he could never be her destined one just as Riordan could never get back the love of his destined one.

"I will not force you to chase me. Punish me as I did my beloved Aine or take me to where your people may punish me."

The resignation in his voice touched Riordan. Yes, he was supposed to follow Aeveren law, but he had never been strictly law abiding.

"Why not simply leave her?" he asked.

The emotion in the Sidhe's voice signaled his anguish. "Have you never loved a woman before? Loved her so much you could think of no other in your arms? Loved her so much the thought of her being in another's arms made you mad?"

Riordan silently nodded. He had loved Sevine like that. And now he was alone, dismissed from her life, a foreigner in a country he now called home.

"What's your name, Sidhe?"

"Gethen."

"Gethen, let us go to your people for your protection or you will be surely punished by mine."

He looked down into the confused face of the Sidhe and felt the connection between them. Fate had brought these two creatures, so very different but so similar too, into one another's lives for a reason Riordan suspected was important.

Amon sat remembering when he learned of Gethen's earlier murders of Aeveren women when he was taken to the Sidhe. However, even two additional killings of his kind couldn't force him to abandon the Sidhe to Aeveren justice. He learned later that he'd murdered those other women out of hatred for destined ones too.

Even now he didn't regret protecting his friend, but the possibility of Thea being his destined one brought the memories of Gethen's crimes back into Amon's mind. In all the lifetimes he'd shared with him, he'd never had a destined one in his life. There had been many Aeveren women, and he'd always kept a close watch on Gethen around them, but none had been his destined one.

He'd heard Gethen threaten Thea when she arrived and wondered if he'd sensed something different about her before even Thea knew what she was. As much as he cared for his friend, he'd protect Thea above all else.

Amon descended the stairs to the front door and looked

around for Gethen and Markku. Arguing all the way down the hallway, they stopped just as they met up with him at the door.

"Amon, Gethen says you insist on coming. Why? I got her once. I can get her again."

"No."

Markku shrugged. "Okay, but are you sure you're strong enough?"

"I'll be fine. Where am I focusing on?"

"Alpine Drive. Hunter, New York."

"Let's go," Amon said gruffly as he grabbed Gethen's arm to teleport him.

THEA SAT WITH HER LEGS crossed under her watching reruns of Charlie's Angels. The tea her sister made her before she'd left was cool enough to finally drink, and she took a mouthful, savoring the lemon and extra honey just as she liked it. Amon was never far from her mind, and she replayed the recent events with him again and again, focusing on the memory of how his body felt under her fingertips.

She had to think of that. She'd lost her job at the daycare, as she'd expected, and thinking of her new status as one of the unemployed masses wasn't how she wanted to spend the rest of her night. She'd loved working with the children, and the loss of her time with them hurt even worse than just being fired.

Usually, when she felt down, she talked things over with Kat to feel better and gain new perspective, but if she talked to her about losing her job, she'd have to talk about what had happened and her feelings for Amon. She barely understood them herself, so how could she explain them to her?

Thea knew in her heart he was her destined one, but this was all so new to her. She'd loved men before in her forty-five lifetimes, but those relationships had developed over time with love being the result of months of shared experiences. Now she felt more in love with Amon than she'd ever felt with any of those men, and she hadn't even known him for a week. Was this what meeting your destined one was like? Or was she just foolish or suffering from a case of Stockholm Syndrome?

All those lifetimes she'd waited for the kind of love she'd seen so many others experience, and now that it seemed she'd finally been blessed with it, she was alone and confused.

The sound of the phone ringing forced her to push aside her thoughts, and she answered it to hear her sister's voice on the other end of the line.

"Thea, I wanted to check on you to make sure you're okay."

"Kat, I'm fine," she answered in a voice she knew wasn't convincing in the least.

"Honey, you don't sound fine. Won't you talk to me? What happened to you, Thea?"

Thea heard the kindness in her sister's voice and something in her made her want to talk about what had happened.

"Kat, I was taken to heal someone."

"Oh, Thea. Not again. This happened before. Why can't

they just leave you alone?"

"Because I'm a healer, Kat. That's what I am in our world."

"That doesn't mean people can just take you whenever they need you! You aren't everyone's personal healer, for Christ's sake!"

Thea remained silent knowing the anger in her sister's voice wasn't directed at her. She loved how wonderfully protective her younger sister was, even if she was wrong.

"Did they at least treat you well after kidnapping you?"

Thea wondered how she should answer that. Markku had threatened her, as had Amon's friend Gethen. But Amon had been kind, even when he was telling her he couldn't be her destined one.

"They were all very kind," she lied.

"So you healed whoever was hurt and they thanked you but couldn't bring you back home, instead leaving you at some greasy spoon in some small town seventy miles away from your house? What the fuck is that about? And you can't charge people for the healing you do? That's just bullshit, Thea."

Kat continued to rail against her sister's Aeveren power and the inconsiderate nature of their kind, but Thea had stopped listening and instead was focused on the three familiar male figures whose faces looked far too serious making their way up the sidewalk to her front door. Jumping off the couch, Thea ran to put her shoes on.

"I have to go, Kat. I'll talk to you later after I get some rest, okay?"

"Okay, Thea. I'm sorry I blew up a bit. I didn't mean to

upset you."

"It's okay. I'll talk to you later. Bye."

Thea hung up and searched frantically for her purse. She raced over to the closet and slipped her coat on, hoping she could sneak out the back door and escape, but the knock on her front door made her freeze in her tracks. If she ran now, they'd catch her, but she couldn't just stand waiting to be kidnapped again.

Her stubborn streak took over and she grabbed her keys on her way toward the back door. As she reached to turn the doorknob, she felt a hand touch her lightly on her shoulder and then heard his voice.

"Hello, Thea."

CHAPTER TEN

A MON FELT THEA'S BODY STIFFEN at his touch and even without probing her mind he knew he needed to brace himself for the onslaught of her emotions. As she turned around slowly to face him, he was secretly thrilled to notice she was still wearing his shirt.

Maybe this won't be so bad.

"How the hell did you get in here? And who invited you in?" she snapped as she stood toe to toe with him, her hands on her hips and her blue eyes blazing.

Amon saw the genuine displeasure he'd caused and rethought the joke he wanted to make about not having to be invited in like a vampire. It was going to be as bad as he'd anticipated. And as painful if she continued to be angry.

"I'm sorry, Thea. I didn't mean to frighten you." In the hopes of diffusing the situation, he intentionally focused on softening his tone.

"Frighten me? Is that what you think you did? First, you have your goon kidnap me as if I'm your personal healer created just to heal you, and now you're back to kidnap me yourself! Frightened? I'm so past frightened, Amon."

If her emotions weren't beginning to take their toll on him physically, he might be turned on by Thea's outburst. He liked her like this. Feisty. Brave. A perfect match for him. Her emotions were beginning to cause him great pain, though, and in his still weakened state, he knew he wouldn't be able to sustain much more of her anger.

"Please, Thea. Don't be angry. I missed you."

As he spoke, he took her hand in his and stroked his thumb over the soft skin of her knuckles.

"Amon, you broke into my house."

Smiling happily as he felt her anger abate just a little, he answered, "Technically, I didn't break in because I didn't use the door."

Thea looked at him with a confused look that made him want to explain, if only because it seemed to have calmed her down.

"I teleported in. So no breaking, really."

"Teleported?"

"Yes, it's one of my powers."

"One?" Thea seemed to consider what he'd said and then continued. "I don't care. You can't just come into my house without being invited in."

"I'm sorry. Can we sit down and talk?"

Amon saw her resolve weaken and knew he'd won her over for the moment. Still holding her hand, he walked with her to the couch and sat down next to her.

"Your house is very nice." His words were predictable, but

he hoped to avoid another emotional outburst from her that would be sure to hurt.

Thea turned her body toward him. "Amon, why are you here, if it's not to kidnap me again?"

Her refusal to let him set the pace made him smile. He was going to have to tell her about Sevine.

"I missed you. I wish you hadn't left."

"Amon, I can't just stay at your house for the rest of my life. I have a job…"

Thea caught herself and corrected what she'd said. "Well, I had a job before you sent that man to kidnap me and you held me captive."

Amon felt her sadness cover him, and he felt truly sorry for what had happened. "I never intended for that to happen. I will compensate you well to make up for everything. I promise."

While he spoke, he looked directly into her eyes and wished they were back at his house together. Or better yet, at his home in Greece, somewhere he was sure she'd enjoy.

"You can't just do things that hurt others and then simply throw money at the problem. I loved my job, and now I've lost it."

Thea's sadness stabbed at him now, and he closed his eyes to ward off the pain. Unlike before, this was more an ache than searing pain.

"Are you okay, Amon?" he heard her say and he opened his eyes.

Wincing, he nodded, but she placed her hands on his and

held them. "Where is the pain located?" she asked when she couldn't figure out how to heal him.

"You can't heal this, Thea. This is the pain I explained to you before."

Gently squeezing his hands, she said quietly, "I can heal your pain. Please tell me where it's coming from."

There would be no explaining this away, so he decided to tell her the truth.

"Thea, you can't heal it because you cause it. Or more specifically, your unhappiness causes it. My destined one cursed me to feel unrelenting pain each time I make you unhappy."

"Why? I thought you said you hadn't even seen her in lifetimes."

"I haven't."

"Then why curse you with something from me?"

Amon sighed and knew he couldn't avoid telling her the most important part of Sevine's curse.

"She didn't. The curse is more general than that. It affects me with anyone I love."

Lifetimes of confidence seemed to evaporate in seconds as he watched Thea's face darken.

"Love me? Is that what you think coming to my house to take me away is? Love?"

"You don't understand. I found out…"

Thea cut him off in mid-sentence and put her hand up. "I understand perfectly. You want me back at your house to heal you, and you think the way to soften me up into accepting being kidnapped a second time is to tell me you love me. You must think I'm pretty pathetic if you believe that will work."

Pain once again raged through his body and Amon silently reached out to Gethen to call for help. Moments later, he and Markku entered through the front door and Thea leaped from her seat on the couch.

"Don't either of you have any manners either? Get out of my house now!"

Both men stood still waiting for instructions from Amon and appeared to almost look right through her. With each word, Amon felt weaker, and he leaned back against the couch, twisted in pain.

In a strangled voice, he whispered, "Thea, please listen. They're here to help me. Your emotions are killing me."

Turning to see his face drained of all color, she asked, "You're serious, aren't you?"

Quietly, he said, "Yes. Can we please just talk?"

With his hand, he gestured to Gethen and Markku to leave and the two men quickly exited. Amon remained silent for a minute as the ache ebbed out of him. When he was sure he had the strength to finish what he'd started, he inhaled deeply and let the air out in a sigh.

"Thea, I found out my destined one has moved on. When I told you what you were feeling wasn't possible, I didn't know. Then when I experienced pain when we were together in your room, I realized the spell she put on me that causes me to suffer when I make someone I love unhappy was affecting me and that I'd fallen in love with you. But even then I didn't think anything was possible, so I sent Markku to investigate the possibility of Sevine's moving on, hoping but never thinking that I'd actually be blessed with you as my destined one."

Amon watched as she listened intently and then closed her eyes when he finished. As he waited nervously to hear her response, he thought in desperation of gently probing her mind to understand her thoughts about what he'd just said and end the uncertainty he felt. Never before had he felt so unprepared to hear another's answer.

Opening her eyes, Thea said tearfully, "Is this true? Have I been blessed with a destined one finally after all these lifetimes?"

Smiling, he took her hands in his and brought them to his lips to kiss them softly. "Yes, Thea. I'm yours and you're mine."

"I wasn't wrong," she said in astonishment.

"No, I was. I'm sorry you were hurt by my not knowing she'd moved on."

Thea grew silent and then said sheepishly, "Amon, we may be destined ones and love each other in some way, but we don't even know each other. This seems all backwards."

Cradling her face in his hands, he smiled. "We know everything we need to know. We know I love you and you love me. And we know you look incredibly sexy in my shirts."

Unconvinced, she squinted her eyes into tiny slits in fake anger and wrinkled her nose. "You know what I mean."

"No, I don't. Those seem to be the most important things,

as far as I can tell."

Thea's blue eyes stared back at him, and he leaned in and kissed the tip of her nose. "Okay. What do you want to know?"

"Everything. Where have you lived other than the house I've been in? How many destined ones have you had? Do you like extra cheese on your pizza?" She stopped and hesitated before asking another question. "Do you like children?"

Amon lifted both his eyebrows and wrinkled his forehead. "Want to jump right in? Okay. I've lived in many places. Greece, Italy, Britain, Ireland, Mexico, Norway, in addition to other places in the United States. I have homes in many of them that I can't wait for you to see. I've had three destined ones before you. I do like extra cheese on my pizza, in addition to sausage and green peppers. And yes, I like children."

He knew the last answer was the most important, so he made sure to smile when he said it. After, he leaned in and softly pressed his lips to hers.

Thea pulled away and studied his face. "What would you like to know about me?" she asked in a hopeful voice.

"What makes you happy?"

Thea wrinkled her nose again. "Because you don't want to feel that pain again, right?"

Amon shook his head. "No. Because I want to make you happy."

OUTSIDE, GETHEN SULLENLY WATCHED THE comings and goings of Thea's neighbors. Markku stood next to him smiling as he surveyed the same scene, albeit from a different perspective.

"Gethen, do you ever wonder what it would be like to be one of them? To be human?"

"No."

Markku turned to Gethen with a look of amazement. "Never once? C'mon. They seem so interesting."

"For all the years I've been around them, I can't figure out what anyone would find interesting about them," Gethen replied testily as he stared straight ahead.

"Not interesting? That's crazy! They only live one life, old man. One life and it doesn't seem to bother them at all."

Gethen knew he should simply ignore Markku and avoid getting drawn into the conversation, but the man's ignorance irritated him more than being forced to wait on the porch for Amon did.

"I have only one life."

Markku shook his head. "No, that's not the same. Sidhe may only get one life, but they get a much longer life than humans. Christ, they only get about eighty years before it's all over."

Gethen's thoughts trailed off as Markku spoke. One life. Unlike those he spent all his time near, he would cease to exist upon his death, another of his kind sent to the afterlife in the Summerlands. He was nowhere close to the natural end of his life. Three hundred and some odd years was relatively young for his kind, who often lived twice as long. But now, as he felt the early November chill bite at him, his many years away from his world made him suddenly feel old.

He knew what was making him miserable. Inside, Amon was reuniting with the woman he was destined to share his remaining lifetimes with, and outside, he was struggling with jealousy he'd never experienced with Amon. He'd entered his world after his previous destined one had left, so he'd always had Amon to his own, despite the myriad of females who'd been in and out of the Aeveren's life. Now his life would change, and he'd very likely see Gethen as an unnecessary addition. Or more correctly, his destined one would.

Markku jabbed Gethen's side sharply with his elbow. "We got trouble."

Gethen shook off his thoughts and trained his eyes on the man Markku was watching. "Why? What's wrong?"

"He's a bounty hunter, probably the one sent to take Amon back."

Gethen felt the adrenaline pump through him as his body shifted into protection mode. He watched the Aeveren male make his way down the suburban side street, looking distinctly out of place surrounded by housewives loading up minivans with bags and children to go to play dates with other housewives and their children.

He assessed the man's physical character instantly as formidable, and since Amon was still recovering from his escape from the very place the bounty hunter intended him to return, Gethen decided to alert his friend to the potential danger.

As the man came closer to the sidewalk in front of Thea's

house, both Gethen and Markku agreed he was Amon's bounty hunter. In his mind, Gethen heard Amon's response to his alarm, and he grabbed Markku by the arm.

"Amon wants us inside…now."

As they closed the door behind them, Thea hurriedly gathered her things and stuffed them into her purse.

"Is he the man, Markku?" Amon asked as he stood from the couch.

"Yeah. My guy described him to a T. Says he's on a mission."

"What the fuck does that mean?" Gethen snapped.

"I don't know. My guy said that this guy was released from his job at Nil last year and was just recalled for this job."

Amon stood next to Gethen to comfort him, silently reassuring him. "Well, he's going to have to get used to failing, gentlemen." Turning to Thea, he added, "Time to go."

Thea came to Amon's side and molded her body to his as he curved his arm around her shoulders. Placing a kiss on the top of her head, he whispered softly to her to calm her fears.

"Gethen, get back to the house with Markku. Thea, I promise we'll come back again."

Looking up and smiling, she said, "We better. I have things I need."

OUT OF THE CORNER OF his eye, Amon spied the man through the front window. He felt the man's eyes meet his and even from a distance of twenty yards away, there was an almost electric connection. Either he would fail in his task or Amon would return to Nil. There was no middle ground.

Quickly, Amon turned to Markku. "Get Gethen back to the house. Go now!"

Just as fast, he positioned Thea on his other side near Markku and when the magickian began to disappear, thrust her hand into his with the warning, "Hurt her and I'll kill you. Go!"

In seconds, Thea's cry of protest and her eyes full of worry were a memory, and her house was silent. Amon stood in her living room waiting. It didn't take long for the knock he waited for to come, but this meeting would be on his terms.

Before the other man knew what had happened, Amon stood behind him on the porch. When he felt satisfied that he had the upper hand, he cleared his throat and the man spun around. They stood facing one another, each one sizing up the other. Amon spent little time on him before he decided that he wouldn't be much to handle physically. What powers he had was a different story. With a quick look into his mind, Amon knew all he needed to know.

"Leave here and never come back, or I promise you this won't end well for you."

"Amon Kalins, I'm here to take you back to Nil to serve out your sentence."

Amon grinned. "I see. All official? Okay. I've warned you. The next time I see you will be the last."

Moments later, Amon reappeared in his bedroom. Silently, he summoned Gethen to bring Thea to him and waited patiently to see the woman he'd completely fallen head over heals in love with.

Thea burst into his room, her anger obvious by the look on her face.

"What were you thinking? You could have gotten hurt or worse!" she screamed.

Amon was so happy to see her that he'd momentarily forgotten that her emotions could still affect him and was surprised when a stab of pain shot through him. He stumbled backwards toward the bed as Thea and Gethen raced to catch him.

"Amon! I'm so sorry! I forgot," she cried as she clutched at his arm.

Gethen supported him and they guided him to the bed. After helping him into it, Gethen stood back and waited.

With Thea seated next to him stroking his cheek with her fingertips, Amon began to relax. Looking up at his friend, he smiled. "Thank you once again, Gethen. You seem to be always saving me."

Amon saw the pleasure in Gethen's eyes and was happy he understood him so well.

"Always, Amon."

"Let me rest, friend. When I'm ready, I think it's time to see our friends of the Soren. We may need their help with this bounty hunter."

Nodding, Gethen said, "I'll tell Markku," as he left the room.

Thea continued to tenderly trace her fingertips over Amon's cheek as he closed his eyes. Leaning down, she softly touched her lips to his and then whispered, "I am so sorry."

Just the touch of her lips excited him, and he caught her face in his hands to return the kiss.

"Don't be sorry. You had every right to be upset. I should have remembered the effect you have on me."

He slid his tongue into her mouth to mingle with hers and gently sucked her tongue between his lips. "I like this effect better," he teased, his face flush with desire.

Moaning softly, she climbed on top of him and straddled his hips. "And just what effect is that?"

As he ran his hands over her back, he groaned, "The one that makes me want to be inside you."

He pulled her down to him and wrapped his arms around her as he kissed her deeply. At that moment, nothing else mattered. Not what he'd have to do to save himself from being dragged back to Nil. Not the last vestiges of pain he felt slowly leave his body. No, the only thing that mattered was how he felt with Thea.

Amon realized she'd been healing him as she touched his face and now was quietly sleeping with her head on his shoulder. Gently, he stroked her hair as she lay on top of him and thanked fate for sending her to him.

For now, he'd let her sleep and he'd build up his own strength because what they faced was something they'd need all their powers and more to overcome. But even though he was just days away from the hell of Nil, he felt stronger than he had in lifetimes. He had something more than himself to fight for. He had a destined one who'd ended his loneliness. He had Thea.

CHAPTER ELEVEN

—◆◆◆—

R YU JANSEN REMAINED ON THEA'S front porch considering what he'd learned so far. He'd known the girl was important the moment he'd seen her run from Amon's house, but now he needed to find out who she was. The other players in this drama he already knew. The servant/bodyguard named Gethen had watched him approach the house with the magickian Kalins kept on hand.

And Kalins himself? Ryu adjusted his jacket and thought about his prey. Amon Kalins presented a formidable challenge. Physically, he was as big as Ryu had expected. However, it wasn't physical power that concerned him. Kalins possessed more powers than the Council knew if the invasion of his mind was any indication. An almost imperceptible tug but he'd felt it as Kalins had stared at him. Bringing in a tempuster who could teleport and read minds was going to be a bit more difficult than he'd first thought.

Maybe it's time for a visit with the Council.

Two hours later, Ryu once again found himself back in Nil—"home", as they'd called it. As he watched the Council members file into the chamber, he wondered if they were right. Was Nil truly his home? Could a place created for the worst of their kind be where he was most comfortable, where he was meant to always return to? And if that were true, what did that make him?

He'd always told himself that he was different from the people in Nil. He'd done his time and was no longer like them. He was better. He'd convinced himself of that point.

He was better.

"Mr. Jansen, I didn't expect to see you so soon or so alone."

Ryu trained his eyes on the head councilman and the displeasure on the man's face registered in Ryu's mind just as his tone had. A feeling of irritation spiked in him, and he silently complained about the man's impatience, not caring whether or not he possessed the power that would allow him to know his thoughts.

He struggled to calm himself so his tone didn't betray all his thoughts. "You can be confident I'll bring Kalins in."

"I have no doubt, Mr. Jansen. What can we do for you now?"

"Two things. First, he's with a girl. I need to know who she is and what she is to him."

"Give us her name and we'll gather the information you seek."

"I don't have a name. All I have is an address."

"Very well. What is the address?"

Ryu finished giving Thea's address and a page scurried off

to find out what he needed to know.

"While we wait for that, tell us what you've done so far to complete your assignment."

"I met with the Council of New York," Ryu said flatly, remembering the experience with distaste.

"And I'm sure you found them eminently helpful."

Ryu was unsure of how to interpret the councilman's tone, so he said nothing. His experience with the Council system as a bounty hunter had shown him that they tended to protect their own, even if the council members for New York didn't.

"I understand from your silence that your experience with that particular council wasn't entirely successful."

Carefully measuring his words, Ryu said, "Perhaps it was because of my accent."

The councilman laughed loudly. "I doubt that was the problem, Mr. Jansen. I'm afraid you were forced to deal with a council that harbors ill will toward the one seated in front of you."

And obviously you don't intend on helping me with that.

Ryu's anger rose at the bureaucratic nonsense that more and more seemed to be a large part of the bounty hunter's job.

Territorial divas.

"What else have you done to apprehend Kalins?"

"I tracked him to his house in New York. That's where I found the girl. As I arrived, she was running from the house, so I followed her."

"Why didn't you simply capture your man instead of running after some girl?"

"He's got some kind of magick working so no one can get near the house."

"So you aren't even certain he was there?"

Ryu knew by the tone of the questions that the head of the Council wasn't appreciating how he'd done his job so far, and he didn't give a damn.

Between the goddamned Council of New York and whatever fucking magick Kalins has working for him, you should be pleased as fucking punch I've seen him at all.

"Be careful, Mr. Jansen."

"You recalled me for this job because I'm good at what I do. Let me do my job then."

"So have you seen Kalins?"

Ryu knew he had to control his anger. No matter how much they needed him, he had to admit he needed them more.

"Yes."

"Tell us about that."

"As I said, I followed the girl to her house and waited to see if he'd come after her. A few hours later, he showed up with the Sidhe and the other guy—the magickian."

The page returned and handed the councilman a file. "Please continue, Mr. Jansen."

"Well, Kalins went inside as they remained outside and only once did they go inside, but then they came back out. Right after that, they spotted me."

"How could they know who you are or why you were there?"

"That's what I wondered too. My guess is you've got Soren

spies in the Directorate."

Suddenly, the chamber grew quiet. The fear of spies in the Directorate was a constant concern, but proof was always elusive. The Soren was good at what it did when it came to helping its own, and the men and women it sent in to do its spying were professionals.

A female council member spoke up, her voice full of fear. "Are you sure, Mr. Jansen? It couldn't be something you misunderstood?"

"I don't think so, ma'am. As soon as they spotted me, they reentered the house and then by the time I made it to the front door, they were gone with the girl and only Kalins remained. I don't think it's a coincidence. He's got a magickian from that group working for him, so I'm betting the Soren is supplying him with information about your sending me from their spies in the Directorate."

"Then from this point on," she said to the head of the Council, "I think we should be very careful with the information we file concerning Mr. Kalins' case."

The head councilman agreed. "And we need to investigate any recent inquiries regarding Kalins."

Ryu watched in amusement as the Council laid plans to protect itself and foil the efforts of the Soren. He knew the bad guys always had better resources, more ways to get around the law than the good guys had to enforce the laws they made. It was just the way of the world. He didn't believe the fight was a pointless one because good had to triumph over evil if there was to be any order in the world, but he knew that more bureaucratic arm flailing wasn't what was going to help the good guys win. It was up to the feet on the ground, people like him, to make sure good won out.

"Well, Mr. Jansen, it seems an interesting wrinkle has been added to Kalins' case. The girl you saw with him is a healer. I suspect if I asked you to describe his physical well-being, you'd say he appeared in the pink of good health, would you not?"

Ryu nodded. *No doubt he'd had help procuring the services of a healer from the Soren.* "If I may ask, what is known about her? Is it likely she's working for the Soren?"

The councilman studied the pages of Thea's file for some time and lifted his head. "It doesn't appear that she is. Her record shows a long history of forty-five lifetimes as a healer, and there's never been any issue with her following the Council's orders."

"That would explain why she ran from Kalins' house. She was there against her will."

"That might very well be true, Mr. Jansen, but I wouldn't count on her assistance in capturing your man."

Ryu looked up at the Council confused. "Why not? It's a tactic any good bounty hunter would use. If she's being held against her wishes, she's a perfect pawn to use against Kalins. Women don't like being held hostage, and in my experience, they'll turn on their captors just as soon as look at them."

"Not if they're destined ones," the councilman said in a hollow voice that immediately silenced the chamber.

"What?"

"Kalins' healer is his destined one. I don't foresee any

assistance from Miss Althea Forester."

Ryu quickly added up the things Amon Kalins had going for him. Ancient and powerful, possibly with even more powers than the already impressive ones he and the Council knew about. The aid of a Sidhe who had helped him escape from the supposedly impenetrable Nil. The support of the Soren, a group dedicated to working against the laws of their people. A magickian of no small talents. And now his own personal healer.

"I'll need to know everything about this healer if I'm to return him to Nil."

The female council member from just a few minutes earlier spoke up again. "You know we can't do that, Mr. Jansen. Just as with every other Aeveren, you are not permitted to know of her past lives."

Before Ryu could protest that knowledge of her past may be just what he could use to capture Kalins, the head of the Council of Nil gestured to a page to come toward him and said, "Your request is granted, Mr. Jansen."

Several council members gasped at the extraordinary breach of Aeveren laws and ethical principles. The female council member exclaimed, "I protest this action! The right to privacy concerning former lifetimes is one of the most sacred rights in our world. It is long held to be inviolable. No matter what Amon Kalins has done to deserve his sentence in Nil, the ends do not justify the means!"

"Your protest is noted," the head councilman said coolly. Turning to Ryu, he continued, "Mr. Jansen, now you have what you need. Bring Kalins back to Nil."

Ryu stood stunned at the scene he'd just witnessed and barely muttered the words "thank you" as the page handed him a folder containing details of Thea's history. He watched as several members of the Council stormed out of the chamber ahead of the head councilman and those who supported his decision that was sure to be controversial.

AMON AWOKE FROM HIS SHORT nap and found Thea still sleeping on top of him. Her warm breath heated the skin on his neck, and he reveled at how wonderful she felt next to him. Long blond waves fanned out across her back and fell onto his shoulder, and he lifted a handful of hair up to his nose to smell the sweet fragrance of the shampoo she used. The softness of the strands caressed his lips as he inhaled the scent that would be only hers in his mind from that point on.

Thea began to stir and turned her sleepy face toward his. "I must have fallen asleep as you were talking," she said shyly. "I'm sorry."

"No need to be. You were tired from your exciting day and healing me again," he whispered before planting a small kiss on her forehead.

She furrowed her brow. "Amon, I need to call my sister. She's going to worry if she tries to get in touch with me and I'm gone."

"Of course. I'll leave so you can have some privacy."

As he moved to place her on the bed, Thea pushed against

him. "In a little while. I want to stay like this for a while longer," she purred.

Thea found his mouth and kissed him passionately. She felt so good next to him, her body soft in all the right places where his was hard.

Amon buried his hands in her hair and tugged gently as he moaned against her mouth. "We have someplace we have to go, but I promise after that we'll have all the time in the world to do anything and everything we want."

As he sat up to sit on the edge of the bed, he silently called Gethen and instructed him to bring Markku also. In seconds, there was a knock at the door and then all four stood in Amon's bedroom.

"Markku, it's about time I visited my friends in the Soren. I want you to arrange a meeting for tonight."

"Sounds good. They'll be happy to see you."

"Take Gethen with you, and he'll let me know when everything's set."

Amon turned to Gethen and simply smiled. With a nod of his head, Gethen left behind Markku and once again Amon and Thea were alone.

"What did you tell Gethen?" Thea asked as she wrapped her arms around his neck and looked up into his face.

Lifting one eyebrow in mock surprise, he smiled. "What makes you think I told him anything? I didn't say a word."

"I know you can communicate with him without speaking, so you don't have to pretend you don't know what I'm talking about."

Amon ran his hands down the side of Thea's body and let them come to rest on her waist. "Thea, where we're going is unlike anywhere I believe you've ever been. The group Markku works with is full of people who are like I used to be. Do you remember when I told you I'd done some bad things in my forty-seven lifetimes? These people are like that."

Thea ran her fingers over the skin of Amon's neck and shoulders. "Why do we have to go to see these people if you're not like that anymore?" she asked innocently.

"Because if I'm going to stay out of Nil and keep you safe, I'm going to need their help."

Amon hugged her tightly and rested his chin on the top of her head. "I need you to remember something, Thea."

Backing away from him, she looked up with concern on her face and squeezed his hands in hers. "What's wrong, Amon?"

Stroking her cheek gently as he spoke, he whispered softly. "I just need you to remember that the person who loves you, your destined one, is the man I am now. The person you're going to see in a little while is the person I have to be with them. And I need you to keep your emotions under control. I can't let them see me weakened because you're unhappy."

"I promise I'll remember. They won't hurt me, will they?"

Rage at the thought of anyone hurting her spiked inside him. "Thea, I would never let anyone hurt you. I'll kill anyone who makes the mistake of even thinking of harming you. I told you before. You're safe as long as you're with me."

"Okay," she said with a sweet smile. "But you never told

me what you said to Gethen."

"You certainly are a tenacious one, Althea. All I told him was to make sure it's safe before calling me."

Satisfied, she smiled. "I see." However, a moment later, she asked, "But why did you just call me Althea?"

Amon realized his verbal slip up but decided not to choose that moment to explain his ability to see into other people's minds.

"That's your given name, isn't it?" he said with a wink.

"Yes, but it just sounded odd coming out of your mouth since I never told you my full name and I rarely use it."

"Well, then Thea it is from now on unless you instruct me otherwise," he said lazily as he nuzzled her neck. "Are you ready, love? Gethen tells me it's safe."

Thea nodded and wrapped her arms around Amon's back. Holding her tightly to him, he focused on Gethen's location and in seconds, they disappeared from his bedroom on their way to Soren headquarters near London.

MOMENTS LATER, THE COUPLE REAPPEARED just outside the doors to a large meeting room. Upon seeing them, Gethen and Markku began to make their way across the large open vestibule.

Thea immediately turned to Amon, fearful of what lay ahead. "Where is this place?"

"We're right outside London at the Soren's headquarters. Don't worry. Everything is going to be all right. Just remember what I said and promise me you'll keep in mind that this isn't who I am now."

Amon kissed her sweetly, and when she opened her eyes, she saw Gethen standing in front of him and Markku right behind him. "Markku did as you ordered, and they're waiting for you."

"Excellent. Let's go in," he said as he squeezed Thea's hand.

Just before the doors opened, Amon turned to her and mouthed, "Remember, I love you." Before she could say the words back to him, they walked into the room and thoughts of love vanished before her eyes, replaced by fear and horror.

"AMON KALINS! WHAT THE FUCK did they do to you?" a man's voice bellowed from the front of the room. The head of the Soren, Kiril Gault stood on a dais surrounded by three human women naked in shackles. Behind him was a large gilded edged chair with a deep purple cushion that resembled a throne.

Tall and dark with black hair, Kiril's eyes were the most beautiful shade of violet Thea had ever seen. He was striking in a terrifying way, the complete opposite of Amon, and her hand reflexively tightened on his. She tried to keep calm, remembering the effect her emotions had on Amon, but the sight of the three handcuffed and naked women frightened her. But if she was sure of nothing else, she was sure she was safe as long as Amon was by her side.

"Kiril. I live again," Amon said in a voice Thea didn't

recognize. Its timbre sounded far more powerful than she'd ever heard from him. And almost as terrifying as the man who now stood just feet in front of them.

"Of course, I owe it all to Gethen and you," Amon said, turning his head toward his friend behind him and then back to face the Soren leader.

"Gethen, how have you been?" Kiril asked and then without waiting for the answer he obviously cared little to hear, continued, "Why have I never gotten a Sidhe for myself? He seems invaluable to have, does he not?"

Thea watched as Kiril tugged on the shackles of the dark haired human near him, and she hurriedly rose to kneel in front of him. When she began to massage his thigh, Thea averted her glance, afraid of what she might see next and preferring to look at the throngs of men lining the sides of the room seemingly oblivious to anything but Amon and Kiril.

"I would be lost without Gethen. That's true," she heard Amon answer.

"And is this something for me? You know I prefer my slaves human, but she'll do fine. I'm going to need another one soon when I'm down to only two."

Thea's entire body stiffened in terror, and she was sure Amon was beginning to feel the first effects of her emotions. In her mind, she heard the words he'd said.

I promise I won't let anyone hurt you. Trust me.

As her grip on his hand eased, he gently stroked the back of her hand with his thumb, but his voice became even sterner than before.

"She's mine."

Kiril seemed surprised by the tone of the words and laughed nervously, "No problem. I guess that means you won't be partaking of the girls this time?"

Thea's eyes darted from one girl, to the next, and finally to the last one. Partaking of the girls *this* time?

"Not this time."

"So, what can we do for you, old friend? Is Markku serving your needs?"

"He is. But I need a bit more. I have a bounty hunter after me."

Kiril pushed the human off his leg, and as she fell to the floor in a thud, he casually stepped over her and the chain that connected her to her two fellow slaves. One giant step off the riser and he was standing in front of Amon.

"Fucking Council! A bounty hunter, eh? Obviously, we can kill him, but they'll send another and another. Not that I have any problem killing off every single one of the Council's lapdogs, but it's just such a fucking hassle."

"Exactly what I thought. I could've killed him when we met earlier, but then I'll just have to deal with his replacement. I know there's a more efficient way."

Kiril paced back and forth past Thea and Amon, and when his back was turned, Amon snuck a glance at Thea. His blue eyes seemed so intense, but she could see the man she'd grown to care for in them. The quick wink he gave her told her he had everything under control, and Thea gave him a small smile to let him know she understood. Still, the idea of him with any of those women rambled around in her head as she worked to remain strong and believe that the man he was here, in front of this awful man, wasn't the real Amon.

Kiril stopped his pacing and stood in front of Amon. "Well, there certainly are avenues to explore, but they involve magick much darker than you usually prefer."

Thea sensed Amon's apprehension and her own coiled inside her. Darker magick was something she'd heard of many times over her existence, though she'd never known anyone who dared to use it.

"Whatever it takes. Just make sure anything I do is safe for Thea and Gethen." Amon was silent for a moment and added, "And I want Markku to stay with me after we perform the spell. He's good with the magick, and he owes me."

"As you wish."

Amon turned to Gethen and gestured for him to come closer. "Take Thea outside and wait for me. If you feel she's not perfectly safe at any time, call to me and I'll know."

He took Thea's hands in his and squeezed them gently. "I need you to go with Gethen now. Trust me. I'll be out in no time. I promise."

Fear raced through her. "No, Amon! You said I'd only be safe as long as I was with you. Let me stay. I'll be okay. Please."

He cradled her face in his hands and looked deeply into her eyes as he shook his head. "No. I don't want you involved in this. You'll be safe with Gethen. He would never hurt anyone I love. Gethen will let me know if anything happens that you need me."

As he handed her to Gethen, tears begin to well up in her eyes and he caught one with the pad of his thumb as it hit her cheek. "Don't worry. I need to do this for your safety as much as mine."

Gethen began to pull her away, but Thea wrenched her hand free and threw her arms around Amon. "No, please don't do this. Whatever it takes, we can find another way."

Amon pressed his cheek against the top of her head. "Thea, I can't let these people see me weakened, and your emotions are already taking their toll on me."

"But what if the spell calls for doing something…" she said hesitating, "with these women?"

Smiling, he whispered, "There is no other woman I want. I promise I won't do anything that involves any women."

Thea looked up at him and hoped she saw a look of sincerity on his face. Forcing a smile, she nodded. "Please be careful. I'm not okay with the dark magick thing either."

"I promise, love. And when I'm done, we'll celebrate at the house."

As Amon released her hand, Thea reluctantly followed Gethen out of the room without looking back, too afraid to see what Amon was going to do.

CHAPTER TWELVE

———— ∞ ————

B Y THE TIME THEY RETURNED to Amon's, it was late and Thea quickly excused herself to call her sister. The three men sat in Amon's study discussing what would have to be done about the Council's intention of forcing Amon back to Nil. As Markku railed against the dictatorial nature of Aeveren laws, Gethen sat quietly staring out the window.

Needing some peace and quiet, Amon said, "Markku, take the night and go enjoy yourself."

"For real? Amon, thank you!" Markku answered as he leapt out of his chair and made his way toward the door.

"Just be back in the morning," Amon warned.

Markku barely got the words "no problem" out before he vanished, leaving Amon and Gethen alone. Amon studied his friend's face as he sat looking off in the distance. He watched him squint his eyes, as if he were in pain or remembering a painful experience, and the expression accentuated the scar next to his eye.

"What's on your mind, Gethen?"

Gethen slowly closed his eyes and sighed. When he

opened them and turned to face Amon, he looked older than his former master ever remembered seeing him.

"I feel a calling home, Amon. All my years away have been with you, and I remain grateful for your saving me when none of my own kind would. But you don't need me with you anymore."

Amon sat silently, a lump forming in his throat. Even though the seven lifetimes he'd spent with Gethen were a mere fraction of the many he'd enjoyed, he couldn't imagine a lifetime without him in it. The last year had been torture not only because he'd been in Nil but also because he'd been without his friend.

"What's causing this?"

"No matter what I ever have been to you, you've always been more than a master to me, Amon."

Gethen turned back toward the window and continued. "But now you don't need someone to care for you. You're no longer alone, and while the love I feel for you will always be, it's time for me to go home to my world."

Amon struggled to keep his voice even as emotions threatened to overwhelm him. "You're wrong, Gethen. I didn't need someone to take care of me. That was never why I needed you. You have been my closest friend, my confidant. That you appeared as my servant was always a disservice to how much you've truly meant to me over the lifetimes we've known one another."

The two men sat in silence, each consumed by his own thoughts and feelings, until Amon asked the question that both knew the answer to. "When will you leave?"

In a voice that betrayed the pain he felt, Gethen answered, "I think sooner is better than later."

Amon stood from his chair and put a hand on his friend's shoulder. "I'll let Thea know we'll be leaving this week."

UPSTAIRS, AMON FOUND HER IN her bedroom looking at the clothes Gethen had gotten for her. Through the cracked door, he watched her hold each shirt, sweater, and dress up to her as she posed in front of the mirror. Her happiness mixed with the sadness he felt from knowing he was losing his closest friend, and he became lost in thought watching her.

Without him noticing, she opened the door and found him standing there. "Amon? Are you okay?"

Silently, he nodded and took her hand in his as he led her across the hall to his room. Closing the door behind him, he gently pulled Thea to him and bent to kiss her.

"What's wrong, Amon?"

"Nothing. I just missed you," he said quietly as he trailed his lips down her neck to her collarbone.

Stroking his hair, she whispered. "You never have to miss me. I'm all yours."

Amon moaned against her neck as his tongue danced over her skin tasting her. Gently, he scraped his teeth over her neck as he sucked and nibbled at her.

"Thea…" he whispered huskily near her ear, his voice full of desire. "I loved your jealousy earlier."

Feeling her back away from him, he opened his eyes and

searched hers for what troubled her. Suddenly, he felt a wall between them keeping her from him.

Thea dropped her eyes to the floor to avoid his stare.

"What is it? Why won't you look at me?"

Quietly, she said, "I don't know if I can be what you want."

"What are you talking about? You're everything I want."

As she raised her eyes, Amon saw fear and sadness in them.

"I don't want to be jealous of other women. I've waited all these lifetimes for someone meant just for me. I want to know—need to know—that person wants only me."

Slowly, he approached her and took her hands in his. "Thea, I don't want any other women. It's only you."

"And I'm jealous. I can't bear the idea of you with those women from that place today."

As she spoke, her eyes grew wider making her look even more vulnerable as she stood there so small in front of him. But he knew better. He knew the beautiful woman looking up at him had a strength beneath that sweet appearance.

"I told you that I'm not that man I had to be there. Kiril's a pig who enslaves women. And I've never been with any of his slaves. Never."

Amon saw that she remembered every word of what Kiril had said and wasn't entirely convinced by his admission. "Never, Thea."

Bending down, he kissed her lightly on the lips and then whispered, "And anyone else I've ever been with you should just think of as practice for you."

Thea's mouth formed a small pout. "That doesn't help."

Taking her chin between his thumb and forefinger, he smiled. "Now, that's the fire I like."

Squinting her eyes, she made a clucking noise with her tongue. "You're not taking this seriously."

"That's where you're wrong, love. I'd be crazy with jealousy if I thought about you with another man."

Amon bent down to kiss her again and took her face in his hands. "I don't want to think about anyone else tonight, Thea. I want to get lost in you. I want to make love to the woman who's meant for me and show her that I'm the only man for her. And then I want to do it all over again."

Nipping at her ear, he murmured low and deep, wanting to hear her answer. "Tell me what my Thea wants."

THEA KNEW THE ANSWER SHE wanted to give him. She wanted his power, his desire, everything he was. Never before had she craved a man like she craved Amon, but fear held her back. Fear of her desires. Fear of the destined ones who'd come before her. But her body betrayed her as her hands ran across his chiseled stomach and her fingers grazed under his pants, briefly gliding over his erect cock. She felt the hardness under her fingertips and heard his sharp intake of breath near her ear followed by a deep groan that told her she had nothing to fear or doubt with him.

Pushing her insecurities away, she unfastened his pants and reached into them to take him in her hand. As she stroked the fullness in her grip, she watched him close his eyes and let a groan escape his lips. With each movement of her hand, his breathing became deeper with need.

Never interrupting the rhythm of her hand, she slowly slid down his body dragging her tongue over the sharp planes of his chest and abs. When her mouth was level with her target, she lifted her face to see his expression.

Amon's head was thrown back and his brow knitted waiting for her to finally touch her mouth to him. But as her lips met his body, she heard a noise from above her and Amon gently pulled her up by the shoulders to her full height.

"No," he groaned in her ear.

Confused, Thea searched his face but found no answers to explain his apparent disinterest. As the sting of rejection hit her, she opened her mouth to express her hurt, but Amon's mouth was on hers, full of passion. Instantly, she forgot all the words she wanted to say.

For the first time in forty-five lifetimes, she felt the need to be with a man. Never before had she known a feeling like this. As he stood in front of her, she was pulled to him by some deep call from inside him—like no one else in the world could satisfy her like Amon could. The thought was both thrilling and alarming.

Suddenly, she felt like a naive girl in her first lifetime, unsure of everything her heart and body were telling her to do. Amon was so much more than anyone she'd ever met, and he was hers.

Her destined one.

As his kiss deepened, Thea's senses swirled into a jumbled mass of desire. The feel of his soft lips pressing against hers as his tongue swept into her mouth over and over, teasing the tip of her tongue playfully, set her on delicious edge. His strong hands held her to him, hands that would protect her against any danger. The smell of his skin, earthy and musky, filled each breath she took. His deep voice, moaning into her mouth as he showed her just how much he needed her, touched her core.

The potent combination of desire and need threatened to overwhelm her, and she felt like the room was beginning to swim around her. His effect on her was intoxicating as every cell in her body called out to him to satisfy her.

Somewhere deep inside, in a place she'd long forgotten about, a tiny lick of happiness began to grow—the happiness of knowing that in all the world and after so many years of ultimately being alone, she'd finally been blessed with someone who was just for her. No more lifetimes of hoping for something sweet and real that never came to her. No more accepting the hollow nothing to fill the want her Aeveren soul always carried with it.

Finally, she had found the one meant for her.

Even more, she was meant for him. She was the woman destiny had chosen to love and cherish him, one of the most powerful Aeveren to ever live.

THE FEEL OF THEA'S MOUTH and tongue on his skin had been

pure ecstasy, but Amon wanted more. He wanted their first true moments together to be the joining only destined ones could ever know. He'd known that bliss three times already in his many lifetimes, but he knew Thea had never felt the joy of a destined one before him.

Pride and possession grew inside him as he feasted on her mouth, so willing and ready. She was his and only his, meant only for him. Her lips, her body a perfect match for him. And he knew from his time in her mind the day before that she wanted him as he wanted her.

Completely.

In a way he'd only wished for with other women since Sevine.

Memories of Thea's fantasies played in his mind as he stripped her of her clothes, and she stood naked in front of him, her blue eyes sparkling with passion as she looked up at him.

A sexy grin came onto her face, and Thea moved backwards a few steps toward the bed. Amon quickly shed his shirt and moved to follow her, but she turned out of his hold and he found himself looking across the bed at her as she stood facing him, looking sexier than ever before with her silky hair flowing over her breasts and stomach.

Amon bent down and planted his hands on the bed. Looking at her, he thought about how good it was going to feel to be deep inside her. Lifting his left hand, he crooked his index finger and beckoned her to him.

"Come here," he said, his deep voice edgy with need.

His cock stiffened more as Thea crawled on her hands and knees toward him, her eyes focused on his to show she'd play the submissive but not entirely. That was fine with him. He'd never liked a woman to completely play the role of submissive, which seemed just a step above the way Kiril used his slaves. No, he preferred a challenge—something to keep his interest and desire piqued.

Thea kneeled on the bed in front of him with her face turned upward. Gently, he pushed her long hair back to reveal her breasts and pearled pink nipples. As he pressed his lips to hers and slid his tongue into her mouth, his thumb played with a nipple while his hand tenderly cupped the milky white breast around it.

As reward for the gentle pinching of her nipple between his thumb and forefinger, Amon heard a soft moan into his mouth and felt her arch her body into his. Her skin felt so warm pressed against his.

He'd forgotten the perfect pleasure a destined one provided after all those lifetimes alone. How one touch could ignite passions that existed with no other soul on Earth. The sweet taste of her lips danced on his tongue and made him crave her all the more.

Grabbing a fistful of hair, he tugged Thea's head back and buried his face in her neck. The delicious smell of her honeysuckle shampoo filled his nose, exciting yet another sense and building his desire to a higher level. The innocent fragrance contradicted the passionate and knowing actions of her hands as they glided over his flesh to the areas that aroused him most.

Amon slipped his hands down over her back to the fullness of her ass and squeezed the soft flesh, kneading it with his fingers. Thea responded by raking her nails over the healed skin of his back, igniting a need that overtook him.

"Thea, I need you. Now."

He pushed her back gently onto the bed and ran his hands up the smooth skin of her legs as his eyes devoured the sight of her pale pink sex. His fingers reached the desired destination first and carefully explored the soft folds that glistened with moisture. With one finger, he stroked her excited nub and then traced his way to her entrance, wet and eager for him.

Desperate for a taste of her, Amon bent his head to her and touched his tongue to her clitoris, sending waves of pleasure through her body. Her hands held him to her while her fingers trailed over the shells of his ears and the nape of his neck.

A second finger joined the first inside her, and he thrust into her as he sucked her swollen nub between his lips. She tasted so good—sweet but musky—and his mouth worked to satisfy the craving she caused in him.

Beneath him, Thea's body opened to his every stroke and desire. With every nip of his tongue and sweet invasion of his fingers, she melted into him becoming his and his alone. He felt her begin to tighten around his fingers as the walls of her core signaled her approaching climax. He pushed into her faster, his fingers stroking her to completion as his tongue sensually flicked her hardened nub. Thea's fingers pressed against his skin behind his ears, and he heard her mew her pleasure above him.

Seconds later, he felt her come apart and quickly moved to lap up her juices as his tongue slid inside her. He stayed with his mouth savoring her until she ceased quivering, and when he lifted his head, he sucked the taste of her from his fingers with the devilish grin of a man who knew he'd thoroughly pleasured a woman.

Looking down at her, he saw her lazily stretch under him, relaxed but wanting more.

"I'd like these gone," she said as she stared at his pants through half-lidded eyes and tugged at them.

"As you command, my lady."

AMON'S MUCH LARGER BODY LOOMED over hers, and her eyes flowed over his chest and abs. Everything about him signaled his power, from his deep blue eyes to the strong ridges of his muscular body. She'd fantasized about him taking her for his, but the reality of him was even better than anything she could have imagined.

Thea trailed her fingertips over the hardness of his torso and saw him smiling down at her.

"What?"

"Nothing. I was just thinking how beautiful you are."

"I was noticing the same thing," she whispered as her fingers traced the trail of soft blond hair over his chiseled belly and below where his pants had hidden. Looking down, she eyed his rigid cock, even more than what she'd expected from a man so large. As she wrapped her hand around it and fisted its girth, she looked up to see the calm look he wore so often slide from his face, replaced by one full of desire.

"You like?"

Nodding, Amon glided his tongue over his lips until they glistened. "I do—very much."

Thea slid her hand from base to tip, noting with pleasure how thick he sat in her hand. A tiny smile crossed her lips as he spoke.

"You like?"

She looked down and then looked up again, as if she needed to inspect it before making her decision. In a voice far sweeter than she felt, she answered, "I do—very much."

He dipped his mouth to hers, and she tasted herself as his tongue slid over hers. Even more, she smelled the scent she'd loved since the first time she was close to him. His smell was masculine, but now it mixed with desire to produce an incredibly seductive scent.

Amon slid up her body until his fit perfectly with hers, and he positioned himself at her entrance. Cradling her face in his hands, he said, "Thea, I'm your destined one, the man meant for you. Your pleasure is my pleasure. Everything I am I give to you."

His words thrilled her. *The man meant for you.* Kissing him deeply, she opened herself to him to become one with the soul she'd always wished for. Finally, she'd been given a destined one.

Before entering her, he said in a voice hoarse with desire, "Let me show you what it feels like to be with the one meant for you."

As she looked into his eyes, he slid into her, filling her like no other man had in any of her lifetimes. All she could think of was how perfect he felt as he slid in and out of her. Each time he entered her, he touched her somewhere no one ever had, as if he were created to fit into only her. With each thrust, his powerful body slid lightly over hers as Amon kept all his weight in his arms. Never had she thought he could give her the perfect mix of strength and tenderness she'd dreamed of for so long in a lover.

Thea wrapped her legs around his waist and pulled him into her even closer, her arms around his strong back drawing him to her. As much as she loved how thoughtful and considerate he was, she wanted to feel all of him. His strong, muscular legs pressing against hers. His abdomen pushing against hers, the muscles contracting and releasing with each thrust. His powerful chest against hers. She wanted him so close to her that she couldn't breathe. Even an inch away was too far.

More than the physical pleasure was the emotional connection of Amon with her. Just as she'd heard all those times over and over, now, for the first time, she felt that bond between herself and him that had never been there with any other person.

FOR AMON, THE FEEL OF Thea around him was sublime. Each time he plunged into her, she fit him like a glove. After thinking of her fantasy, he'd fantasized about something else and yearned to have her that way, though.

"Thea, roll over," he said as he changed her position from under him to on top of him.

Amon looked up at the woman riding him and saw a goddess. Blond waves fell toward her waist and bounced in time with her breasts as she lowered herself onto him. Half-closed eyes stared down at him, and her pink tongue drew a quick swipe over her lips, swollen from his kisses. His large hands sat on her waist guiding her and setting the pace.

Thea placed her hand on his and nudged it lower. "Amon, touch me, please," she begged in a keening voice.

As she rode him, he slid the pad of his thumb over her tender nub and rubbed in slow circles. The effect was immediate. She bit her lip and moaned as she began to buck wildly on him. Amon knew her release wasn't far off and thrust upward to meet her movements.

"Come for me, Thea," he ordered, and with one last thrust into her, she came as he watched in wonder. She became more beautiful than he thought possible in those moments of sweet surrender as her body released its passion onto him, and he felt his own climax rage through him and into her, flooding her with warmth.

She fell onto him, exhausted, her damp hair blanketing the two of them, and breathed heavily near his ear. He reveled in the pleasure of bringing her satisfaction in addition to enjoying his own. As he softly caressed her back, she kissed his ear.

"Mmmmm, that was wonderful," she cooed.

Amon slowly removed himself from her and placed her next to him on the bed. Turning on her side, she looked at him and smiled sweetly. She looked like an angel with her hands folded under her head and her hair splayed over her body.

His angel.

"I wish I didn't have to wait all those lifetimes to finally meet you," she said quietly with a look of sadness in her eyes.

Smiling, he leaned over and kissed her shoulder. "I don't think you would have liked me before."

"I never had a choice, so it wouldn't have mattered."

Amon was struck by the truth of her statement. As Aeveren, they never had a choice of their destined ones. But she wasn't entirely correct.

"Just because I'm your destined one doesn't mean it was certain you'd like me or want me."

Thea sat up and looked down at him. "You don't understand. I don't love you because you're my destined one. I'm called to you and sexually drawn to you because of Aeveren biology, but that isn't why I love you. Trust me. I have forty-five lifetimes of experience with love."

Raising one eyebrow, he leaned close to her. "Now I think I'm jealous."

"I could say something about them being practice," she teased, "but I won't."

"How nice of you."

"What if I told you that I've never felt like I do for you with anyone else in all my lifetimes?"

"I feel my male ego improving by the second," he said with a smile.

Thea leaned in and kissed him softly on the lips. "How could you be jealous of any man I've ever been with? You're an ancient of our race and a tempuster who can teleport into places, avoiding actually being guilty of breaking and entering."

Thea placed her head on his chest, and in the gentle silence that grew between them as they lay in each other's arms, Amon decided this was the moment to tell her about his other abilities. He just hoped he wouldn't have to end up apologizing and ruining their first lovemaking.

"Thea, I need to talk to you about something. There is something I haven't told you."

Snuggling closer to him, she buried her face in the crook of his neck and mumbled, "You don't have to be jealous. I was just teasing about having that much experience."

"I have other abilities in addition to those you already know about," he began.

Thea lifted her head and looked up at him with a look of confidence on her face. "Like being able to communicate mentally with Gethen?"

"Not exactly."

"What do you mean?"

As he stroked her hair, he continued. "My ability to communicate with Gethen without speaking is more because of him than me. Because he's a Sidhe, he can understand what I'm thinking."

"I'm confused. How do you communicate then?"

"That's where my mental abilities come in. I can know what people are thinking sometimes if I focus. It's easier with some people than others. I've never really been able to master my mental powers." Then, after a long pause, he said with hesitation, "In addition to that power, I can do other things."

"Like?"

"I can plant ideas into people's minds," he confessed.

Thea grew very quiet. "Have you ever done that to me?"

Amon considered how much to tell her and decided against a full confession. "Yes, at Kiril's to calm you."

"That explains why I suddenly felt okay there."

"Yes."

Thea remained silent for a few moments. "Amon, I need you to promise me you'll never use your powers on me, except to help me."

With a twinge of guilt from knowing he'd already used them on her for his own selfish benefit, he agreed. "I promise. Never, unless I think you need my help."

A sly smile crossed her face and her stare drifted down his body. "Any idea what I'm thinking of now?"

Amon watched as Thea slid down his body, her hands following her mouth to his cock. Already hard, it jumped when her tongue flicked over the head.

Looking up at him, she grinned. "Seeing anything good in my mind?"

"Definitely," he groaned as she began to take him into her mouth, the guilt from not telling her the absolute truth about when he'd used his ability on her dissipating with every touch of her lips and tongue on him.

When Thea returned to his side, he kissed her, more in love than he believed he could be. Somehow, he'd been blessed with her, a happiness he knew he didn't deserve. Deep in his heart, he knew he was a different man because she'd rescued him from himself, though. As they drifted off to sleep, he could think only of the happiness she brought him.

CHAPTER THIRTEEN

———— ∾ ————

A MON LAY PEACEFULLY NEXT TO Thea listening to her breathe softly in her sleep. Her head rested on his chest, and he lazily stroked her hair as he let the joy of being in love sink in. Everything about Thea with him felt right. It was more than she was meant for him. It was the way she made him feel love again. Since his time with his last destined one, he'd only loved two women. Callia had brought him back from lifetimes of loneliness, but she hadn't loved him without his manipulation of her. But the woman he'd loved before her— lifetimes earlier—had loved him with all her heart.

Victoria.

The name haunted him still. The guilt of what he'd been as Riordan Blake and what he'd done to her was never far from his mind, no matter how much he worked to bury it. Now, as he began a new life with Thea, he was reminded of Victoria, another woman who'd cared for him all that time ago.

He entered the dance with Frederika on his arm, prepared for yet another uneventful night in Bedfordshire. As a member of the landed gentry, balls like this were part of his social responsibilities, no matter how much he detested them. Frederika, his wife and destined one for seventeen lifetimes, adored social affairs, so at least half the couple presented a pleasant face at such functions.

To the vast majority of those he interacted with in the sleepy hamlet of Hinwick, where his manor Hinwick Hall was located, and the slightly less sleepy county of Bedfordshire, he was Riordan Blake, part of the landed gentry, husband to Frederika, and father to James and Simon. He tended to his business and lands as every other gentleman and lived a generally comfortable life punctuated by frequent social duties, such as the one he found himself attending this August evening.

Inside, however, he yearned for the excitement of his previous lifetimes. As an ancient Aeveren, he'd lived many lifetimes before his reincarnation as an English gentleman, with quite a few ranking higher in interest than his current one. From a Roman in the third century Empire to his lifetime as a Nordic marauder to his time in a position high in Aztec society before the arrival of the Spanish conquistadores, he'd lived lives of daring and action. Now he spent his days doing little more than watching over his fortune.

Worse yet, his destined one for the past seventeen lifetimes and he had grown apart in this lifetime, at least in small part due to his unhappiness with the life he'd been given. For her part, she'd always yearned for a life of stable luxury, so being Frederika Blake of Hinwick Hall was the perfect fulfillment of this wish.

As Riordan made his way through the crowd, smiling

through his obligation to play the content husband, he scanned the faces of his fellow Bedfordshire residents. One blended into the next; from men to women, they all shared a bland common look, no matter how wealthy they were. Even the Aeveren seemed happy to be nothing more than staid English society dictated. Riordan wondered if they might all by some wild coincidence be in their first lifetimes and simply didn't know any better. Whatever their excuse was, he couldn't forgive his kind for their seemingly eager acceptance of such a banal existence.

Dance after dance, he performed his duties knowing at least his destined one would have no quarrel with him on this issue. An hour into the gathering, he spied a face in the crowd that was unfamiliar to him. She stood on the opposite side of the hall, immediately noticeable by her blaze of red hair. Next to her stood a man Riordan had only met on a few occasions but had quickly written off as a complete bore.

Mr. Harold Adams was a fellow Aeveren and from what Riordan could judge, he was one of the worst offenders in accepting his lot in this lifetime. Perfectly happy in his life as a landed gentleman, he'd moved to the county recently and appeared to gleefully enjoy every job of his social position, if his endless prattling about grounds and tenants was any indication. Riordan had made a solemn pledge to himself after their second meeting to avoid him as much as possible.

Now as he watched the beautiful woman standing next to him, he wondered if an adjustment to that idea was in order. Unable to gain her attention through the throng of people who stood between him on one side of the hall and her on the other, Riordan began to make his way through the crowd, his gaze never wavering from her face.

As he inched closer, he saw that distance had not improved her looks. She wore a pale blue dress that highlighted her pale, white skin and stunning green eyes. Blessed with an ample décolletage, this beauty made the odious Harold Adams all the more a beast and certainly unworthy of such a woman.

He finally caught her eye and saw he had the same effect on her that she had on him. As he approached her and Adams, a pink blush colored her cheeks and told him of her interest.

"Harold Adams, a delight seeing you here," Riordan announced with a strong pat on the man's shoulder, knowing it would take only these few words to begin a conversation.

"Riordan Blake. How have you been? I haven't seen you since before I left for London."

"Very well, thank you. Do your responsibilities call you away from Bedfordshire often?"

"Yes, it looks like my time away from here will be increasing in the near future. How about you?"

"No, I find few reasons to leave the county."

As he spoke, he kept an eye on the woman who now looked at him intently with those pale green eyes.

"Mr. Blake, please let me introduce my wife, Victoria. Dear, this is Riordan Blake of Hinwick Hall."

Riordan bowed and let his gaze settle on the lovely area of milky white skin just above her dress's neckline when she curtsied. Even before she'd spoken a word, he knew he wanted her.

"Mr. Blake, I believe I met your wife earlier in the other room with Lady Russell."

"Yes, Frederika enjoys her time at these balls."

Hearing the music end, Riordan turned to Harold Adams. "Would you mind, Adams?" he asked as he indicated to Victoria his desire for the next dance.

"Please do. My poor wife would never dance if she relied on me," Harold Adams said with a tone of relief in his voice.

Riordan led Victoria to the dance floor and despite his almost total disinterest in dancing, waited in anticipation for the music to begin again. She stood across from him in her line and after curtsying, reached out to place her hand gently in his to begin the intricate steps of the chosen country dance.

He noted how small her hand felt in his as he completed the first pass of the dance. She barely touched him, but her effect on him was tremendous. He struggled to keep his composure in the room full of his country neighbors while his mind raced with ideas of what he hoped to enjoy with her in the future when it would be just the two of them.

"I haven't seen you smile much tonight, sir. Do you not enjoy gatherings like this?"

Her words brought him out of his fantasy, and he was pleased by the sound of her voice.

"No, I do not. And I'm afraid I leave much to be desired as a dance partner."

His attempt at being self-effacing was successful, and she smiled warmly at him. "Not at all. But perhaps I'm a poor judge as I rarely have the opportunity to enjoy events like this either because I cannot attend or because my husband dislikes dancing."

Riordan pressed his palms to hers and turned away before the dance returned them to face one another. "Perhaps we should make a pact to entertain one another as you seem to be tolerant of my abilities."

As the music ended, Victoria looked into his eyes as she leaned in to a respectful distance and whispered, "And what do you get out of such an agreement?"

Remembering where he was, he pushed aside the plans he had for her and grinned. "The pleasure of spending time with you, Victoria," he said quietly as they walked back to her husband's side.

Riordan knew he'd taken a great liberty by using her first name, but the result was exactly what he'd hoped for. The enchanting blush from earlier returned to her cheeks but extended to the skin above her lovely breasts, a clear indication that his flaunting convention hadn't offended her in the least.

As he returned her to her husband, he thanked her with a bow and planted a subtle idea of his desire for her in her mind before he turned to walk back to his original position next to the hall's opposite wall. By the time he'd turned around, he knew she'd watched him cross the room. With little effort, he entered her mind and enjoyed finding the idea of him uppermost in her thoughts for the rest of the night.

Amon wished he could keep his memory of his time with

Victoria confined to a single dance at a ball, but his conscience, which seemed in the last year to enjoy a renewed power to affect him after many lifetimes, pressed him to relive his compete memories of her.

Within weeks of his meeting her, Riordan had made sure to find ways to see Victoria. The constraints of eighteenth century English society made approaching a married woman difficult, but in that area, Harold Adams had been quite helpful. A chance meeting with him permitted Riordan to pry concerning his travel plans, and he happily allowed the man to extract a promise from him to look in on Victoria and his young daughter in his absence.

Before the end of November and just days after making his promise to her husband, he made his way to their home just a short distance from his home in Hinwick. As if fate blessed and aided his endeavors, as he rode his horse to their home, the skies opened up and a torrential downpour soaked him to the bone. Their maid opened the door to find the man she greeted looking like a drowned rat. After leaving his name, he was allowed entry into the home and within minutes, the lady of the house was attending to him to ensure he didn't succumb to a cold.

As she talked about the effect of chill on the body, she led him to a bedroom where he could change into some of her husband's dry clothes. Other than looking forward to shedding his soaked clothes, he cared little for the polite conversation. He was far more interested in her.

Away from the ball, she wore plainer dress, but she was no less stunning. Her red hair, pinned up, framed her oval face beautifully, and her green eyes were just as gorgeous next to a pale pink dress as they had been next to her blue ball gown.

"Mr. Blake, if you'll wait in this room, I'll return with a set of dry clothes."

Riordan walked past her into the bedroom and began to undress after she closed the door. By the time she returned, he wore only his breeches and boots, his broad chest bare. She knocked softly on the door and when he intentionally didn't answer, she opened the door and entered the room.

Stepping out from behind the door, he blocked her exit and smiled at her embarrassment at seeing him half undressed.

"Thank you, Victoria," he said quietly as he reached out to take the clothes from her hand. Instead of merely taking the garments, he grabbed her arm and pulled her to his naked chest.

"Victoria," he said almost as a groan.

"Mr. Blake, please let me go. This isn't right."

Riordan heard none of the true protest or fear that would be present in her voice if she truly wanted him to let go of her.

"Riordan. You may call me Riordan, Victoria."

Shyly, she lifted her eyes to his. There was desire in those beautiful eyes.

"Riordan, please don't," she begged.

He let go of his hold on her arm, and when she made no move away from him, he put his hand to her face and stroked her cheek tenderly. Closing her eyes, she sighed and a tiny moan escaped her lips.

His hand left her cheek and trailed down her neck to the swell of her breasts. Her breathing quickened, and they rose and *fell as he watched them.*

"Please, Riordan. Don't do this. I'm weak from being alone so much and can't tell you no."

Dropping his head to softly press a kiss into the tender flesh at the top of each full breast, he looked up and smiled devilishly. "That's exactly what I want to hear."

Before she could protest any further, Riordan's mouth covered hers, his desire to have her surprising even him. Her hesitancy spurred him on, exciting him to take her hurriedly right there in a bedroom of her home, only a wall separating their coupling from the rest of the household.

To his pleasant surprise, the beautiful wife of Bedfordshire's most tedious gentleman was a smoldering woman with a deeply passionate side. Never truly uttering any real protestations against his actions, Victoria quickly met his desire with her own.

Their first time together was a rushed affair, but Riordan knew it wouldn't be their last. As he left wearing the other man's clothes, he knew he had something far more valuable of Harold Adams'.

By the spring, Riordan no longer had to pretend to check in on Victoria to see her. Left alone so often, she basked in the attention Riordan paid her and eagerly sought him out. A tiny cottage on the outer fringes of his estate provided him with a place for their trysts. Often up to three times a week, she'd come in response to his summons, always happy to see him and thankful for their time together.

But the reasons for her husband's frequent absences disappeared by the time summer had begun, and Victoria couldn't be at Riordan's beck and call. This change angered him and his unwillingness to understand that she was another man's wife above all else more than once threatened to expose her behavior to the world.

Amon clenched his jaw at the thought of how he'd treated Victoria. Forced to admit his behavior at his trial before being sent to Nil and having a full year to think about his deeds, his memories now forced him to admit that his callous mistreatment and later her death were the culmination of over a year of selfish actions toward a kind heart that had genuinely loved him. The truth of who he'd been to her tormented him and turned his stomach.

"The cottage is big enough to feel like a tiny home away from home," he heard her say as he slipped his breeches back on.

"Compared to Hinwick Hall, this is nothing, Victoria," he said dismissively.

He saw the crestfallen look cross her features and the tears begin to well up in her eyes. Too late, he realized what his words had sounded like to her.

He fastened his breeches and reluctantly walked over to the settee where she sat looking dejected. "You know I didn't mean that the way you took it," he said, lifting her chin with his finger. "You know what I think of you, Victoria."

A pout formed on her mouth, and he frowned. He hated when she pouted—hated the effect it always had on him.

"What do you think of me, Riordan?" Her green eyes stared at him as they did when she wanted the truth.

"Do we have to do this now? Why do we have to ruin a nice afternoon together?"

"Riordan, I know the reality of who we are. Harold is my destined one as Frederika is yours. I don't expect permanence or even marriage in this lifetime, but I need to know how you feel about me."

She'd freely expressed her love for him often, and he'd long ago taken for granted that she truly did feel love for him. He'd never told her he'd loved her even once because he didn't think of their time together in those terms. She made him happy and broke up the boredom of a life he was forced to live. If there was more to them, he never thought about it.

"You're my Victoria. That's what I think of you," he said as he placed a kiss on her forehead.

After she'd gone, Riordan thought about ending his time with her. She was beautiful and gave his body more pleasure than he'd had in years with his wife, but perhaps her feelings were becoming a problem. However, as he had each time he'd considered giving her up, he decided she was worth having enough to tolerate her occasional outbursts of emotion.

Riordan continued to take her for granted while his behavior with the woman he'd known for seventeen lifetimes grew less and less acceptable. Frederika had come to him as Sevine, a young Aeveren instantly in love with a more experienced Aeveren, but his abuse of his powers finally pushed her away, and no amount of land or money would make her remain with him. Lifetimes of manipulation of those closest to him finally came back to haunt him when Frederika did what *few Aeveren destined ones ever did: refuse their mate.*

Unable to manipulate her one last time, Riordan found himself alone in the world, refused by the one Aeveren biology had chosen for him. Turning to Victoria, he took all he desired, even convincing her to leave her husband and daughter for him. In love, she was an easy target, and it took few promises to make her leave those she loved for him. But she wasn't enough. After years of nothing, he wanted everything—gambling, drinking, and women. Above all, women.

Amon held Thea to him as his mind replayed the day he left Victoria. The vision of her standing in front of him, as she begged him to stay with her and he callously disregarded her, a woman who'd given her heart and soul to him wholly and willingly, gnawed at his conscience.

As he thought about those last moments with Victoria, Amon's chest tightened. His eyes closed, he saw the face of a woman who'd loved him wracked with sadness as he heard the cavalier words he'd used to let her know just how little he'd truly cared about their time together. Those words had haunted him in Nil after learning at his trial that alone, cast aside by him and without her husband and daughter, she'd taken her own life.

Now, as he experienced the loss of Victoria through his memories, he felt hollow inside. He looked down at Thea and questioned whether any man had ever treated her as he had Victoria.

Had she loved unconditionally and been abused in return?

Had the selfishness of another destroyed her sometime as

his had destroyed Victoria?

Amon felt his heart harden at the thought of Thea's kindness turned against her like that. Holding her to him, he silently begged forgiveness from the woman he'd mistreated all those lifetimes ago and the woman who innocently lay sleeping near him.

CHAPTER FOURTEEN

K IRIL HEARD THE PHONE RING but chose to ignore it and instead rolled over and buried his head in the pillow. When it stopped ringing, he promised himself to put the ringer on silent at night in the future and closed his eyes hoping to get back to sleep. Seconds later, it rang again, and he angrily rolled onto his back and grabbed the phone from the night table.

Before he could get the nasty words he planned to say out of his mouth, a voice came through loud and clear. "Gault, when I call you, you'd better pick up by the second ring, not the second call. Do you understand me?"

He understood clearly the man on the other end of the line was powerful enough to rightfully make the demand, so he quietly agreed to it. He listened as the news he'd expected came through. Knowing his allegiance to the caller trumped any favor he held for anyone else, he accepted his instructions without protest and slowly closed the phone.

Dressing quickly in a robe, he called for his aides, and as he waited for them, he considered the task just assigned to him. Messing with powerful Aeveren was dangerous and something he preferred not to do. He'd, therefore, worked very hard to ensure the Soren remained on friendly terms with them. Now he'd be forced to abandon that policy.

His aides filed in, took their places in front of him, and awaited their orders. Kiril folded his arms across his chest and smiled. Today, he'd give orders unlike any he'd ever given.

"Cancel the new girl for today. I've got another one coming. She's not human, so I'll let you know the particular details about how I want her handled before she gets here."

The group of men stared back in confusion as he finished speaking. "Not a human? Then what?" one of the aides asked.

Kiril's grin grew wider. "An Aeveren, gentlemen, and not just any Aeveren. A healer."

RYU ENTERED THE ROOMS OF the head councilman with more than a little trepidation. He'd never been summoned to meet privately with the head of the Council at Nil and was sure this first time wouldn't set a good precedent.

The room he was escorted to was the councilman's office immediately adjacent to his living quarters. It looked like any office would with a desk, bookshelves, and filing cabinets, but Ryu was struck with the opulence of the setting. He slowly ran his fingers over the top of the mahogany desk and admired the craftsmanship of the piece. His eyes traveled to the leather office chair behind the desk and the matching couch on the far side of the room before he saw the floor to ceiling mahogany bookcases full of obviously rare and expensive editions of famous Aeveren works and priceless art pieces.

Not a bad life, if you can get it.

"I'd trade it all for the only treasure that ever meant anything to me," a voice said sadly behind him.

Ryu turned to see the councilman standing in the doorway to his office. The man's usually stern features seemed softened for a moment but quickly changed back to their usual appearance, and Ryu's gaze was met with a flinty stare from cold, gray eyes.

"Please be seated, Mr. Jansen."

Across the desk, the most powerful man in Nil sat with his hands folded in front of his face, fingers steepled. Ryu studied his pose and waited for him to explain about the offer he'd not been able to refuse.

"I called you here to enlist your help in an additional aspect of the Amon Kalins case."

"Additional?" Ryu asked confused. "Is there something more the Council would like me to do beyond capturing him and returning him to Nil?"

"Mr. Jansen, your file indicates you spent a lifetime in the British Isles. How did you find that life?"

Unsure of where this was leading, he generically answered, "Fine," and waited for the councilman to continue.

"Nineteenth century England, if I'm not incorrect."

Uneasily, Ryu's mind ran through the major events of that lifetime as he nodded in agreement. A lifetime as an industrial worker, it had been nondescript compared to others he'd had and certainly not a worthy topic of discussion for his first private meeting with the head of the Council of Nil.

"I so wish I could have seen the greatness of the empire," the councilman said in a faraway voice.

The men sat in silence, and Ryu watched the other man's features soften and then harden once again. When the councilman spoke again, his voice sounded as harsh as his expression looked.

"In addition to capturing Kalins, you are to take his destined one to a location to which I'll provide directions."

"The healer?" Ryu asked in a voice that only partially told how shocked he was.

"Yes. You will transport her to the location I give you."

"Before or after I capture Kalins?"

The councilman smiled. "This is why I had you recalled, Mr. Jansen—for your superior abilities. Before you get Kalins, if you will."

Ryu took a moment to once again go through the list of advantages Kalins possessed. Sighing, he wondered why the councilman seemed intent on making the job harder than it needed to be.

The councilman squinted his eyes angrily and answered Ryu's unspoken question.

"Amon Kalins needs to feel the pain of losing his destined one because of something other than his return to Nil."

Ryu chastised himself for forgetting the man's ability to read thoughts, and the councilman's face broke out in a smile.

"Mr. Jansen, there is really nothing I can't know about you

with the power I've been given here. It's an indispensable tool for the head of the Council to possess."

Lulled into forgetting where he was for a moment by the man's change, Ryu asked, "You didn't possess this power in your lifetimes before here?"

"No. I was a very common Aeveren for my time before I was offered a position on the Council of Nil. As many of us even after the twentieth lifetime, all I could boast of was a heightened sense of awareness with others, but even that I can't say I used as effectively as I should have."

As he listened to the man, Ryu felt as if he were intruding on a memory. Hoping to escape what had become an uncomfortable situation, he carefully guided the conversation back to the new requirement that had been imposed.

"Other than finding the healer and taking her where you want me to, is there anything else I should do?"

The councilman shook himself out of his thoughts and rejoined Ryu in the present. "Make haste, Mr. Jansen, in your fulfillment of this council's demands. Get Amon Kalins back to Nil where he belongs."

When he finished, he slid a paper with the location Ryu was to take Thea to. As Ryu took the paper, the councilman rose from behind the desk.

"Mr. Jansen, complete this assignment quickly and I'll ensure your future with the Aeveren council of your choosing."

As Ryu left the Council of Nil, he removed the paper from his jacket and looked at the address.

London.

AMON OPENED HIS EYES AND looked over at Thea still sleeping quietly next to him. Hours of tossing and turning over his past left him exhausted, but worse was the fact that today was the day he was to take Gethen home. This day had been a long time coming, he knew, but that didn't mean he didn't dread it all the same.

Thea awoke and took his hand in hers. Raising it to her lips, she kissed the back of it as she looked into his eyes. "What's on your mind that's bothering you?"

Amon remained silent for a moment and then said, "We leave soon to take Gethen back to his people."

Stroking his cheek, she seemed to understand his pain. "I'm sorry, Amon. I know Gethen is dear to you."

He smiled briefly and let out a sigh.

"Amon, what else is bothering you?"

A dozen things ran through his mind that he couldn't tell her. He'd always heard that at some point everyone's past catches up to him and for the first time in forty-seven lifetimes, he saw how true this was. And it was different than having to answer for his crimes to the Council. Then his biggest fear had been the loss of his freedom. Now with Thea, he felt a different fear. Now he feared losing her—her love—because of who he'd been all those lifetimes.

How could she remain with a man who'd done the things he'd done?

He couldn't let her find out. Now, more than ever before, he needed the present to be more important than the past.

He ran his fingers gently over the lock of hair that rested near her cheek and silently pledged to do whatever he had to do for her to never know the truth of whom he'd actually been.

"Nothing else, Thea. Just Gethen's leaving."

Slowly, he rose to his feet and extended his hand to her. "Time to get ready."

Pulling her close to him, he kissed her head and hugged her. The feel of her arms around his body made him forget for just a moment everything that tortured his mind.

"I'd stay here, like this, holding you for the rest of time if I could," he whispered.

AS THEA LEFT FOR A shower, Amon thought about where they'd be going, a place he hadn't been since right after he'd left England lifetimes ago. Almost two hundred years had passed since he'd set foot in the Irish countryside, and while the land of humans and Aeveren had changed greatly, he knew the world of the Sidhe had remained as it had been throughout time. A place of magick, the kingdom of the Sidhe was forever untouched by the changes of the outside world.

How much Gethen had changed in his time away from his people, though. Shunned for his crimes, Gethen had been a wild, young Sidhe when he'd taken him. Since then, through each lifetime, Gethen had found him, each time older and wiser after their separation.

With a stab of shame, Amon admitted to himself that he

knew little of what Gethen did in the years apart from him, other than safeguard his homes and wealth. Had he spent all those years alone?

As he walked down the stairs to prepare to travel with Gethen one last time, he selfishly wished he'd change his mind and stay. But he'd made his choice.

He found Gethen alone in the study, still pensive as he'd been before. With sadness, he tried to imagine this home—a home he'd only had in his current lifetime—without Gethen's presence. Remembering what he'd thought about his homes being empty, lonely places without a destined one to share them with, he quietly chuckled at his mistake.

"Sit and talk to me, Gethen."

As the two men had done so many times before, they took their customary seats facing one another. Knowing he may not have another opportunity to say his goodbye alone with Gethen, Amon swallowed hard and readied himself to bid farewell to the one being who he'd spent more time with in the past seven lifetimes than any other.

"Gethen, I need to know you're sure about this."

A look he hadn't seen for lifetimes passed over the Sidhe's face, and Gethen said in a measured voice, "It's better for everyone involved if I return to my people...safer."

Immediately, Amon understood his friend's choice. No reason for Gethen's murder of the women before Aine had ever been given, and Amon had long considered whatever had been the reason to be a part of his friend's past. But he had to admit that Thea's being his destined one had given him pause recently and had brought those long forgotten crimes back into his thoughts.

As he stared at the scar on Gethen's face, proof of his past savagery, Amon's protective nature reared up inside him.

Gethen saw the change in him and quickly explained. "I've felt nothing of the urges I once had, Amon. My loyalty to you simply makes me want to leave before anything possibly changes in me. Please know I would never harm your destined one."

Pushing down his concerns, Amon nodded. "I know, friend. Your loyalty to our friendship was never in doubt."

Silent again, Amon began to say his goodbye to his friend the best way he knew. When he was finished, Gethen smiled. "It has been the joy of my life to know you, Amon."

Thea's descent from the floor above ended the meeting, and by the time she entered the study, both men were standing and ready to leave. Gethen left to find Markku, and Thea stepped next to Amon and put her arms around him. "Everything okay?"

Half lying and his stomach in knots, Amon forced a smile. "Yes. Are you ready?"

Thea nodded. "Exactly where are we going?"

"Ireland."

Tilting her face up toward him, she laughed. "You and I have different ideas on just what the word exactly means. I was looking for a little more specificity than the name of a country."

Amon, charmed by her way of bringing him out of his

sadness, smiled. "Specificity?" he asked in a mocking tone.

"Yes, as in maybe the name of the town we're going to. Or since it's Ireland, a county name would work," she teased.

Amon looked up to see Gethen and Markku walking down the hall toward them. In her ear, he whispered, "It's a surprise, but I think you'll like the house."

Thea's face looked surprised. "What house?"

"Our house. Or to be more specific, one of our houses."

"One of *our* houses?"

Winking at her, he joined Gethen to discuss what Markku was to do upon arriving. With one final look, Amon held Thea as they disappeared from his study, followed by Markku with Gethen.

AMON WATCHED AS THEA SLOWLY opened her eyes to see the beautiful countryside of southern Ireland. The charm of the land here amazed even him, and the wonder in her expression told him she was just as impressed.

"Welcome to your home in County Cork, my lady."

Thea stepped back away from him, opened her arms, and began to spin around, her long blond hair fanning out around her.

"This is one of the most beautiful places I've ever been!" she squealed as she continued to spin.

"I'm glad you like it."

"Like it? I love it!"

As Thea slowed her turning, she staggered and tumbled to the ground, landing on her back. Amon held out his hand to help her up, but she pulled him down to the ground next to her, giggling her delight. The sound of her happiness thrilled him more than he thought possible, and there, on the grassy hillside, he pulled her close to him and stared up at the cloudless blue sky, for the first time believing everything would be fine.

Softly, she whispered in his ear, "Amon, I only hope I make you as happy as you make me."

Kissing her, he showed her just how happy she made him, but moments later, he heard Gethen's voice in his head warning him of trouble. Looking up, he saw the bounty hunter walking toward them up the grassy hill.

"Thea, get to the house now."

Frightened, she jumped to her feet and saw the man Amon was now staring at. "Who is he?"

"Thea, he's a bounty hunter. I need you to get to the house. I'll be there when I'm done with him. Go now!"

Thea ran as fast as she could toward the large Georgian home a few hundred yards away. In horror, Amon watched as Ryu turned to chase Thea instead of him. He was faster than she and would catch her before she reached the house!

In seconds, Amon had teleported in front of Ryu, and he stopped him dead with a fist to his chest. From behind him, he heard Thea scream and when he turned to see if she'd made it safely to the house, Ryu disappeared from sight.

Enraged, Amon stormed into the house behind Thea, bellowing for Markku. "Find out why the fuck the bounty hunter sent for me just went after Thea. And find out fast. Go!"

Markku quickly obeyed Amon's orders and vanished. Still in a rage, Amon sat down on the couch in the living room to figure out what had happened. *Why would the bounty hunter attempt to take an innocent woman? The Council is a bunch of bureaucratic bastards, but even they don't take women hostages. But Kiril isn't opposed to doing that and worse.*

Amon dismissed the idea that Kiril Gault and the Soren would be behind Ryu's attempt to take Thea. He and his group had always been allies of Amon's, so it made no sense that they'd want to make an enemy now, after they'd just helped him escape from Nil. And the bounty hunter worked for the Council, not the Soren.

Thea's voice broke his focus on the question of who had tried to take her, and he looked up to see her standing in front of him. The fear that remained in her expression caused the anger to melt away from him, and he pulled her down onto his lap.

She nestled her face in the space between his neck and shoulder. "What happened back there?"

Amon stroked her hair and back, sensing how frightened she was. "I don't know, but I told you what I'd do to anyone who even made the mistake of thinking of hurting you."

"Will it always be this way, Amon?"

That was a question he couldn't answer. Until now, he'd only thought about how he'd need to evade the Council, but now he saw that they intended to make his destined one a target too.

Kissing her softly on the lips, he quietly said, "Don't worry. I told you. You're safe with me."

CHAPTER FIFTEEN

HOURS LATER, THEA LAY IN bed, still shaken from what had happened earlier. Quietly, Amon entered the room and slid into bed next to her.

"I missed you," Thea whispered softly.

Amon wrapped his arms around her and held her close. "I don't ever want you to feel that way. I'll always be here with you."

"But what if the bounty hunter gets you? Or me?"

Shaking his head, he kissed her. "No more about that."

"But," she began and was interrupted.

"Obviously, I'm going to have to do something with your mouth so you can't talk any more about that," he teased.

Kissing her, he sensually flicked his tongue over hers and moaned into her mouth. Near her hip, she felt his cock begin to harden.

"Got any ideas about what else to do with my mouth?" she whispered seductively.

"A couple," he said before kissing her again. "But for right now, I like where it is."

Thea felt like time stopped when Amon kissed her like this. His tongue created sensations that raced straight to between her legs when he teased the inside of her mouth. As if he knew how she felt, his hands slid under her clothes, and he pulled her on top of him.

Tugging at her pants, he slid them off her and ran his hands over her skin before rolling her back onto the bed. In seconds, he'd stripped out of his clothes and returned to her. He looked like a hungry man whose eyes devoured the sights of a banquet laid in front of him. Removing her shirt, she lay back naked, waiting for him.

"Open up for me," he groaned as he gently pushed her legs open and began to stroke her soft flesh.

Thea closed her eyes and waited in sweet anticipation for him to press his lips to her. Before he did, he slid a finger down her wet slit and into her, groaning, "Angel, when I make love to you, it'll be slow, but now I need to taste you on my tongue and feel you explode into my mouth."

As he spoke, he moved his finger slowly in and out of her, stroking the spot she so desperately loved him to touch.

"Please....hurry, Amon."

Dipping his head between her legs, his mouth kissed every part of her core as his finger continued its slow torture. In no time, Thea had her hips off the bed, her body begging for release.

"Amon…"

"Come for me, Thea," he commanded.

From deep inside her, it began as a tendril of need

blossomed into her orgasm. When she came, his tongue replaced his finger, and as he fucked her with his tongue, she whimpered into the spasms his mouth caused.

When he sat up to face her, he sucked his still moist finger into his mouth with a grin. "I love the taste of you on my lips."

Thea moaned. "Roll over. Turnabout is fair play."

With Amon on his back, Thea kissed down his stomach and lingered on the spot near his hip that was one of her favorite parts on his body. So silky soft, yet so powerful and strong. Wrapping her hand around his long, thick cock, she slowly began to stroke him. His groans told her he loved what she did to him as much as she loved doing it. She teased the tip with a flick of her tongue, tasting the salty dampness that waited for her, making him moan more. As she stroked, she teased the length of him with tiny flicks and kisses but never took him in her mouth.

"Don't tease me, angel. You're playing a dangerous game," he growled seductively.

"Dangerous, huh? You don't seem to have a firm grasp on who's in control here," she said smiling up at him.

Before she knew what had happened, Thea found herself under him with him pressing into her from behind. Leaning over, he nipped at her ear. "I think your assessment of control was flawed, love."

Teasing her, he slid through her moist folds to her excited nub and back, not quite ready to give in to her pushing back toward him. "Let's work on that idea of control," he groaned as he turned her onto her back.

LOOKING DOWN AT HER, WITH her half-closed eyes and face that looked almost too innocent for what he had in mind, he bent down to kiss her. "If I do anything you don't like, just tell me. We're only playing, Thea."

He knew she was unsure of what he meant, though she agreed with silent nod.

From the closet, he took two red silk neckties and returned to the bed to dangle them over her, dragging them over one breast and then the other.

"Do you know what these are for, angel?"

Thea's eyes grew wide, and she shook her head as she mouthed, "No."

"A little lesson in control."

Carefully, he took one hand and tied her wrist to the bedpost. "Do you trust me?"

"Of course."

As he made his way over to her other hand, he stopped to kiss her, slipping his tongue sensually into her mouth as he held himself over her. With her free hand, she pulled his head to her, wanting so much more than teasing.

Pulling away to focus on tying her hand, he said, "Good things come to those who wait, angel."

When he'd fastened both hands to the wooden posts, he returned to hovering over her and began kissing her again. After a few moments, he rolled off the bed to return to the closet to retrieve another tie.

"Amon, I don't have three hands," she joked.

He returned to the bed and kneeled over her. "Three hands. You're going to get it for that," he said sweetly. "Lift your head."

Thea did as he ordered, and he slipped a third tie around her head as a blindfold. When he'd finished tying it, he knew she couldn't see a thing through the black fabric.

Immobilized and effectively blinded to his next move, her voice suddenly showed her fear. "Amon?"

Kneeling over her, he bent down to softly tease her lips with his. "Yes?"

"Please, don't do…"

"Don't worry, love. I would never hurt you. Trust me."

"I've never done this," she said in a worried voice and then bit her lower lip nervously.

Next to her ear he whispered, "Then I'll have to make sure you love it enough to want it again."

Standing next to the bed, Amon watched as her breasts rose and fell and wished it was more because of desire than fear. But he'd soon change that.

Thea turned her head toward the side and seemed to search for him. "Amon?"

"Yes?"

"What are you doing?"

"Just looking."

He placed his finger on her lips and began to lightly trace a line down over the column of her neck and between her breasts. Slowly, he slid his finger around one nipple and then the other, loving how they hardened into excited peaks. Thea arched her body to gain more contact with his touch, but he pulled back and watched as she lay back down on the bed, waiting in anticipation for him to make his next move.

He knew she'd be waiting for him to touch her breasts again, but instead he reached over to her right thigh and lightly grazed it with his knuckle. Instinctively, she opened her legs for him, eager for him to touch her more.

"Not yet, love," he said as he leaned next to her ear. "First, we have to get back to where we were before."

Amon crouched next to the bed and gently turned her head toward him. "Remember, if you don't like something, tell me and I'll stop."

Leaning against the bed, he guided his cock to her mouth. Tentatively, she licked her lips and then parted them, wrapping them around the head to gently suck him into her mouth.

Amon watched as Thea took him in slowly and then released him when he retreated from the sensual feel of her mouth. He knew she must be anxious as she was entirely dependent on the pace he set, but as she eagerly pleasured him she gave no sign of this fear. He reentered her mouth and slowly pushed his cock in toward her throat, ready to back out quickly if she began to struggle. Inch by inch, he gently leaned in until he felt the smaller passage of her throat push up against the tip. The feel of her taking him so far into her mouth almost made his knees give out, and he slowly backed out of her. Empty again, she licked her lips and waited for him to return once more.

He stood there for a long moment just watching her and noting how sensual she looked as she waited to taste his cock again. From somewhere deep in his memory the vision of Kiril's slaves helplessly chained and shackled rushed into his mind, and suddenly he felt sick at the scene in front of him. Slowly, he leaned down to kiss her cheek.

"That's enough for now," he said quietly.

"Amon, is something wrong?"

"No. Nothing," he said as he reached over to untie her hands.

When she was free, she sat up and began to unfasten the blindfold. He quickly stopped her, and she let her hands fall to her sides as her body sagged with a look of disappointment.

"Did I do something wrong?" she asked in a voice full of dejection.

Pulling her onto his lap, he placed her above his rigid cock and entered her as he whispered, "Not a thing."

Thea wrapped her arms around his neck and pressed her body close to his. With his hand, he braced her lower back as she began to ride him, his cock filling her. Still blindfolded, she kissed his neck as he moved inside her, murmuring softly against his skin. Her tenderness touched him, and he responded with a gentleness he hadn't known for a long time.

As she moved against him, he watched her blond hair, still bound by the black tie, bounce almost playfully over her shoulders. As he edged closer to his climax, he slid the blindfold from her head. For a moment, Thea stopped in surprise, her eyes wide as they readjusted to the light of the room.

"Hi," she said sweetly, her smile reaching all the way to her eyes.

Amon couldn't help but kiss her when she was being so cute. She had no idea that the memories of Kiril and his women had nearly ruined this for him. A darker thought crossed his mind. She had no idea of many of the memories that threatened to ruin their life together. Holding her close to his chest, he hugged her tightly as he silently swore to not let his past touch her.

"I love you, Thea. Don't ever doubt that."

CHAPTER SIXTEEN

T HEA AWOKE FEELING WONDERFUL ABOUT life after
making love with Amon. She had a destined one who
loved her and whom she loved. And it appeared he came along
with houses, in addition to incredible looks, tremendous sex
appeal, and everything else he was. After forty-five lifetimes,
she finally had what so many other women she'd known had
been given, and no bounty hunter was going to take it away
from her. Not if she had anything to say about it.

With her renewed spirit, she climbed out of bed, slipped
on one of her new dresses, and made her way to the kitchen.
As she took her first good look at the house, she wondered if
she was still dreaming. The Georgian home was furnished with
the best of everything, from the furniture, window coverings,
and hardwood floors to the appliances in the kitchen, which
were all state of the art. It was all so much nicer than she'd ever
had.

Amon seemed to be nowhere in the house, which Thea
thought odd, but she trusted him. It did concern her, however,
that after what had happened when they'd arrived that she

appeared to be alone.

From behind her, she heard footsteps and turned to see Gethen but no Amon. He looked more serious than usual, and Thea sensed an uneasiness about him that worried her.

"Hello, Gethen. Is everything okay?"

Thea watched his face grow darker in the moments before he answered, but when he spoke, his voice was the same timbre as it had been from the moment she'd met him—formal and slightly intimidating.

"Everything's fine, miss."

Although she wanted to know where Amon had gone, Gethen's expression made her reluctant to ask. The man had a foreboding look that Thea decided came from the scar that transected one side of this face. She wondered what could have happened to him to cause such a wound.

The look on his face morphed into something frightening right before her eyes, and she suddenly remembered with guilt what Amon had told her about his communication with the Sidhe.

"I'm sorry for that, Gethen. That was inconsiderate of me."

Instantly, his mood seemed to lighten, and Thea could have sworn a tiny smile crept onto his face.

"Excuse me. I'm going to find Amon," she said, hoping to escape the uncomfortable situation her thoughts had created.

As she walked past him, Gethen caught her arm by the elbow and stopped her. The lightened mood she thought she'd noticed seconds ago was now gone, and the man she faced seemed imposing and dangerous in front of her.

Gethen's dark green eyes studied Thea's face, scanning her features as if he were looking at a woman for the first time and deciding if he liked what he saw. Panic rose inside her, and her heart pounded against her chest. For the first time, she truly feared him, even more than at the moment she'd met him.

"I can read your mind. I know you're frightened."

Thea felt his hand loosen its grip on her arm and some of her fear subsided, but he didn't let go.

"There is no reason for you to be frightened. You are Amon's destined one, and what Amon cherishes, I cherish," he said in a low voice as he looked deeply into her eyes.

"Why are you leaving? Is it because of me?"

Thea felt his hand leave her arm, and Gethen stepped back away from her.

"In one way, yes, it is. For lifetimes, I've been Amon's servant taking care of him. While I didn't have a choice as I owed him my life for taking me when no other creature on Earth would accept me, my life was freely given to him from that first day. My place in this world was to take care of him. But he no longer needs me because he has you."

Sadness filled Thea's heart. "But I can't replace the friendship he has with you."

"I am Sidhe. I am not one of your kind. Amon belongs with you without having me to think of. It's time I returned to my people, to my kind."

"You said Amon was the only one to accept you. What if they won't take you back?"

Gethen's expression grew softer and a real smile formed,

brightening his eyes so they appeared to dance and sparkle. "Much time has passed since I was cast out of my world, albeit less time for the Sidhe. My penance has been fulfilled for many years. Amon knew this lifetimes ago."

Thea wondered why Amon hadn't returned Gethen to his world before now. Before she could voice her question, Gethen answered.

"Don't think poorly of Amon for keeping me as his servant. Solitude is a choice few of us would willingly make."

Gethen stepped out of Thea's way to let her pass. Touched by the knowledge of his love for the man she cared so much for, she stood on her toes and placed a kiss on his scarred face.

"Thank you for this, Gethen."

As she moved to walk away, he once again caught her arm and she turned to see not anger but kindness.

"Take care of him. Even when he seems to be a man you don't recognize, don't forget who he is."

Thea smiled but wondered what this meant. How could she ever not recognize her destined one?

Out of the corner of her eye, she saw Amon and Gethen's warning quickly left her mind. "Amon!" she said as she put her arms around him. "Where have you been?"

"Thea, I need to speak to Gethen. Can you excuse us?" He placed a small kiss on her lips and winked. "Wait for me upstairs, okay?"

Thea made her way to the stairs and stopped before she reached the top, curious to know what the two men discussed.

"I'm concerned about Markku, Gethen."

"Why?"

"That bounty hunter knew we were coming here and knew when. The only way he could know that would be through Markku."

"Amon, as much as the man irritates me, I have a hard time believing he would betray you again."

"Then how did the bounty hunter know?"

Neither man answered the question, and Thea hurried upstairs before she was caught spying, just as concerned about the man who was their connection to the Soren.

THEA SAT ON THE BED and looked out the window at the Irish countryside. The lawn seemed to go on forever, changing shades from pale to deep green as the grass ran over the rolling hills. The scene looked like one from a postcard she'd received from a friend who'd visited this beautiful land years before. Outside the bedroom door, she heard footsteps and waited for Amon's embrace. A hand touched her face and instantly she knew it wasn't Amon's, but it was too late. Before she could scream, her mouth was covered and Ryu Jansen had taken her.

When she focused her eyes moments later, she didn't need to be told she was far away from County Cork and the man she loved. Everything that surrounded her felt foreign.

Ryu's hands pressed on her shoulders, holding her still so she couldn't struggle. Forced to remain in place, she scanned the room she stood in for any clue of her whereabouts. The walls around her were plain white and provided no indication of where she was. The small room was nondescript, a room that could have been in any building in a thousand locations in the world.

"This will go a whole lot easier if you stay calm," Ryu said coldly behind her.

"Where am I?" she demanded as she craned her neck to face him.

In front of her the door opened and Thea heard a voice that immediately struck fear in her heart. She spun her head back to see Kiril Gault standing in the doorway.

"How wonderful it is to see you again so soon, Thea," he purred as his eyes roamed over her body suggestively.

Around him, his hulking bodyguards mimicked his actions, their greedy eyes devouring everything she was.

"Why have you kidnapped me?"

Ignoring her, Kiril focused on Ryu. "You can go. I'll take this from here."

Kiril winked knowingly at Thea and grinned. "We're going to have a wonderful time. Gentlemen, take her to the room with the other girls."

Thea thrashed wildly as Ryu loosened his hold on her and two of Kiril's men grabbed her, squeezing her upper arms with their thick fingers.

"Let go of me! You're hurting me!"

Each move she made in a futile attempt to be free led to tighter squeezing on her arms, bringing tears to her eyes.

"Mr. Gault, please make them stop!" she cried as tears rolled down her face.

Kiril waved his hand casually, and the men released her

and stepped back. Thea rubbed her arms where painful bruises began to form and prayed that Amon would be able to find her before they did even worse to her.

As the leader of the Soren stepped in front of her, Thea watched his violet eyes zero in on her face. His piercing gaze made her shrink back, but Ryu stopped her. Kiril slowly ran the back of his index finger down her jaw line to her chin and tilted her face up toward his. The feel of his skin on hers made her shiver, something that seemed to please him immensely.

"Thea, the more you fight me, the worse this will be. Now be a pet and go with these men."

His touch lingered on her as he spoke, and Thea sensed all too clearly that the sweetness in his voice was temporary and easily replaced with the viciousness she'd heard days earlier.

She saw the men return to her side, but this time she put up no fight. They led her down a dark hallway to a room far dimmer than the one before. As her eyes focused, she was horrified to see she was to be held with Kiril Gault's slaves. Unable to back away, she froze in place.

Oh my God! Amon, can you hear me? Kiril has me!

Hands shoved her into the room, and she stumbled to the floor in front of the three women who sat chained together. When she looked up, she saw the fear in their eyes and her instincts as a healer kicked in. Struggling to get to her feet, she crouched down in front of them.

"It's okay. I won't hurt you. Please don't be afraid."

One of them looked at her with tears in her eyes. "You're here to replace one of us!" she cried.

"No! Don't be afraid. Please," Thea said softly.

"Then why are you here?" another one asked.

"I don't know. Do you remember me? I visited here, I think, with my destined one."

The women nodded but said nothing.

"He'll find me and rescue us."

The one who hadn't spoken snorted in disgust. "You don't know much about Amon Kalins, do you?"

Thea looked at her innocently, but inside she feared the woman was right. Amon was friends with Kiril Gault, but now she was a prisoner of his, which made no sense.

"No, you're wrong. Amon won't rest until he finds me. I'm his destined one. He loves me."

"Honey, I don't care what you Aeveren claim about these destined ones. Amon Kalins is as vicious as Kiril, even more because of how powerful he is. And he's close to Kiril, so how do you explain why you're here with us?"

Thea couldn't explain why one of Amon's friends had kidnapped her, but she believed in her destined one. She had to.

AMON LOOKED FORWARD TO A few moments of relaxation with Thea and smiled to himself as he thought about something he'd like to do that would take far longer than just a few moments. Just the thought of making love to her again lightened his mood. He looked forward to giving her every one of his homes as gifts to show her how much he loved her. The thrill he'd seen on her face and the excitement she'd shown him when they'd arrived at just this one house made him actually care about the places he owned.

For a brief moment, he remembered Callia's thrill when she first saw his Italian villa and cringed with regret at what he'd done. By the time he reached the bedroom, he'd pushed those memories out of his mind, though. He was a different man now—a man with a destined one he adored and who made him better than he ever could be alone.

"Thea?" he called as he stood looking into the empty bedroom. No response came, and he called her name again, in case she'd gone for a shower.

Instinctively, he knew something was wrong. He raced to the bathroom but found it empty too. Teleporting downstairs, he quickly found Gethen.

"Have you seen Thea?" he asked as he attempted to tamp down the fear that was growing inside him by the second.

Gethen shook his head. "She isn't upstairs?"

"No. You look in here. Search every room. I'll look outside."

Amon looked frantically, but she was nowhere in sight. With every step he took, his fear mixed with rage. It didn't take long before he admitted to himself that the bounty hunter had gotten her. By the time he found Gethen inside the house, he was nearly blinded by anger.

"The fucking bounty hunter has her. I swear to God, I'll kill him and every member of the Council for this. Where the fuck is Markku?"

"I don't know. I called him, but I got his voicemail."

"I want him here, now! Markku!"

Amon's voice shook the walls and windows. "Markku!"

Almost as if he'd heard his name across the miles, Markku appeared in the room before Amon and Gethen, unaware of what awaited him. Before he could ask any questions, Amon seized him by the throat with one hand and lifted him the almost nine inches to his eye level, almost crushing his larynx.

"Where is she?" Amon demanded.

Markku's arms grasped at the hand choking his throat as he croaked out the words, "I don't know."

"Amon," Gethen cautioned in a forced calm voice, "perhaps he can tell us more if you put him down."

Although he knew his friend was right, he didn't want to release Markku. He wanted to kill someone, and the man hanging from his right hand would do until he got a hold of that bounty hunter or the members of the Council.

Gethen's judgment prevailed and Amon dropped Markku to the floor. As he lay there in a heap, gasping for breath, Amon returned to questioning him.

"The bounty hunter has taken Thea. Something tells me you had something to do with it. So start talking or the next time I put my hand around your neck, I'll fucking choke the life out of you."

Markku cowered on the floor as Amon waited to follow through with his threat. Fear made him avoid Amon's eyes, making him look guiltier than ever.

"Amon, I swear I had nothing to do with it. I swear."

"Then how the hell did he know we were coming here and the exact time to arrive?" he shouted.

Markku had regained the ability to breathe, if not to swallow, and he attempted to rise to his feet, all the while shielding his face with his hand to protect from the attack that could come at any moment. Once standing, he wisely stepped back from Amon and began to speak, his raspy voice barely audible.

"I did as you ordered and went to find out why the bounty hunter had targeted Thea. Amon, something big is going down. That guy has been seen at the Soren headquarters before. What the fuck would a bounty hunter for the Council be doing with anyone at the Soren? Nobody at my level knew, but that's not all. There's something going on with the Council. My guy at the Directorate told me they're using people's past lifetimes against them."

Amon knew all too well how serious a breach of Aeveren ethics this was. In fact, the inability of any Aeveren, even those on the Council of Nil, to know an Aeveren's past lifetimes for any reason other than legal ones was one of the few rules of their world he'd generally agreed with.

"Why?"

"I don't know about anyone else, but they gave Thea's record to the bounty hunter. I'm guessing to help him get to you."

"He knows about her past lifetimes?"

"Yeah. The head of the Council at Nil ordered it. But I'm hearing his actions are causing a problem with the other members. At least one officially went on record to protest his giving the bounty hunter Thea's past lifetimes information."

Amon paced back and forth past Markku as he thought about what he'd said. Pausing in front of him, he asked, "What the hell is this man's issue with me? Did I dishonor his family or something lifetimes ago? It's got to be something big if he's willing to break one of our most solemn laws. Find out from your guy in the Directorate who he was before he went to the Council."

"Okay, I will."

"And find out whatever else you can about why a bounty hunter would be visiting the Soren."

"Okay, Amon. Okay."

After Markku left, Amon turned to Gethen. "You believe him?"

Gethen appeared to think about the question for a few seconds. "Yes, I do. But if this is what's going on, then it's possible that Kiril isn't the friend you thought he was."

"Do you think he's foolish enough to fuck with me? I've availed myself of the Soren's services in the few areas I've found them useful, but I have no feelings of loyalty to him or that group that would take precedence over Thea's safety."

"Amon, if a Council of Nil bounty hunter has been seen at the Soren headquarters, I think you need to accept the fact that Kiril Gault may not be anything he's claimed to be."

"I think the bigger concern should be Kiril's if I find out he had anything to do with Thea being taken."

Gethen began to speak but hesitated.

"What is it?"

"Amon, do you remember what Kiril said when he saw Thea with us as Soren headquarters?"

Images of Kiril Gault's slaves flashed through Amon's mind and the thought of Thea chained up, enslaved to service Kiril made him want to kill someone.

"I think it's time I went to see my good friend at the Soren."

"Be careful. If Kiril and the Council are working together, you're walking into a trap, and they're using Thea as bait."

Amon walked outside to the spot where he'd watched Thea innocently twirl around and focused his mind on hers. He knew it was unlikely she could sense him because he couldn't sense her, but he had to try. He had to let her know he would move heaven and earth to find her and kill any man or woman who got in his way.

And God help anyone who harmed her.

Thea, I'm coming for you. Don't be frightened. I will find you.

As he walked back to the house, another thought stayed in his mind.

I'm going to kill you, Kiril.

CHAPTER SEVENTEEN

⸺⸺❧⸺⸺

T HEA GENTLY PLACED HER HANDS on the brunette's arms to help alleviate the painful soreness Kiril's chains caused her. He was particularly cruel to her, often tugging her into positions that hurt her and seemed to delight him. Slowly, the woman's arm began to heal, and Thea was awarded with a smile for her care.

"Why would they make you a slave? You're one of them."

Thea wondered the same thing. While she'd never condone slavery in any way, she'd never heard of any group of Aeveren enslaving their own.

"I don't know, Suzanne. But the man who brought me here is a bounty hunter after my destined one."

"Why did he kidnap you?"

"I don't know that either," Thea said sadly.

Suzanne lifted her hand to comfort her, causing her shackles and chain to make a hollow, metallic sound. As she gently touched Thea's cheek, the restraints knocked against her shoulder.

"It'll be okay. I'm sure your husband will come soon."

Thea smiled at the mention of Amon as her husband. She thought for a moment about how much she'd grown to love him in the short time she'd known him.

"He's not my husband yet. But he is my destined one."

"Tell me about destined ones. It sounds so romantic."

"I admit I don't know much about it, Suzanne. Amon is my first. See, I'm a healer for my people, and they rarely are blessed with the gift of a destined one to love."

"Why? I can't imagine anyone deserving love more than someone who helps people."

"Because we need to be devoted to those we care for, I guess."

"Are you your destined one's first?"

Blushing, Thea shook her head. "No. He's had others before me."

From a few feet away, one of the other women laughed. "You have no idea, sweetie."

"Cherie, stop it! Thea doesn't need to hear your awful comments."

Thea knew Cherie had seen or heard about something Amon had done, and she hated the idea of what it might have been. She quickly reminded herself that he'd warned her that he'd done some terrible things in his forty-seven lifetimes.

"It's okay, Suzanne. I know Amon may have been a different kind of man before meeting me. Part of who we are as Aeveren is our pasts."

"That's the way to think. Your knight in shining armor will be here any time now."

Thea found it difficult to understand how anyone who'd been as mistreated as Suzanne had been at Kiril's hands could be so optimistic. Even she, as a healer, seemed to feel more despondent than Suzanne.

"How can you remain so kind and good after what's happened?" she asked.

Suzanne smiled and Thea saw the sweetness in her eyes grow. "I'm not the person Kiril Gault keeps here as a slave. That person has to satisfy him in all of his sexual appetites, but she's no one. A machine."

Touching her fingertips to the area above her heart, she continued. "Who I really am is in here, somewhere Kiril has no interest in. In here, I'm still the girl who worked in a London office, the daughter of John and Sharon, the sister of Carrie and Chrissy, the person I was before he took me one night on my way home and turned me into this."

Thea's heart wrenched as she listened to the details of who Suzanne truly was. "Oh, Suzanne. I'm so sorry. How could this happen?"

Shrugging her shoulders, she answered, "The same way it's happened to you. There are bad people in this world, Thea."

AMON APPEARED IN THE SOREN meeting hall but found few members there. Those who were seemed the same as they always had, but Amon knew that it was probable something important had changed in the group if its leader had any connections with the Council at Nil, so he was alert and ready to deal with Kiril's goons.

He walked slowly through the headquarters' halls looking for Kiril and searching for any evidence Thea was there. It didn't take him long to find the Soren leader. In his private conference room, he sat playing with a whip as his other hand rifled through papers.

"Kiril," he said announcing his presence as he entered the room.

"Amon Kalins. To what do I owe the pleasure of this visit? You weren't announced," Kiril said nervously.

As he approached the table Kiril sat at, Amon watched him stand and understood instantly that something had altered the relationship between them. Kiril's stance was defensive, and his demeanor telegraphed his guilt.

"I'm here to find out what you know about my destined one's kidnapping."

"Your destined one has disappeared?"

"No. She was kidnapped by a Council of Nil bounty hunter. You know anything about that?"

Kiril shifted his position anxiously and shook his head. "How the fuck would I know anything concerning one of their fucking employees?"

"That's what I wondered when I heard that the same bounty hunter had been seen here at the Soren headquarters."

As Amon spoke, he listened carefully for any of Kiril's men. He also attempted to probe the Soren leader's mind for answers, but Soren magick made it impossible to penetrate his thoughts.

Then he sensed Thea and in one swift move grabbed Kiril and slammed him into the wall. "Where is she, Kiril?"

"Sorry, pal. Someone had to be sacrificed. This is bigger than you and your current piece of ass."

"What do you mean sacrificed? Tell me where she is now or I swear I'll kill you."

Amon knew she was still alive as he sensed her nearby. But what did he mean someone had to be sacrificed?

Before he could carry out his threat, Kiril's bodyguards were in the room and on top of him. Pushing each of them off him, he knew he had to get out of there. As he prepared to teleport, he heard Kiril boast, "I hope she likes it rough."

THEA SENSED AMON NEARBY AND ran to the door. Pounding loudly, she screamed his name to let him know where she was.

"Amon! I'm in here!"

Over and over she screamed his name but to no avail. He never came, and although she continued to sense his presence, within a few minutes she knew he was no longer close by.

Amon, where are you? Why did you leave me here?

Dejected and confused, she slid down the door to the cold floor. Had he been captured or killed by Kiril and his men? Thea couldn't believe he would simply leave her to be tortured.

Minutes later, she felt someone push against the door and her heart leapt for joy. He'd come for her! He'd rescue her and the women trapped with her, just as she'd promised he would. When the door opened, she saw Kiril and the bodyguards instead.

"Get the girls. I'll take this one myself," Kiril said as he bent down to pull Thea to her feet.

"Time to go, pet."

"Where? Where are you taking us?"

Panicked, Thea wondered if he was moving her to a different location Amon wouldn't be able to find.

Kiril gave a sinister laugh. "Don't worry. You'll only have to watch."

Thea turned to look at her three fellow captives, but all of them kept their eyes toward the floor. Terrified, she pleaded with him, "Please don't do this. I beg of you."

Kiril ran his finger over her lips. "Sweetheart, you're only exciting me by begging and I promised I wouldn't harm you, but if you keep this up, I may have to renege on that promise."

Thea's mind raced to figure out who he'd promised not to hurt her more than kidnapping and holding her hostage. It made no sense to consider that Amon had done this to her, but Markku or Gethen? Could either of them have done this?

As Kiril led her by the arm to his room, she considered the possibility of their involvement and decided Gethen loved Amon too much to hurt him like this. Markku, however, she couldn't rule out. She'd already experienced his nasty streak. Before she could think about it more, she saw Kiril's room. Obviously designed as his own private sex chamber, it looked like a nightmare with shackles and chains, in addition to whips and metal implements Thea couldn't place but was sure were painful.

Frightened, she tried to back out of the room, but Kiril held her tightly, squeezing her arm. "Don't worry, pet. I told you you'd only have to watch."

Kiril excused the men and began to undress. Moments later, he stood in front of them, naked with a silver cock ring on. Thea's surprise at the sight of it quickly turned to disgust. Sickened to think of what was to come next, she buried her face in her hands as she sat down in the furthest spot away from him.

She heard the hollow clang of the chains and looked up to see Suzanne being freed. As she was lead to the bed, the other two women moved away to sit on a bench against the wall. Behind her, Kiril knelt on the bed and ran his hands over her shoulders. It looked almost loving, but Thea knew it was anything but.

"Thea, look at Suzanne. No one is hurting her." Kiril grasped her chin and pulled her head back toward him. "Tell her."

Suzanne's brown eyes grew wide and then closed. When she reopened them, she spoke more quietly than when they'd talked before, but her voice was the same sweet tone Thea had been comforted by.

"I am not hurt, Thea. Please don't worry about me."

As she heard her words and watched Kiril enter her from behind, Thea knew she'd lied. Shielding her eyes, she hid her face in her hands again and tried in vain to block out the terrible sounds of what was happening in front of her.

AMON RETURNED TO THE HOUSE in Ireland to figure out how he'd save Thea. He knew she was at the Soren headquarters somewhere in the building and hoped she'd heard his promise to come back for her. Gethen was waiting for him and expressed no surprise that Kiril was involved in Thea's kidnapping. Always the helpful servant, even if Amon had freed him, he offered his assistance in any way Amon required.

"Thank you, but none of our combined powers other than my teleporting will work. And that's going to be dicey since they'll be waiting for me next time."

"Amon, do you think you should approach this from another angle? If the Soren and the Council are working together, maybe you need to work the Council."

"I've thought of that. I need to find out who the member is that Markku said is against the head of the Council at Nil."

"Markku should be back any moment. Hopefully, he can tell us."

Amon stood and walked toward the window. Looking out, he said, "I don't have time to wait for him. Every second Thea's with Kiril is killing me. I'll have to find someone else who'd know the answers."

"Who?"

"An old friend who probably hates me, but I have to try. If Markku comes back with news, try to contact me but I'll be far away."

Gethen shot him a confused look, but Amon didn't bother to explain before he disappeared from his house seconds later.

HE REAPPEARED ON THE FRONT steps of a white, suburban home like many found throughout the United States. The leaves that had fallen from the maple tree in the front yard made a crunching noise under his feet as he shifted his weight anxiously. He rang the doorbell and second-guessed his choice to come at all, but his alternatives were decidedly worse.

The face of the woman who opened the door registered first shock and then anger. "You've got a lot of nerve coming here."

Before she could slam the door shut, Amon wedged his boot in between it and the door frame and leaned in to begin the pleading he knew he'd need to do to get her help.

"Please don't shut the door. I need your help. I know I have no right to ask, but I am. Please Jean, I need your help to save someone."

The elderly woman looking back at him grimaced and sighed before slowly opening the door. She said nothing but extended her arm to welcome him in, and he cautiously walked past her into a room full of white lace doilies and flower patterned furniture. He turned back to face her and felt the sting of her hand as she slapped him across the face.

Wincing, he said, "I guess I deserved that."

Walking past him into the kitchen, she said angrily, "You deserve that and more. You stole Callia from her destined one and manipulated time to make sure she fell in love with you. You're a real bastard and now you want my help? You haven't changed, Deimos."

Amon smiled, knowing that her use of the name she'd

known him by all those lifetimes ago meant she'd help him. Or at least he hoped that's what it meant.

"I haven't heard that name in so long, I'd almost forgotten it, Elan."

"I didn't use your Greek name so you'd use mine. We're not having a past life walk down memory lane here. Sit down and don't think just because I still think fondly of you because you were the brother of my destined one once that I'll help you."

Amon sat as ordered as she thumbed through items on the kitchen counter. When she'd found what she was searching for, she turned toward him and handed him something. In his hand he saw a picture of Callia with Varek, a small girl, and a baby. He stared at it and then handed it back to her saying nothing. He knew why she'd shown him it.

"Isn't that a beautiful family? The little girl is his daughter Tia he'd thought he'd lost after what happened with his first destined one, and the baby is named Tanner."

Amon sat silently knowing he deserved Jean's punishment. Nothing he could say could change what he'd done.

Jean sat down at the table across from him, her arms folded. "Well, I'm sure you didn't come here to see pictures of my grandniece and her lovely family, so why are you here?"

"I need your help concerning an issue with the Council."

"That seems strange since if I remember correctly you were sentenced to spend the remainder of your lifetimes in Nil. If I'd known you were so bad, I wouldn't have sent Callia and Varek to you for help, Amon."

His gaze meeting hers, he said quietly, "Elan, I never meant to hurt her. I loved her."

Jean was silent for a few moments and then sighed. "I think you did in your own way. Okay, I've tortured you enough. I'll let fate do the rest. So, what's your problem with the Council, other than its desire to return you to their hell for the rest of your existence?"

"My destined one has been taken, and I think the Council and the Soren are involved. The bounty hunter sent for me took her, but he's been seen at the Soren headquarters. I confronted Kiril Gault about it. I know he's holding her. All the signs point to something going on between someone on the Council at Nil and Kiril."

Her eyes closed, Jean listened and then after a long silence asked, "Why would anyone on the Council get together with the biggest enemy of the Council?"

"I don't know, but I know the actions of the head of the Council at Nil have moved into the illegal realm and at least one member had filed a formal protest."

"Dissention among the ranks of the most powerful council? What did he do?"

"He's authorized the use of my destined one's past to capture me."

Jean whistled and stood up from the table. "That's a big no-no. Obviously, he wants you returned pretty badly. So the question I'm sure you've asked yourself must be, 'What did I do to him to deserve such an overzealous prosecution?'"

Amon nodded. "Jean, I need to know the council member who filed the protest. And I need to know fast. Thea's in danger every minute she's near Kiril."

Nodding, Jean moved into action. "Wait here. This could take a bit, but I think I can find what you need."

While he waited for her to return, Amon picked up the picture of Callia and her family. As he studied their faces, he had to admit that they were happy. He'd hoped for that kind of happiness for lifetimes, and now it was within his reach if he could save Thea and expose the Council's corruption.

Amon knew fate had always favored him. Born with powers in his first lifetime that other Aeveren could only dream of possessing, he'd had the world on a string for most of his existence. He'd had three destined ones who'd loved him probably long after he'd deserved it, another blessing many of his fellow Aeveren would trade almost anything for. He'd been fortunate, no doubt.

But he'd squandered much of his time abusing his powers at the expense of others and his destined ones, finding out all too late how mistaken he'd been with them.

It wasn't in his nature to wallow in regret, though. If his time on Earth had taught him anything, it was that there was no time like the present. No, he wouldn't make the same mistakes of his past. Destiny had given him another chance in Thea, and he'd take it like he'd done with every chance in his forty-seven lifetimes.

By the time Jean returned, Amon had found the focus he'd lost when Ryu took Thea. He knew what he had to do.

"All right, the council member's name is Naomi Cooper.

And it seems she's got a cabal around her that has definite reservations about the head councilman's actions."

Amon rose to leave and Jean caught him by the arm. "Be careful with this group. You've made an enemy in the head of that council. Even if this woman wants to help, you're going up against the two biggest power centers of our world."

"Is that concern I hear in your voice?" he asked in a teasing tone.

"I promised Dmitri lifetimes ago when he was ready to move on that I'd keep an eye on you. He knew what you were and worried about you. I'd like to be able to tell him when I move on and see him again that you were happy and had finally grown into what you were meant to be."

"Are you saying you broke the rule about finding people from past lifetimes, Elan?"

Jean smiled. "I'm an ancient one like you, Amon. All of us have broken a rule or two in the number of lifetimes we've lived."

Amon laughed and hugged her. "Some of us more than others."

"Take care of yourself, Amon."

"You too. And when you see Dmitri again, tell him I finally have what he always wished for me."

Outside Jean's home, Amon stood on her front porch while the early November chill bit at his skin. Armed with Naomi Cooper's name, Amon once again sent out his silent promise to Thea that he'd come for her and prayed to God he wouldn't be too late.

CHAPTER EIGHTEEN

FTER FINISHING WITH THE OTHER two slaves, Kiril seemed to be sated, and Thea prayed he would remember his pledge not to hurt her. Despite Suzanne's words, she knew she'd suffered, and it took every ounce of willpower not to take her in her arms and soothe the pain of what he'd done right out of her. But Thea suspected any kindness offered would only serve to incense him.

She'd only heard the painful sounds of their coupling, each sharp intake of Suzanne's breath like a knife to her heart. When he cast her aside to her place on the floor and took one of the blondes, Thea had raised her eyes from the shield of her hands to look at Suzanne, sure that what she'd heard had broken the woman's spirit. What she saw was a smile, faint but there, that had told her he hadn't taken away everything she remained inside yet.

Suzanne's strength inspired Thea, and she'd watched as Kiril took first the blond who hadn't spoken to her and then Cherie. It had been the most vicious sex she'd ever seen, but she'd met his violet stare from the first thrust and never wavered until he fell back onto the bed and closed his eyes.

More than once as she watched him rest she considered using one of the torture devices hanging from the wall near his bed to attack him, but that would've required walking past him, and she had no idea if he was sleeping or merely resting. Even if she succeeded in grabbing one, she had no assurance she'd be able to kill him and his retribution on Suzanne and the others would no doubt be deadly if she didn't succeed.

No, Thea knew she had to be more than strong. She had to be smart. Amon would come soon, but until then, she had to take care of herself. The problem was that at any moment Kiril could sit up and order her onto the bed believing that his brand of sex didn't constitute harm. She had to devise a way to distract him. She had to make him think of something other than sex—in his bedroom, where he'd just had sex with three other women. If she couldn't, she only had the same fate waiting for her.

Looking around the room she saw little that didn't have something to do with sex. The enormous, intricately carved bed looked like it was straight from a brothel, and the deep red silk sheets screamed sex. Even the lighting, with three ceiling lights pointed directly at his bed, looked geared toward highlighting the act. And then there were the metal implements hanging near his head, which she was sure he used for sex, although she didn't want to imagine how.

She needed some way to focus his attention elsewhere and soon because he was beginning to stir. She quickly ran through ideas in her mind and decided he didn't look like a sports fan, unfortunately. However, slowly a memory from her lifetime at the court of Louis XIV of France bubbled up and she remembered reading a French translation of *One Thousand and One Nights*. That was it! She would act like Scheherazade and hope Kiril fell for her ploy just as the Persian king had fallen for hers.

She would have to improvise, though. Thea decided to do as her sister always suggested doing for a successful date, ironically—"Ask questions, Thea. People love to talk about themselves."

Kiril rolled over to face her and opened his eyes. Inside, the same butterflies she had every time she performed danced in her stomach, but she took a deep breath and reminded herself that she was a smart Aeveren woman with forty-five lifetimes of experience to help her. Something in all those years would be sure to interest him besides sex.

"Did anyone come to the door?"

Thea shook her head.

Kiril stretched his long legs, slowly kicking the sheets from his naked body and smiling at her small reaction to the sight of his once again erect cock. Instantly, Thea regretted letting her focus fall from his eyes, but she quickly made sure her face showed no more surprise or revulsion and once again stared into his piercing eyes.

"See anything you like?" he seductively teased as he folded his arms behind his head and crossed his legs at the ankles.

She hesitated for just a moment and then began what she hoped would be a very long conversation with the most dangerous person she'd met in lifetimes, ended by Amon's arrival and her leaving this place for good.

"Your eyes are the most unique color. I don't think I've ever seen eyes such a beautiful shade of violet," she answered in a voice far calmer than she actually was.

In fact, she wasn't being insincere. His eyes were beautiful, even if they did belong to a sadistic psychopath. She worried he'd either misinterpret her statement as evidence of her attraction or see right through her ruse, though.

Instead, she found him pleased by the compliment and surprised, as if she'd caught him off guard or he'd not heard anything like it in ages. But quickly all that showed in his expression was pleasure and not the sinister kind that often dominated his features. However, when he spoke, Thea knew she was by no means safe yet.

"My eyes? You want to talk about the color of my eyes?"

"Well, no. I just think they're quite unique and striking."

Kiril grinned and rolled over to press a button next to his bed. In seconds, his men were in the room and with nothing but a wave of his hand, he instructed them to remove Suzanne and the two other women.

As Thea watched them walk out, their eyes down and chains clanging against one another, she was thankful her ploy had at least provided them with a reprieve. Now it remained to be seen if she could distract him long enough for Amon to arrive.

Amon. How she missed him! She had no idea where he was or why he hadn't rescued her yet, but her faith in him remained. He was her destined one and would cross miles to save her because of that.

The bedroom door shut, and she was alone with Kiril. Again, she focused her gaze on his, but communicating across the room had lost its interest for him and he ordered, "Come here," as he motioned to the area next to him on the bed.

Fear quickly escalated to terror as Thea stood from the chair. There had been some sense of safety when she sat across the room, but now that rapidly evaporated as she walked toward the bed. Now she'd be within striking distance with no barrier, no matter how illusory, between them.

Thea stood at the edge of the bed looking down at his upturned face that appeared more pleased than ever. With a silent plea to Amon to please hurry, she sat down on the bed next to Kiril.

"I thought if you wanted to discuss my eyes you should be close enough to see them," he said in a low voice that told her she had a long way to go until he thought of something other than sex.

Uncomfortably, she stared into his eyes. "They are quite beautiful. Do either of your parents have eyes like yours?"

Thea knew she was possibly treading on dangerous ground introducing parents into the conversation. Psychopaths like Kiril Gault often had poor relationships with their parents. Happily, she saw no evidence of upset in him.

Shaking his head, he explained, "No, neither. I guess I'm one of a kind."

Disappointed and shaken that he hadn't chosen to talk

more about himself, she remained undeterred. She'd just have to find something else to draw him out, but she'd leave the flattery behind, if possible. It seemed too close to flirting, which was a far too dangerous tactic with a man like him.

To her relief, though, he continued to talk, turning the conversation to her eye color. "Your eyes are quite beautiful too, Thea."

Unlike him, she was more than willing to explain chapter and verse about who she'd gotten her eye color from and any other detail she could think of that had even the slightest connection to the subject of her eyes.

"That's very nice of you to say. I get my eyes from my mother, but hers are a tiny bit darker than mine. I've noticed as she aged, hers became lighter. I imagine mine will lighten too. Perhaps yours will too, although I don't know if the same applies to violet."

Thea realized she was even boring herself, but Kiril seemed enchanted by her words so she continued with a description of her sister's and father's eye colors, never breaking her stare into his eyes.

When she finished, he smiled. "I don't think I've ever talked so much about eye color with a woman, particularly one sitting with me in bed as I lay naked next to her."

"Actually, you've said very little during this conversation. Now it's your turn."

Kiril licked his lips and smacked them together. "My turn?"

"To talk."

He seemed to consider the idea and then discard it as something distasteful. "I don't want to talk."

Thea felt her control of the situation slipping away and frantically searched her mind for another topic of conversation. As her mind raced, Kiril moved his hand to her leg and rested it on her knee.

"You don't have an English accent. Why is that?" she asked as she struggled to keep her voice steady while his fingers slid back and forth over her skin.

"More questions? Ok, I'll play this game but only because I like you. You're a nice change from my usual."

Sure her ploy was on its way to success, Thea relaxed, but then he added, "And I want you willing when I put you in Suzanne's place."

Forgetting her plan momentarily, she blurted out, "Why do you hate her so much more than the other two?"

Thea feared she'd made a mistake, but Kiril's response surprised her. In what sounded like a hurt tone, he said, "I don't hate Suzanne. She's my favorite. I always choose her first."

"You abuse her far more than the other two. The bruises you leave on her body don't show you prefer her."

Squeezing her leg, Kiril looked directly into her eyes. "She's a fucking human. Am I supposed to take care of her?"

As he spoke, he squeezed harder, causing tears to come to her eyes from the pain.

"Is that how you'll treat me when she's gone?" she said through gritted teeth.

Seeing the tears in her eyes, he released her leg from his grip and almost purred his answer. "No, pet. You're Aeveren. I'll take care of you like you've never had before in any lifetime."

Looking down, she ran her hands over her knee to ease the pain. Red spots marked where his fingers had pressed into her skin.

"Can you heal yourself in addition to others?"

Nodding, Thea stilled her hands over her leg to release the last of the pain.

"So you can't truly be hurt?"

Snapping her head right to face him, she dropped all pretense of her plan and said angrily, "Of course I can be hurt! You just brought tears to my eyes squeezing my leg!"

Thea waited in fear for the retribution her words would bring, but none came. Instead, he merely returned his hand to her leg, pushing her hands out of the way, and continued stroking as he'd done before.

"I don't have an English accent because I'm not English. I'm Albanian. I've lived in London for much of this lifetime after coming here when I was fifteen years old."

Stunned by his quick mood change, Thea was unsure what to say next. She was sure she'd never been so frightened in her life or in so unstable a situation. Believing it was just a matter of time before he grew tired of talking to her and simply forced her to do as he desired, she only hoped Amon would arrive before her time ran out or that he could someday forgive her.

"What lifetime are you in, Thea?"

"Forty-fifth," she said quietly, confused as to where he was going with this new conversation.

"Do you know I'm only in my twenty-third? Does that surprise you?"

"No. Greatness can occur in any lifetime."

Thea watched as Kiril moved his hand up her leg to the middle of her thigh. Her time had run out, and she hadn't even made it one night.

Looking at his hand, she couldn't help but see his erection and shiver. He was excited even after she'd tried to distract him with mundane conversation. Nothing had worked. As he stroked the inside of her thigh, she prepared herself for what she'd feared since arriving. If she didn't fight, perhaps she'd survive.

Kiril's hand continued its movement up her thigh until it reached the seam of her leg. She watched his eyes travel the path his hand had and waited for his next move. When he looked up at her and spoke, she was stunned.

"You're Aeveren, so I won't take what you won't freely give."

"You'll respect our heritage but not my having a destined one?"

Sitting up, he sat face to face with her and smiled. "It's just a matter of time before your destined one is returned to Nil for the rest of his time on Earth. So you having a destined one isn't a concern of mine."

"No! Destiny wouldn't do that to me after making me wait so many lifetimes!" she cried.

"Well, pet, she's been a bitch to you then because he's going. His fate is sealed."

Thea turned toward him. "Why are you doing this? Aren't you friends with Amon?"

Kiril's stare slid down her body and when it stopped on her breasts, he reached out to twirl her hair around his finger. "Amon's a sacrifice I'm willing to make. That you're part of the package is just a bonus."

As he spoke, he tugged her hair and pulled her closer to him. Thea closed her eyes and felt his warm breath near her face. Any second now, he would kiss her, and even if she believed his claim that he wouldn't force her, she had a feeling his definition of consensual and willing were quite different from hers.

The moment his lips touched her she froze in terror. Over and over, she silently begged Amon to hurry to her as Kiril held her by the back of the head and slipped his tongue back and forth through her stiff lips. Passionless, she waited for him to tire of her but nothing seemed to deter him.

In her ear, he whispered, "Soon you'll beg me to fuck you, Thea, like you begged before. When you do, you won't have to sleep with my slaves. And I don't think it will take long after I get rid of Suzanne."

"Get rid of her? What are you going to do?" Thea asked as she jumped up off the bed.

Kiril didn't bother to answer, his grin showing how obviously he was enjoying her reaction.

"Please don't do that to her, Kiril. I beg you."

"Your darling has to go. She's too much trouble," he said calmly.

"But you said she was your favorite. Why would you get rid of your favorite?"

"Because you're my new favorite. And I don't need her."

Thea stood in tears as Kiril remained unmoved by her sadness. Suzanne was going to suffer in part because of her, and even if it wasn't her fault, she couldn't stand by as another suffered any more.

Please forgive me, Amon.

Hanging her head, she quietly said, "Kiril, please don't. I'll do anything you want if you just spare her."

Leaning over, he pressed the button to summon his guards. Then he stood up and grabbed her by the hair and yanked her head back. Looking down into her eyes, he spoke, his voice ice cold. "You'll do whatever I fucking want regardless of what I choose to do with that cunt. Do you understand me?"

Thea's eyes grew wide in terror at the sight of his rage and the vicious sound of his words. As she stood there, pain radiating from where he pulled her hair, his men entered the room and waited by the door for instructions.

Never breaking his cold stare into her eyes, he hissed, "Take this one back to the others. And bring Suzanne."

RETURNING FROM JEAN'S HOUSE, AMON knew he'd have to ask Gethen to do him yet another favor. There was no way he could go to Nil to speak to Naomi Cooper. No, he'd have to ask his friend to once again make the dangerous trip to Nil and pray he'd make it out successfully, knowing Gethen's fate if he didn't.

He found him outside and joined him in the garden behind the house. The sun was just setting and something in the way the former servant looked off into the distance reminded Amon of the reason they'd returned to Ireland.

"I'm sorry, my friend. I'd forgotten we came here to take you home."

Gethen turned to face him and in the fading light of twilight, Amon saw the loyalty he'd enjoyed for lifetimes.

"What did you find out?" he asked, quickly sidestepping the conversation Amon had begun.

"I need your help, Gethen. I can't get to the councilwoman in Nil. Only you can."

Gethen nodded slowly. "I know."

"I'm sorry I have to ask you to make this trip again. If there was any other way…"

"There is no other way. I know that as well as you do. Only the Sidhe can travel between worlds safely."

As the sunlight disappeared, the two men talked of the task ahead. Gethen would have to find Naomi Cooper and convince her to read Amon's letter explaining the connection between the head of the Council at Nil and Kiril Gault. If she believed him, she could be the one person to begin the investigation that would expose the corruption of the head councilman.

All the while Amon explained what he needed, Gethen listened and when he'd finished, asked, "What about Thea?"

Taking a deep breath, Amon closed his eyes and once more sent a thought of love to her. He hadn't sensed that she was in true danger yet and told himself that meant she must be okay. But a nagging doubt troubled him. He hadn't known of his other destined one's moving on, so what if he simply couldn't sense danger to Thea until he returned to the Soren headquarters, when it could be too late?

"I have to believe she's all right. She's smart. And she's Aeveren. I don't think Kiril would harm one of our own. It's humans he hates."

Quietly, Gethen said, "Amon, if that bounty hunter has been anywhere near their headquarters, Gault is involved in kidnapping her."

"I know, but I don't think he'll harm her. She's too valuable to him and not just as bait to lure me. She's a healer, and Kiril would see that as an asset to the Soren. Having a healer in his back pocket is a nice addition to the rest of the members and their talents."

"I hope you're right."

"I know I'm right. I used to be like him, remember? And that's exactly how I'd have seen her," Amon answered, hoping to God he was right.

An awkward silence rose between them as they both knew Amon's assessment of himself was the truth. He had been like Kiril Gault in many ways for lifetimes.

"Gethen, it's time we got this going. I'll write the letter I need you to deliver to her while you get ready. We don't have any time to waste. Thea might not be in physical danger, but she needs to come home."

When Amon finished the letter, he returned outside to Gethen. As he handed it to him, he pressed it into his palm. "Be careful, friend. You know what they'll do if they catch you."

"Have faith. Remember, we're in Ireland, the land of my people."

As Amon watched, Gethen took a few steps backwards and slowly dissolved into mist.

CHAPTER NINETEEN

GETHEN REAPPEARED IN THE EXACT location Amon had told him the councilwoman's quarters could be found. Jean's contact had warned of the sentry who stood guard outside her rooms and had suggested her private chambers as the perfect place to rematerialize. The room was dimly lit by only wall sconces, and as he listened for the sound of voices, he heard nothing. She was alone. Carefully, he began his search of Naomi Cooper's quarters.

It didn't take him long to find her. In an ante room of her office, she sat alone reading a book. Gethen stood silently in the doorway and waited, hoping not to frighten her into sending up the alarm.

Lifting her head from the book, the councilwoman trained her gaze on him as if she were deciding if he were real or an apparition. Slowly, she closed her book and placed it on the table next to her.

"You're a long way from home, my Sidhe friend," she said in a soft voice.

"You know what I am?"

Nodding, Naomi Cooper stood and walked toward him. When she'd reached him, she placed her hand on his and smiled.

"No matter how long I'm gone from the world outside, I can't forget your people. Once, lifetimes ago, a Sidhe rescued me from the clutches of one of my people and took care of me. Your presence affects me just as his did."

Gethen attempted to move his hand from hers, unable to control the emotions she caused in him, but she refused to release him.

Looking away, he pleaded, "Please don't."

The councilwoman saw the scar on the side of his face and gently touched it with her fingertips. "Who did this to you, Sidhe?" she asked as she felt the raised scar.

Fighting the emotions welling up inside him, he whispered hoarsely, "One of your people."

Her face grew sad and she dropped her hand. "I'm sorry. Even friends like Aeveren and Sidhe sometimes wrong each other."

Looking back at her, he said seriously, "I deserved this mark. It was I who wronged her, madam."

Nodding her understanding, Naomi Cooper gestured toward a chair near hers to offer him a seat. When they'd sat down, Gethen remained quiet for a moment and then removed the letter from his coat.

"What is your name, Sidhe?"

"I am called Gethen."

"Gethen, please call me Naomi."

Gethen let a small smile appear on his face, and he handed her the letter. "I'm here on behalf of Amon Kalins."

The councilwoman raised her eyebrows in surprise but said nothing. Gethen waited for her to alert her sentry, but she remained still.

"He needs your help. He's uncovered something going on between the head of the Council here and the head of the Soren."

"Amon Kalins is an escaped prisoner from Nil. It's my duty to inform you that I sit on the council that convicted him and sentenced him to spend his remaining lifetimes here in Nil as punishment for his many crimes. Why would I help him against the head of my council? What proof does he have to substantiate these wild claims?"

Gethen handed her Amon's letter and watched as she read it and folded it again.

"This bounty hunter he refers to—Ryu Jansen. He's been a loyal employee of this council for years."

"He took Amon's destined one. Why would a bounty hunter from your council kidnap a woman instead of taking the man he's supposed to bring back here?"

The councilwoman appeared to consider Gethen's question for a moment and then turned to face him. "Thea? And he can prove this man took her to the Soren head-quarters?"

"Yes."

"I must admit I find it hard to believe any member of my council would associate with anyone from that group, least of all Kiril Gault."

Gethen waited, hoping her next move wouldn't now be to call the guard.

"However, Gethen, your friend is correct when he writes that I have been an outspoken opponent of some of the choices my council head has made. I believe in Aeveren laws, and his decision to conduct a no-holds-barred mission to return Amon Kalins to Nil by using his destined one's past is one I believe to be very wrong. It is, however, a great leap to say that this means the head of the Council at Nil is in collusion with the head of the Soren."

As he waited for her to continue, Gethen knew he had to make his point stronger or he'd fail Amon.

"I know better than anyone else as Amon's servant for the past seven lifetimes what he's done to belong here. But his destined one has done nothing, and your leader has placed her in the hands of a man who possesses female slaves for the sole purpose of his pleasure. Every moment Kiril Gault is free to do as he pleases because of his association with the head of your council is another moment Thea may be serving as his slave."

As she listened to the information Gethen gave her, Naomi's face showed her sorrow at the idea of Thea's fate. When she'd said nothing for a few minutes, Gethen rose to leave, saddened by his failure to help his friend this one last time.

"What should I tell Amon?" he asked, hopeful she'd answer that she'd at least look into the allegations made.

"Where is your friend now, Gethen?"

When she saw the look of suspicion in his face, she explained, "I won't give him up yet. You may trust me."

Unsure if he was signing Amon's death warrant, he said slowly, "Ireland, at his house in County Cork."

Standing, she held her hand out to take his and smiled. "Then that's where we'll be going."

Gethen's look of surprise amused her, but quickly he remembered the trip back and became concerned. "I can't be sure you'll handle the trip. Aeveren don't travel well between the worlds."

"Not to worry, my Sidhe friend. Now take me to him."

Gethen looked down at Naomi Cooper's hand in his and focused his mind on Ireland as they both dissolved from her rooms in Nil.

AMON STOOD IN THE ROOM where just hours before he and Thea had made love and tried to focus his mind on hers. Each time he felt a connection, it was broken just seconds later. He felt relief as he received no clear sense that she'd come to any harm, but he knew his words to Gethen earlier may have been merely wishful thinking.

But they were all he had for now.

Gethen's voice in his head called to him excitedly, and Amon quickly teleported to the living room downstairs to find his friend standing with a woman. Stunned, he silently asked Gethen if he'd taken her against her will, but quickly saw no fear in her expression.

"Amon, this is Councilwoman Naomi Cooper."

Extending his hand to greet her, Amon shook hers and offered her a seat. As he sat across from her, he realized what he was seeing was supposed to be impossible.

"Ms. Cooper, how is it that a council member is able to leave Nil?"

Smiling, she explained, "We may leave when we choose. It is just assumed we can't leave because we do so infrequently. To spend time outside of Nil will only encourage us to want what we left behind when we chose to accept a position on the Council. I felt this was a situation that called for me to return to this world, however."

"Gethen gave you my letter?"

"Yes, your Sidhe friend gave me your letter and explained about your destined one's kidnapping. I admit, it's more out of concern for her than belief in you that I chose to come here."

"I'm grateful for whatever reason brought you here," he replied as he looked over at Gethen and silently thanked him.

Nodding, Gethen excused himself and left Amon to speak to the councilwoman alone.

Naomi watched him leave and turned to Amon. "You have been very fortunate, Mr. Kalins. You've been blessed with the loyal friendship of a Sidhe and a fourth destined one. A healer, no less. And yet I remember quite clearly the crimes you were convicted of. You seemed to be favored by fate."

"I have. But the one who will suffer the most if the head of the Council at Nil has his way is my destined one. I may not deserve Thea, but she doesn't deserve to be held by Kiril

Gault."

Amon listened as she apologized, and then they sat quietly studying each other until he broke the silence. "May I assume by the way you're looking at me and the slight tug I just felt in my mind that you possess the power of telepathy and you're using it on me?"

The councilwoman folded her arms across her chest and sat back in her chair. "Yes to both. You didn't think I'd simply trust a convicted prisoner, did you?"

Amon watched as Naomi's skepticism faded with her look into his thoughts. Stroking his chin, he said, "Then you know I'm telling the truth, or at least what I believe to be the truth. If I may be frank, Ms. Cooper, I don't have time to pass any more of your tests. Every minute I spend here with you is another minute Thea may be in danger. So if you don't mind, let's cut to the chase."

"Fine. I believe you're telling the truth, and I do find the idea that one of our bounty hunters has been to the Soren headquarters rather damning, but to him, not the head of the Council. Are you sure it isn't this bounty hunter that has an ax to grind with you and wants to punish you through your destined one?"

"That only makes sense if I'd ever met him, which I don't think I have."

"How would you know? Unless one is your destined one, you can't recognize them from one life to the next."

Amon couldn't disagree with her logic and preferred not to explain how easy it was to bribe a Directorate worker for that information, but he was sure it wasn't Ryu Jansen who had the ax to grind.

"Don't you think if he wanted revenge on me he'd had said something about it to me? No, your bounty hunter isn't the person calling the shots. I know Kiril Gault. He wouldn't be bothered associating with one of your lapdogs."

"Yes, you know Kiril Gault, Mr. Kalins. Kiril Gault, the head of the main opposition to all Aeveren hold dear—the laws of our world. A man who wants to subjugate all humans and a man who's behind much of the darker side of our world."

Amon was growing impatient with Naomi Cooper's need to discuss his past. "Yes, I've associated with Gault and hundreds like him over the lifetimes. Yes, I've done some bad things in my past. If you came here to conduct your own personal hearing and retry me, you're wasting your time and mine. I'm every bit as bad as you think I am and more. And if anything has happened to Thea because of the head of your fucking council, I'll make sure the rest of his time is full of more pain than you could ever imagine. He'll die by a thousand cuts as I slowly drain the life from him drop by drop in as many lifetimes as I can."

Silently, he called to Gethen to take the councilwoman back to her quarters in Nil. When he'd returned, Amon stood and said curtly, "The councilwoman needs to go back. Take her."

Dutifully, Gethen approached Naomi to take her back to Nil. She stood and faced Amon, who looked down at her warily.

"And no matter what happens, I won't be going back to Nil, and if that means I have to kill every bounty hunter you send after me, then so be it."

"You've convinced me, Mr. Kalins. I'll look into what you allege about Councilman Adams." Turning to Gethen, she asked, "May I rely on you to convey any information, Sidhe?"

Gethen nodded and Naomi turned back to face Amon. "Godspeed, Mr. Kalins. I'll do what I can to find the truth and help your destined one. I only pray that what you believe isn't true."

ALONE AGAIN, AMON WALKED BACK upstairs and sat on the bed. His heart was filled with regret for getting Thea involved in his life. While he knew Aeveren biology would have eventually brought them together, he blamed himself for selfishly not walking away when she'd run from him.

She'd be safe now.

Even that he couldn't be sure of. If the head of the Council at Nil was willing to break Aeveren law and give a bounty hunter details on her lifetimes, would he have sent him to detain her hoping she'd provide the information he wanted? And she'd disobeyed the council's edict not to help him, from the head of the council no doubt, so possibly she'd have been punished for that.

He ran his hand over the pillow she'd rested her head on and thought of her blond hair fanned out over it as she slept.

Before he could stop himself, he thought about Kiril's sex slaves and how he'd seen him pull them around by their hair as they wailed in pain. His hands curled into tight fists as his mind raced with images of Thea being abused by Kiril—his hands tearing at her long hair as she crawled across the floor behind him, tears streaming from her eyes as she cried out in pain.

I'll kill him. So help me God, I'll kill him.

Amon knew he couldn't think about what Kiril could be doing and still keep his sanity. Just the idea of what he might do made murderous rage build inside him. He'd take care of his former friend when the time came, but for now, he had to believe Thea was unharmed.

To distract his mind, he focused on the head of the council, replaying his trial and the councilman's words. At the time, he thought he'd been a bit too pleased at his capture, but over time he'd decided it had probably been no different with any other prisoner. But why did the head of the Council at Nil seem hell bent on punishing him? Had they known one another in a previous lifetime?

Amon ran through lifetimes of experiences cataloguing men and women he'd known, but he knew the futility of this. No matter how many things he'd torture himself with, he'd never be able to know for certain why this one man despised him so much.

While he thought about this, he heard someone call his name from downstairs. Recognizing Markku's voice, he made his way down to the kitchen where he found the magickian helping himself to something to eat. Amon wondered if the man simply didn't respect him or if he didn't remember how angry he'd been just a short time earlier.

Peaking his head out from inside the refrigerator, Markku began rambling on about what he'd found out. "Amon, it's huge. Much bigger than we thought. I can't even get near the Soren headquarters. Fuck, they saw me coming! And I just got back in, goddamnit!"

Before Markku could get lost in self-pity, Amon closed the door and guided him to the table.

"Slow down, Markku. Tell me everything."

Markku sat down, took a deep breath, and began again. "I did just what you said to. I went to my guy at the Directorate to find out who this head of the Council was before but no dice. Council members' information is impossible to retrieve. So I asked him to check on any connection between you and the bounty hunter."

"And?"

Shaking his head, Markku continued. "Nothing. Fuck, you've never even been in the same country at the same time until this lifetime."

"I knew it."

Taking a bite of an apple, Markku continued. "But here's something interesting. Your bounty hunter lost his job at Nil last year. They let him go after he failed to bring someone in."

"I guess he's become a dedicated civil servant again," Amon said sarcastically.

"Well, something like that. They brought him back

specifically to get you."

"Why? Why him?"

"No idea. My guy couldn't find one reason why this particular bounty hunter would be brought back at all. Fuck, they routinely fire hunters who fail to bring in their assignment, but they don't recall them after only one year."

"Markku, there must be something."

"Amon, I'm telling you. Nothing. He doesn't even have any serious power. He can heal faster than others. Every other power he needs to catch someone like you he has to get from the goddamned council."

"Any idea who recalled him?"

Chewing another bite of apple, he answered, "The head of the Council of Nil himself."

"Mr. Adams."

"How'd you know his name?"

Amon leaned back on his chair. "I've been to Nil, Markku."

"Well, the interesting part of his recall is that this Adams didn't offer it up for a vote with his fellow council members. It was all him."

"So something about Ryu Jansen makes him such a great bounty hunter that he needs to be the one to bring me in? But he's fired for not doing his job, and his only power is that he can heal fast?"

Amon continued, "Anything in his past that we can connect to Adams?"

Markku shook his head. "Sorry, Amon. My guy couldn't

get anywhere near the head councilman's files. Security's tighter than a drum on that."

Amon stood up from the table and patted Markku's shoulder as he passed. "Thanks, Markku. Don't go anywhere. I'm going to need you to get Thea. None of my powers work well inside Soren headquarters."

"I'll do what I can, but I'm back to being the bastard at the family reunion as far as they're concerned. That's what I don't get. They wanted you out of Nil. Fuck, I spent the last year on the outside looking in for what I did..."

Markku realized what he'd said and stopped. "I'm sorry, Amon. I never intended for you to go to Nil."

Amon nodded but said nothing. The truth was he was sent to Nil for the things he'd done, not because of Markku or anyone else, and he knew it.

As he silently sat thinking about this fact, Gethen returned from escorting Naomi Cooper back to Nil. Pale and weak, he fell onto the couch immediately after reappearing in the living room.

Struck by how fragile he looked, Amon went to his side and knelt down next to him. "Gethen, what happened? Were you captured?"

"No," he answered weakly. "I'm fine."

After a few minutes of rest, he began to speak again, but his voice was still strained. "Naomi wants you to know the council members like her, who don't like how the head councilman is conducting the Council's business, are mobilizing behind her. She's started an inquiry, but she warned that these bureaucratic decisions can take a long time."

"Once more, you've been a lifesaver. Thank you."

Amon stood up and turned to Markku. "We can't wait anymore. I need you to get me into the Soren headquarters so I can get Thea the hell out of there. Adams will have to be the Council's problem."

Markku got ready to leave. "What do you plan to do about Kiril and his men?"

A vision of what he'd do to Kiril Gault when he got his hands on him flashed through Amon's mind. "Leave Kiril to me."

CHAPTER TWENTY

THEA LIFTED HER ARM AND the heavy chain that dangled from it and angrily slammed her hand down on the floor. The sound of metal hitting concrete jarred her but didn't seem to faze her two fellow captives in the least. Numb from their months in Kiril's possession, they kept their eyes firmly fixed on the floor as ordered. Their lack of defiance—of any resistance at all—saddened Thea.

She stared at their deadened expressions and compared them to the memory of Suzanne's still vibrant face with her gentle eyes and sweet smile. She'd watched with tears in her eyes as Kiril's men had led her away. How long had passed since then? An hour? Three? Thea couldn't be sure. She imagined the torture Kiril was inflicting on her, and her stomach tightened in knots at the thought of Suzanne's caring eyes wide in terror as she bore his attack. If it was the last thing she did in this lifetime, she'd see Kiril punished for what he'd done to Suzanne and every other human woman he'd harmed.

The words 'this lifetime' rang in her head. This lifetime, in which she'd finally been given a destined one. Thea began to fear that Amon's absence wasn't because he was devising a way to save her. She began to think that just as she'd been given him, he'd been taken away either back to Nil or to his next lifetime after being murdered by Kiril.

The thought of Amon gone from her world, perhaps forever if he was back in Nil, broke her. Unable to muster up anger or resistance anymore, she lay down on the hard floor and curled up in a ball. The cold wrist shackles pressed next to her face as she rested her head on her hands. This would be how the rest of her forty-fifth lifetime would be—an empty, hard existence at the hands of a vicious psychopath.

Tears rolled down her cheeks as sadness consumed her. Over and over, she sent the same thought to Amon in the desperate hope that he was still coming for her.

Amon, please don't leave me.

Nothing—no sense he was near came back to her. Closing her eyes, she let the memory of their time together play in her mind as she struggled to hold on to some hope. She didn't know how long she lay there, but as the door opened now, she saw Kiril beckon to her.

KIRIL GAULT STEPPED INTO THE main meeting room of the Soren headquarters and walked to his seat on the dais, Thea trailing close behind him.

"Thea, today is the day I finally become what I've wanted for so long. Today, I become more than just the leader of the Soren, and like a ruler, I'll have my queen next to me."

As he spoke, Thea wondered if he had lost his mind. A ruler? A queen? What was he talking about?

"Once I hear the words that tell me Amon Kalins is back in Nil where he belongs, I'll be given the go ahead to claim you as mine. I'll also be as powerful as the Council."

"Amon will never let you get away with this, Kiril. I'm his destined one. When he finds me, he's going to kill you."

Thea knew instantly that voicing those words had been a mistake. Kiril's hand shot out violently and came down on the side of her face. Pain radiated from her cheekbone to her eyes, and she couldn't stop the tears that began to flow over her stinging cheek.

"I thought a few hours in chains had showed you how preferable the alternative of giving yourself willingly was to toying with me with endless questions and pleading for a human's safety. Now, instead of being more pliant, you're just as insistent on making me hurt you. I don't want to hurt you, Thea. Won't you be a nice girl so I don't have to?"

As she stood silently staring up into his maniacal expression, Thea wondered if she would ever make it out of there alive. Every moment that went by seemed to make Kiril madder.

"I had a destined one. Did you know that?"

Quietly, she answered, "No."

"I did. I do still, but she didn't believe in what the Soren was, so she refused me. She said I had a traitorous nature, I think is how she put it." Kiril fell silent for a long time and then mumbled, "Puritanical bitch."

The idea of Kiril being given a destined one while she'd been basically alone for every lifetime until this one hurt, and as Thea carefully kept her gaze focused toward the floor, she thought that the fate of Aeveren like herself was even crueler than she'd ever imagined.

"Thea, look at me," Kiril ordered, his voice softer now.

As she slowly drew her head up to look at him, he reached out to dry her tear-stained face and spiky eyelashes still wet from crying. "I want you to look far more content for this meeting. It wouldn't do to have a sulking woman standing next to me if I hope to get approval to claim another man's destined one, even if that man is Amon Kalins and is consigned to Nil for the rest of his lifetimes."

"Kiril, please don't do this. Please. It's not too late."

Cupping her aching cheek, he stroked her face. "Would it make you happier to know I released Suzanne?" he asked in a sweet voice intended to convince her to believe his lie.

Thea knew she had to go along with this act and forced a tiny smile onto her face. "That's my Thea," he cooed as he saw her mood improve. "Now come. I want you to sit."

He guided her to his chair and unlocked the shackles and chains that bound her wrists. Tossing them away from him in disgust, he gently massaged the skin on her arms where the restraints had sat.

"Does that feel better?"

Thea nodded. It was futile to do anything other than acquiesce at this point. She faked another small smile that seemed to thrill him.

"Thea, you and I are meeting someone today. You may remain seated as he and I talk, but I want you to promise you won't speak. Do you understand me?"

Quietly, she said, "Yes, Kiril. I understand."

But she didn't understand at all. Why did he want her at one of his meetings? And why did he care if she looked happy or not to this particular person? If he'd ever met Kiril, he'd seen at least one unhappy woman in chains near him before.

Kiril finished rubbing her wrists and stepped back away from her. Thea watched as he seemed to enjoy looking at her in his chair. Unsure if he'd meant she couldn't speak while he met with the man or not at all, Thea hesitantly asked, "Why did you take the chains off if I'm Suzanne's replacement?"

She instantly saw the anger grow in his face and feared his response.

"Thea, you're Aeveren. I would never enslave an Aeveren woman. And you aren't the replacement for any human. Do you understand me?"

Nodding, Thea was thankful for the moment that she'd escaped his wrath. He moved behind her, and she felt him rest one hand on her shoulder as he stroked her hair with the other.

The man he was to meet entered a few minutes later, and Thea wondered how such an ordinary man could inspire such subservient behavior in one as brutal as Kiril. As soon as she saw him, she felt Kiril's hand tense up on her shoulder, not out of cruelty but apprehension.

Who was this average Aeveren?

She watched him approach them confidently with a look of amusement on his face and decided he must be someone far more powerful than Kiril to make him respond as he was.

"Kiril," he said in a voice as common as he looked. "Are you ready for our meeting?"

Thea immediately felt like an intruder, but Kiril's hand smoothed her shoulder as if to reassure her.

"Councilman, I'd like you to meet Thea."

She saw a flicker of recognition cross his face at the mention of her name, and she worked to remember if she'd ever met this stranger. But what council did he work for? London?

"Thea, how nice to finally meet you. I've been curious to meet the healer who disobeyed my edict and helped Amon Kalins."

Recoiling in horror, she realized the man in front of her was the most powerful Aeveren in their world—the head of the Council at Nil, the ruling council above all others. He was the man who'd imprisoned her destined one and had sent a bounty hunter to kidnap her and give her to Kiril.

Smiling, the man said, "No need to fear me, young lady. All will be rectified soon."

Kiril bent down and touched his lips to the side of her face he'd hit just minutes ago. "Thea, stay here, and I'll be back in a bit."

As she watched them walk to the opposite side of the room, she began to breathe normally again. Her mind racing, she attempted to understand why the head of the Council at

Nil would be meeting with the head of the Soren, a group that was the Council's worst enemy. And then she realized the first sign of hope since she'd been brought here—the councilman had said all would be rectified soon.

Amon's alive and still free!

"KIRIL, I NEED TO KNOW everything is ready here. I don't want Kalins escaping another time."

"I know. He won't. His powers won't work here next time."

"And he'd better show like you think he will, Kiril."

Looking back at Thea sitting quietly as she waited for him, he said confidently, "He'll show. Even if she weren't his destined one, he'd come for her."

"Kiril, you seem very attached to Kalins' destined one. I'd hate to have to use my influence with the Directorate and see you end up losing her."

Turning back toward the councilman, Kiril silently cursed the power he held over his life. "I won't let anything go wrong this time. When he comes to get her, my men will capture him and he'll be yours to take back to Nil or do whatever you want. Fuck, I don't care if you kill him."

Kiril saw the hatred that appeared on the councilman's face any time Amon was mentioned. He'd never explained what he'd done to him, but Kiril imagined it had something to do with the man's last lifetime in the outside world before he'd accepted an offer to serve in Nil. Whatever had happened, his need for vengeance was as raw as Kiril had ever seen in another.

"I have your word you'll help me with my claim for Thea when this is all over?"

"I told you that would be your reward, if you choose it. Claiming another man's destined one is only allowed in very special cases. But as the head of the Council at Nil, I'll happily attest to the impossibility of him ever fulfilling the role of destined one for her."

"Something's concerned me about this, though. How will you get my claim approved knowing who I am? I don't see the Directorate approving anything for the leader of the biggest outlaw group in our world."

The councilman brushed off Kiril's fear with a wave of his hand. "Don't worry. I'll take care of it. Now how are we doing with the humans?"

Kiril remained concerned about how he'd get past the Directorate but was forced to answer his question. "We're fine. On track with what we planned. I just sent another one to our place outside the city today. I've got my people working around the globe, but they're fucking stubborn creatures."

"I've only seen you with females, Kiril. Do you handle the males too?"

Kiril couldn't contain the look of disgust that crossed his face. "No. I've got others who like it that way."

The councilman let out a sinister laugh. "Of course. What was I thinking?" Looking around, he asked, "Where are your usual girls? I was hoping to see the one I had last time."

"Nope. She's the one I got rid of today."

Not trying to conceal the anger in his voice, the councilman said, "Even though you knew I was coming?"

Kiril saw that he'd made a serious mistake and quickly added, "I have two others I keep and dozens I could have here in a matter of minutes. Just tell me what you want."

As he saw the other man walk back toward Thea, he knew exactly what he wanted. Hurrying to catch up to him, he continued, "Suzanne was a brunette. I can have one just like her here whenever your want. Do you want me to get one now? All it takes is a phone call."

All he could do was watch as the councilman walked up to where Thea sat and stood over her grinning. "C…Council-man…" he stammered. "She's Aeveren."

Kiril saw the councilman's grin grow even wider. "I know exactly what and who she is, Kiril."

"Come with me, Thea. I'd like to spend some time with you."

THEA TOOK HIS HAND AND rose from the seat, so nervous she felt her legs might give out at any moment. She had no idea where the head councilman from Nil was taking her, but the look on Kiril's face told her everything about what he intended to do with her.

"Kiril, I'm going to use my usual room. And I don't want to be disturbed."

Thea walked with the man she hated as much as Kiril to a

bedroom close to the room she'd been in with Suzanne and the others. As he closed the door behind her, she waited for the horror to begin, understanding now why he'd chosen to disrespect Aeveren ethics once again.

"You can do whatever you want to me, just like Kiril, but it won't change anything. I am Amon's destined one. I love him and belong with him. What you're about to do is against everything we are. How can you do this?"

"I have no intention of raping you, dear. What am I? A pig like Kiril? No. I did that to punish him for doing something against my wishes."

The councilman sat on the bed and motioned for Thea to sit in a nearby chair. When she had, he began talking to her almost as a father would to a daughter.

"I'd like to tell you a story, Thea, and I'd like you to pay very careful attention. Unlike you, I'm a relatively young Aeveren not even in my thirtieth lifetime. Until my twenty-fifth lifetime, I'd lived as other Aeveren had, meeting my destined one in my fifteenth lifetime and dealing with the everyday joys and sorrows of life."

Thea watched as he breathed deeply before continuing, as if the next part of his story was far more important.

"We were happy—as happy as anyone else. We'd lived through bad times and good, and by my twenty-fifth lifetime, I was fortunate enough to be part of the English landed gentry. We had a beautiful little girl, and life was good."

"Sir, I've heard enough stories like this one to know something happened. But what does this have to do with me?"

"Thea, I've read your history. What happened in your thirteenth lifetime?"

Memories that had been buried for lifetimes flooded her mind. "No, please don't do this."

"You were a healer, as you are now, in a small village near Rome."

"Please don't do this. You have no right to know my past."

"I'm doing this for your own good, dear. What happened?"

Thea buried her face in her hands. She hadn't thought about anything of that lifetime in so long. She'd worked so hard to forget everything she'd suffered. Now it was back, a memory as fresh as if it had happened only a lifetime ago.

"He killed me."

"Who, Thea? Who killed you?"

"My lover. I'd been with a man who was married to someone who wasn't his destined one, and I'd let him convince me that we weren't wrong to see each other," she cried.

"And why did he murder you?"

Thea began to sob remembering the moment she'd realized the man she'd loved planned to leave her. "I was pregnant with his child. He said he couldn't hurt his wife that way."

The councilman sat silently as Thea struggled to continue. "He was furious at what had brought me such happiness and told me I had to get rid of it. Get rid of our child! When I refused, he told me he was leaving me and never wanted to see me again. But I loved him! I couldn't just let him go. I was having his child."

Shaking, she remembered the last time she saw him, the last day of her thirteenth lifetime. "Why are you doing this? Why would you want me to remember this?"

"Because it's important to your future, dear Thea."

Confused, she shook her head in disbelief. "How can causing me to remember one of the most painful memories of my existence help me?"

"What happened, Thea?"

"He murdered me! He pretended he wanted to reconcile with me and had me meet him in a secluded spot. After professing his love and his apologies for his behavior, he took out a piece of cloth and held it to my face. As I scratched and clawed to get away from him, he smothered me! He killed me and the child he didn't want!"

Thea wept uncontrollably as she said the words she hadn't spoken in more than twenty lifetimes. The painful memory hurt as much as it had all those lifetimes ago when she'd realized how she'd died in her thirteenth lifetime.

"Why would you do this to me?" she asked as she wiped the tears from her face.

As if he hadn't been affected by her story, he continued what he'd begun earlier. "What do you know of your destined one?"

Defiantly, she answered, "I know he loves me."

"Yes, I'm sure."

"I know what you're going to say. Amon's done some

awful things. I know. He told me. But that's not the man I know."

Rising from the bed, the councilman walked past Thea to stand near the wall. "So Amon Kalins has become a new man since last year when he manipulated time and took a woman away from the man he knew to be her destined one?"

Thea sat silently not knowing what to say.

"Or he's become a new man since he was very much like our friend Kiril fucking enslaved human females?"

Thea couldn't control the shock at hearing this accusation and knew her face showed it.

"I guess he didn't tell you about that, or did he deny it?"

"Amon wouldn't do that! He's not like Kiril!"

"Maybe you're right, but I've never seen anyone who associates with Kiril Gault who didn't take part in his particular brand of entertainment."

"No....no," she muttered sadly, wishing more than anything else in the world at that moment to not hear anything more the councilman had to say about the man she loved.

"Perhaps he's become a new man since he abandoned a young woman foolish enough to get involved with him, a woman who then took her own life, leaving her child and husband behind?"

Thea shook her head violently, unable to listen anymore. "No! Stop this!"

The councilman folded his arms across his chest. "This woman loved her husband dearly. A devoted wife and mother, she was too innocent to realize what your destined one was before it was too late. He used his powers to manipulate her—to make her fall in love with him and steal her away from her loving husband and destined one, just like he did last year."

"You're wrong. He wouldn't hurt someone he loved."

"And when he was done with her, he left her alone, shunned by society and with no one to take care of her, she took her own life."

Thea sat dumbstruck as he finished, unwilling to believe the man she loved in Amon could do the things she'd heard. Amon had said he'd done some terrible things in his past, but she couldn't bring herself to accept what the councilman had told her.

As she struggled to keep her faith in Amon, Thea sensed him nearby. He'd come for her! But he was walking into a trap with Kiril and the councilman waiting for him. She had to help him. No matter who he'd been or what he'd done, he was her destined one.

Just as she opened her mouth to yell, Kiril burst into the room. "He's here! My men spotted him in one of the lower corridors."

Turning toward Thea, the councilman warned, "Behave yourself, dear, and you might just get to hear your beloved himself admit to his crimes."

CHAPTER TWENTY-ONE

AMON, MARKKU, AND GETHEN QUIETLY made their way through the lower level of the Soren headquarters building prepared to kill those who just a week ago they'd counted as friends. Amon was relying on Markku's magick to help them since his own powers were rendered useless by Kiril's magickians and their enchantments that safeguarded the Soren members from anyone looking to infiltrate the organization. Already Markku had proven himself invaluable by getting them inside the building. Now Amon needed him to pinpoint where Kiril was holding Thea.

Each step brought him closer to her; at least that's what he tried to convince himself of. He couldn't think about what Kiril might have done to her without becoming blinded by rage, so he chose instead to concentrate simply on finding her. After that, he'd let his wrath seek out its victim.

Voices from a nearby hallway in front of them put them on alert, and all three men readied their guns at their sides. Backs against the stone wall, they slid toward the intersection of hallways, ready to kill if they had to.

The two unarmed guards they came upon never saw them, and with a sharp hit to the back of each one's head, they had made it past the first hurdle to getting Thea out safely.

"What do you want to do with them?" Markku asked as he looked down at the two unconscious guards.

"Check them for anything that we can use and then leave them."

"Amon, do you sense her anywhere nearby?" Gethen asked as they began down the cross hallway.

"I can't get anything, but hopefully I'll know when we're close. I only hope she can hear me."

"Markku, where are we?"

Pointing to a stairwell at the end of the hallway, he said, "Those stairs go to the main level."

"I'm not feeling good about being trapped in a stairwell. Any other way we can get upstairs?"

Markku pointed to a freight elevator. "Feel better about that?"

Amon shook his head. "No."

"Then stairs it is."

Gethen grabbed Amon's sleeve to stop him. "I could rematerialize upstairs and make sure it's safe."

"Are you feeling better? The last time you did that you looked like hell afterward."

"And felt like it, but that was traveling between worlds from Nil. I'm not much of a Sidhe if I can't disappear and rematerialize one floor up."

Turning to Markku, who was about to enter the stairwell,

Amon said, "Hold up. Gethen is going to check things out while we wait here."

"Gonna try a little Sidhe hocus pocus, huh, old man? Sounds good to me."

Gethen disappeared before their eyes and the two men waited and watched for more of Kiril's guards. When the Sidhe reappeared, he looked pale and troubled.

"He's got guards all along the main hallways to the central room where he holds meetings. But none seem to have any weapons either. We're going to have to get through a few sets of them before we can get to Kiril."

As Gethen finished, his breathing was labored and he leaned up against the wall to support himself.

Amon reached out to touch his shoulder. "No more of that. We'll find another way to do this. Understand?"

Nodding, Gethen took a deep breath. "Amon, he's got her in the main room. He's waiting for you and using her as bait."

In a low voice, Amon growled, "That's just another fucking reason I'm going to kill him."

"Okay, guys. We need to get upstairs if we expect to get your lady out of here. No time like the present."

"Let's go. Markku, you take the rear. Gethen, stay near me. And this time we might not be able to get past them by just knocking them out. Sorry, Markku. I hope none of these guys are your friends."

"No need to be sorry. They cut me out like cancer at a moment's notice. Kill 'em all."

As they climbed the stairs to the floor above, Amon and

Gethen turned to see Markku stopped on the landing and mumbling something. As he joined them and they hit the top of the stairs, they heard a series of successive thuds. Once the noise had stopped, Amon opened the heavy metal door and looked up and down the hallway. In both directions, the floor was littered with the bodies of unconscious guards.

Looking back, Amon smiled at Markku.

"I'm a lover, not a killer. That back there was just bravado. I'm surprised as shit that it worked, though. But it's only for a short time, big guy, so you can thank me later when we're all back at the house and I'm enjoying some whiskey."

All three stepped out into the hallway and walked to the main room. They were walking into an ambush, but they had little choice.

Amon braced himself as he grabbed the handle to the door. Just days earlier, he'd come here with Thea and the men who stood behind him now to seek help from the Soren. Now he hoped what lay behind the door didn't break his heart.

The three stepped in not knowing what to expect, but what they saw was even more shocking than anything they could've imagined. On the dais sat Thea in Kiril's chair and behind her stood the head of the Council at Nil. To their right, lay Kiril, unconscious on the ground.

"Come in, gentlemen. Come in. And my compliments to you, magickian. Whatever you did affected even your leader. That's some talent you possess."

Silently, Amon instructed Gethen to guard the door and shoot on sight anyone who tried to get in. He and Markku approached the stage Thea sat on, and as he walked Amon attempted to gently insert in her mind that everything would be okay. He only hoped Markku's magick had made it possible for his powers to work now.

"So we meet once again, Mr. Kalins. I thought the last time we met would be the last, but fate serves you well. Thankfully, very few of my prisoners can count a Sidhe as a close associate willing to risk his life to free them from Nil."

"Let her go, Adams. I'm who you want."

A flash of surprise crossed the councilman's face. "You remember my name? Then have you yet figured out why I've hunted you for lifetimes, used your friends against you, and even had my bounty hunter kidnap a woman to get you?"

Amon studied the face of the man who could truthfully be called his enemy. Nothing about him sparked even the slightest memory. Average height, average features told him nothing. His attempt to read the man's mind gave him nothing.

"Don't bother trying to find out. I'll willingly tell you. I've hated you for so long, it seems there has never been a time when I didn't want to see you suffer. But even when I sentenced you to spend the rest of your time on Earth in Nil, it wasn't enough. And it won't be enough when I do it again, but no matter. It will have to suffice."

Amon focused on Thea. *Angel, I don't know if you can hear me, but I promise I'll get you out of here safely. I promise.*

Thea smiled and closed her eyes, but Adams tugged on her hair sharply. "No fair telling her things without letting everyone else hear, Mr. Kalins. Thea, dear, tell your beloved what we talked about just a short time ago."

Amon watched in horror as Thea tried but said nothing. The councilman tugged on her hair again, this time even harder. "Come now, Thea. Do as you're told."

Amon fought the urge to tear Adams in two as he feared he'd hurt Thea if he even took a step. "Let her go," he warned. "I'm sure it's not your style to harm an innocent woman."

The councilman barked out a sharp laugh. "No, I'd say that's better suited to you."

Amon heard Gethen's warning interrupting his thoughts to remind him that the odds were in their favor as long as Kiril and his guards were out, but that would change soon. But with Adams standing so close to Thea, Amon knew his options were limited. Unfortunately, the councilman seemed in the mood to talk.

"Adams, you've gotten me confused with someone else. Let her go."

"I admit it took me a while to find you, and then when I did, you were involved with Gault and his group and they protected you. Then that murderer in New Hope did me a huge favor. There was no way a prisoner with no powers could catch you, but then fate smiled on me for once. His destined one was related to an ancient one, and knowing you ancients, I could bet on her knowing you. But even better, she'd been related to you at one time. It was perfect."

Amon took a step toward the stage and Adams yanked Thea out of the chair. "No further, Kalins. One more step and

I hurt her."

"Amon, please," Thea pleaded. "Please do what he wants."

It broke his heart to hear the sadness in Thea's voice. "Fine, Adams. I won't move from here."

As the councilman explained how his selfish desire for another man's destined one had almost ruined a young couple in love, Amon realized he wasn't in pain because of Thea's emotions.

"You're wasting your time. Thea already knows what I did last year."

"Ah, the love of a destined one. Tell me, does she know about your other crimes?"

Bluffing and hoping Thea would do the same and forgive him later, Amon smirked and shrugged his shoulders. "We're destined ones, Adams. She knows about my past."

"Does she? She didn't seem to know earlier when I was explaining what you did to poor Victoria."

At the sound of that one name, Amon felt like he'd been hit in the chest with a sledgehammer. Of all the names he'd hoped Adams wouldn't say, that was the one. He knew by the look on Thea's face that he'd told her the story and she desperately wanted to believe he'd lied.

"Let's hear it. How you convinced her to leave her husband, the man she truly loved, her destined one. Explain to your current destined one how you cheated on your destined one then—Frederika, wasn't it?—and took Victoria away from the man who loved her and the life she had with him. Explain how you used her until she didn't interest you anymore and left her alone, so lost she took her own life."

Dumbfounded, Amon tried to remember how much he'd said about Victoria at his trial to explain how the councilman knew so much. Sure he hadn't said enough to allow him to know such intimate details, he stood confused.

"Adams, you've made your point. I'm a fucker. You don't have to say any more of what you've read in my file."

"What did she look like when you told her you were done with her, those beautiful green eyes full of sadness when she realized too late what you truly were?"

The description of what Victoria had looked like when he'd last seen her that day in the English countryside nearly knocked Amon off his feet. The councilman's details were too perfect to be from a Directorate file.

"How?" he stammered.

"How do you think? She was my wife! My destined one!" Adams roared.

Amon stepped back, reeling from the knowledge that the husband of Victoria Adams stood in front of him prepared to once again be judge and jury, but this time punishing Thea also. Thea's shocked look devastated Amon, and for a moment he swore he felt her pain from finding out about this dark part of his past.

"And now, I'll let you watch as I make your lovely destined one pay for your crimes," Harold Adams said as he squeezed his hands around Thea's neck and began to tighten his hold.

Amon's rage took over, and he launched onto the stage and Harold Adams. He pulled his hands from her neck, and as she crumpled to the ground gasping for air, Amon began to pummel the man's face repeatedly, the feel of breaking bones under his hands as he beat him into unconsciousness.

From behind him, he heard Thea scream and he turned to see Kiril, awake and on his feet, taking her away through a side door.

"Markku, watch him!" Amon boomed as he chased after Kiril.

Amon followed the sound of Thea's frightened screams to Kiril's bedroom. He'd been there before, so he knew of all the possible weapons his walls provided. Adrenaline coursing through his body, he easily kicked the door in and found Kiril standing next to his wall of weapons and shielding himself with Thea.

"Kiril, you're a fucking coward. Let her go. Either way, I'm sending you on to your next life, right now, in this room."

Reaching up, Kiril grabbed a dagger from the wall and held it to Thea's neck, making her cry out in pain as the blade pressed against her skin.

"Not unless you're planning to send her on too," he said as he pushed the blade into her neck and blood began to trickle down her chest.

Thea, trust me. I need you to scream, honey, when I tell you to. Loud. And then stomp your foot. When he releases you, drop to the floor and get the hell out here. Now, Thea!

Exactly as he'd instructed, Thea screamed as loud as she could and stomped on Kiril's foot. As a stunned Kiril released his hold on her, Amon pushed her out of the way and lunged at Kiril, taking him down onto the bed.

THEA WATCHED IN HORROR AS Kiril jabbed the knife at Amon as the men rolled around on the bed, cutting his neck and chest. Amon pinned his arms and forced the knife out of his hand, causing it to drop to the bed.

For a moment, Amon stopped fighting, but she knew only one of them would be able to leave this place alive. Picking the dagger up, he drove it into Kiril's chest. Exhausted and losing blood from his wounds, Amon collapsed onto the bed.

"Amon!" Thea screamed as she watched him fall.

As she gently turned him over, she saw his wounds. Kiril had cut him with a gash across the neck, but the deeper cut was on his chest. The red stain on his shirt was spreading with each passing second. Carefully, she placed her hands over his chest wound and prayed he wasn't too far gone. If his injuries were mortal, her ability to heal would mean nothing. If he was meant to die, she'd lose him no matter how much she tried to save him.

She pressed gently against his chest, but the blood continued to flow over her hands. Pushing harder, she called out to him to open his eyes. She couldn't lose him!

"Amon, please open your eyes. Don't leave me! Please, God, don't take him yet. Please!"

Slowly, he opened his eyes and focused on her face. "Thea, find Gethen. Everything I have is yours," he whispered.

"No! I don't want houses in dozens of places. I want you!

Please don't leave me."

Amon closed his eyes, and Thea focused her healing like she'd never done before. The pain was excruciating and she slowly felt herself slipping away, unable to fight it.

Please. Don't leave me.

MARKKU REMAINED STANDING OVER THE head councilman, ready to continue the beating Amon had begun. Each time he stirred, Markku prepared his foot to kick him back into unconsciousness.

Gethen stood guarding the door, but no one attempted to enter. As they waited for Amon and Thea to return, he reached out with his mind to search for his former master's but felt nothing.

"Markku, something's wrong. Stay here. I need to find Amon."

As he made his way toward where Kiril and Amon had gone, he sensed Naomi Cooper trying to contact him. Before he could answer, she was standing in front of him over Harold Adams. Within seconds, she was joined by other members of the council who stood near her examining the scene around them.

"Gethen, I'm here to tell your friend his accusations were correct, that Mr. Adams' presence here is just the beginning of the proof against him."

Shaking his head, he quietly said, "I can't sense Amon," before he left to search for Amon and Thea.

"I'm sorry, friend," she said sadly.

Turning toward her fellow council members, she said, "Ladies and gentlemen, my investigation has uncovered a close relationship between the head of our council and the leader of the rebel group, the Soren, Kiril Gault. Mr. Adams' presence here and the testimony I believe we'll receive from not only the Sidhe but this man will show the exact nature of that relationship to be against Aeveren law and everything we hold ethical."

Slowly, Harold Adams began to regain consciousness and awoke to see his fellow council members standing in judgment of him.

"Mr. Adams, this council formally charges you with the illegal use of your position to terrorize and incarcerate your fellow Aeveren. You will be tried in a separate council but know that each of us here will be willing witnesses against you. You've abused your power and even more than that, you've cooperated with an organization that goes against every principle we council members pledge to uphold."

Naomi Cooper motioned to Markku to lift Harold Adams from the floor. He rose, bloodied and bruised, to face his colleagues and immediately hung his head.

"What is your name?" she asked Markku. When he remained silent, she continued. "Sir, while I'm sure if I did some checking I'd find your past to be rather unsavory, we have no wish to punish you. We've bigger fish to fry. So tell me your name."

"Markku Dunning, ma'am," he said, his voice full of

respect, and then added, "I'm here with Gethen and Amon to rescue Thea."

Naomi Cooper smiled. "Something tells me you're a very clever man to have around, Mr. Dunning. Please tell your Sidhe friend I'm thankful for his help. And my apologies for any loss you've suffered because of the actions of this council."

Markku's smile at her compliment faded and he rushed to locate Gethen, finally finding him standing in the doorway to a room halfway down the hall. He looked pale and sad and held himself up against the doorframe.

"Gethen?"

Silently, the Sidhe moved aside to allow Markku to enter the room. Two steps in he saw what had turned Gethen pale. Kiril Gault lay dead in a pool of blood with a dagger stuck in his chest. To his left, next to him on the bed lay Amon, his shirt soaked in blood, and on top of him was Thea, covered in blood.

CHAPTER TWENTY-TWO

S LOWLY, AMON BECAME CONSCIOUS, FEELING Thea on his chest, and looked down to see her covered in his blood, her long, blond hair sticky and pale red. On her face, arms, and hands showed the effort she'd made to save him.

He waited to feel her breathe, his heart in his throat at the idea that she'd given her life for his and would be gone from this life at any moment.

"Thea?" he asked, his voice almost pleading with her to still be alive.

Rubbing her back, he repeated her name as fear gripped him. But almost imperceptibly, her chest rose and fell against his, and he wrapped his arms around her as fear was replaced with purer joy than he'd ever felt in all his lifetimes.

Beside him, Kiril Gault began to fade from this lifetime, and Amon watched as the man he'd killed went on to await his next lifetime, his violet eyes still wide with terror from his last moments in this one.

"Amon?"

Turning his head to face the door, he saw Gethen and

Markku both with worried looks on their faces. They looked at Thea, not knowing she'd survived and waiting for the sad moment when she'd slowly begin to vanish just as Kiril just had, as all Aeveren did after death.

"Gethen, she's going to be okay. Come here and help me."

"Thea, honey. Open your eyes for me," Amon whispered next to her ear as he stroked her blood soaked hair.

"Help me lay her on her back, Gethen," he said looking up at him.

Carefully, he rolled Thea over and placed her on the bed. Her eyes remained closed, and as Amon sat next to her pushing her hair away from her face, he saw just how much like an angel she truly looked.

My angel.

"Markku, get me something to clean the blood off her," Amon said looking up at him as he remained in the doorway. "There's got to be something in Kiril's bathroom."

Nodding, Markku seemed to come out of his shock at Amon's command, and he scurried into the adjacent bathroom to do as he'd been told.

Amon's gaze returned to Thea's face. He stroked her cheek tenderly as he waited for her to regain consciousness.

"What happened with Kiril?" Gethen asked quietly.

Staring at the placid face of the woman he loved, Amon answered coldly, "I did what I said I would."

Gethen sighed, and Amon continued. "I know what you're worrying about. Don't. If they want to punish me for Kiril's death, they'll have to catch me first."

Markku returned and quickly handed Amon a wet cloth. Turning to Gethen, he asked in a nervous voice, "I thought she was okay. What happened?"

Amon looked up as he cleaned Thea's face. "Markku, I'm going to need to take Thea out of here my way. I need you to get rid of any spells or whatever else Kiril had that would prevent me from teleporting."

"No problem, Amon. It'll only take me a few minutes." Then quietly, Markku said, "I hope she's going to be okay."

Amon gave him a slight smile and returned his attention to Thea. When he'd almost finished cleaning her face, her eyelids begin to flutter and slowly she opened her eyes.

Whispering, she said his name, as if she were unsure if she were dreaming or truly awake.

Bending to kiss her, he felt her press her hand to his chest where Kiril had stabbed him. He covered her hand with his and smiled.

"Once again, you saved me. But I'm more concerned about you. As soon as Markku does his thing, I'm taking you home."

Thea tried to sit up, but even with help she immediately sat back and closed her eyes.

"Don't try to move. Just be calm. We'll leave soon."

"Home?" she whispered.

"Yes, home. For now, Ireland. When you feel better, we can go anywhere you want," he said as he ran his finger over her lips.

"But what about the Council?" she asked in a worried

voice.

Amon shook his head. "Don't worry about that."

Before she could voice any protest, Markku returned to proudly announce that the Soren headquarters was a charm-free zone.

Pulling Thea to his chest, Amon said, "Markku, I want you to get Gethen back to the house in Ireland. Once I get Thea settled, I'll meet with both of you."

Gently kissing Thea's ear, he whispered, "Hold on. We'll be home soon," before they vanished from Kiril Gault's bedroom, leaving everything there behind them.

Amon made sure to arrive in their bedroom and carefully set Thea on the bed. Seated next to her, he returned to stroking her face as he silently thanked God for letting her stay with him.

Almost fully recovered, Thea caught his hand in hers and repeated her concern from earlier. "Amon, what about the Council? I'm worried."

Leaning in to kiss her, he cradled her face in his hands. "I told you not to worry. I have no intention of letting them take me away from you."

Concern clouded her eyes. "But all the things he said."

Amon knew she meant what Adams had said about Victoria. As much as he wished he could deny everything, he kept his focus on her eyes and said the words he dreaded.

"Thea, it's true. I did what Adams said I did. I can't deny that."

Thea closed her eyes as he continued.

"I've never wished more that I wasn't the kind of man he described, but I was for lifetimes. I know that."

Amon watched in sadness as a tear slid down the side of her face. She was breaking his heart. As he kissed her cheek, he whispered, "I'm sorry. All I can promise is that the man I am now isn't that person anymore."

He waited for what seemed like years until she opened her eyes again. What he saw was worse than any punishment they could devise for him in Nil. Unable to look at the distance that had settled into her eyes, he focused on his fingers as they stroked her hair.

"Let's get you cleaned up."

THEA STOOD IN THE SHOWER and let the hot water run over her body. Pinkish colored water pooled at her feet as Amon's blood left her hair. The gentle pelting of the jetted spray on her back felt good on her aching and bruised body.

As much as she wished her mind would just go blank, thoughts of what the councilman and Amon said ran around her brain. Her destined one had callously discarded a woman who loved him—another man's destined one.

She knew Amon stood just outside the shower, ready if she felt weak and needed help. Everything she knew about the man he was told her he wasn't the man he'd been with Victoria Adams.

Amon made a noise and she looked out to see him as he kicked off his shoes and peeled off his socks before climbing into the shower to stand behind her.

"Amon, what are you doing?"

He filled his palm with shampoo and began massaging it into her hair. As he lathered her up, he said all the things she knew he had to if she were to fully accept him again.

"Victoria was sweet and kind. She loved me, and I mistreated her. What I did makes me cringe when I think of someone doing that to you."

Thea closed her eyes as he continued.

"I was selfish. It doesn't matter why."

Amon gently pushed Thea toward the water and waited until the soap was rinsed from her hair before he pulled her back toward him and wrapped his arms around her, whispering into her ear. "Thea, I can't change who I've been. But for whatever reason, you've been given me as your destined one. All I can promise is that I will do whatever it takes to make you happy."

Opening her eyes, she saw he stood behind her fully clothed and soaked to the skin. She turned to face him and wrapped her arms around him. As she looked up toward him, he carefully pushed the hair from her face.

"I believe you're not the man you were. But I need you to promise me there will be no more killing."

Shaking his head, he grimaced. "I can't promise that, my angel. Anyone who tries to hurt you will be in grave danger. Your safety has to be my primary concern."

Thea accepted his answer, even if she didn't like it, and turned off the water. Looking at his soaked shirt and pants, she smiled at the difference between what she knew of Amon's past compared to the man who stood in front of her looking foolish after a shower with his clothes on.

As she stepped past him, she said with a chuckle, "Maybe next time you might try it with your clothes off."

Arching one eyebrow, he put on an irritated face as he followed her and began peeling off his wet shirt. As she watched, she wrapped herself in a towel and for just a moment, she stopped to admire his body.

AMON LOOKED UP FROM UNDOING his pants when he realized she was staring at him. She looked beautiful standing in only a towel and he so much wanted to just reach out to draw her body to his, but what he heard in her mind stopped him.

"Yes, I loved her. Not the way I love you, but I think I did love her."

"Oh. How did you know I was thinking that?"

"It seems I've been given another power since Nil."

"Another power? Just how many do you have?"

He stepped toward her smiling. "Let's just say I'm not lacking in that department."

"That's one of the things I love most about you, Amon. Your humility."

Thea pushed by him to leave the bathroom, but he had other ideas. Hooking an arm around her waist, he pulled her back to him and held her close. As he feathered kisses down her neck, he whispered, "My humility? I think I have to remind you of the other things that are far more interesting than that."

The feel of her damp skin against his lips excited him, and as a tiny moan escaped her lips, he pressed his hard erection into her back. He slid his free hand to where she'd knotted the towel and freed it from her body. As the towel fell to a heap at her feet, he ran his hand over her breast and cupped it while his thumb and forefinger squeezed her excited nipple.

"Good, but I think you need more reminding," he teased as the hand that had held her to him slid down to tease her sex.

Her head fell back against his chest, and he heard the hitch in her breathing when he slid his finger down her moist slit. As his fingers played, she covered his hands with hers, guiding him to the spot that with just his touch would deliver sweet release.

"Not yet, love. I want to remind you some more," he said as he slid a finger inside her.

In a keening voice, she said his name and turned to free his cock, wanting what stood proudly behind the fabric of his pants. He watched her efforts eagerly, licking his lips for a delicious taste of her and waiting for the touch of her hand on him.

He didn't have to wait long, and at the first touch as she gripped him, wrapping her fingers around him, his thick cock kicked in her hand. Looking down, he watched as she stroked the full length of him, aroused even more by how erotic her hand looked as it created waves of pleasure with each glide over his skin.

He dipped his head to nudge her face up toward his and kissed her mouth impatiently as she continued to pleasure him with her hand. Sliding his tongue into her mouth to mingle with hers, he began to back up toward the bathtub and broke away from her mouth to quickly turn the water on.

"You're not planning to take a bath now with your pants on, are you?" she teased as she tugged his pants toward his thighs.

Amon said nothing but smiled and shook his head as she undressed him. Knowing she wanted what he wanted, he stepped out of his pants and sat down on the edge of the oversized tub. Thea kneeled in front of him and pushed his legs open as she ran her palms over his thighs, exciting him even more.

Thea looked up at him, her eyes full of desire, and licked her lips. "Remind me again why you like me to do this?"

"Because the feel of your mouth sucking my cock is better than almost anything in this world. When you run your tongue…"

Amon abruptly stopped talking and sighed deeply when Thea's mouth covered the head and she began to tease him with her softly flicking tongue. Slowly, she sucked him into her mouth and then retreated, sliding back up to the swollen crown. He watched as she became more aroused with each movement she made. Breaking his stare at the erotic scene between his legs, he turned to shut off the water.

Touching her jaw with his hand, he motioned to the water. "Come here."

Thea rose and climbed into the tub after him. Amon sat with his back against the cool marble above the water and stretched his long legs out in front of him. From across the tub, she stared at him.

He looked down to see the spot on his chest that still bore a pink scar where Kiril had stabbed him, where she'd healed him taking every ounce of pain from his body with her touch. She crawled onto his lap and softly ran her fingers over the fading scar as she stared into his eyes. Her other hand held on to his broad shoulders, hardness under her gentle grip. But her focus was on the soft skin where she could have lost him.

"Amon, I was so afraid I was going to lose you."

He slowly traced his hands down her sides as she spoke. "When I thought you were gone, my heart felt like it had broken. I've never loved anyone like I love you. I know having a destined one isn't new to you, but I've never felt like this. I can take the life that comes with you, and even the past, but the thought of losing you hurts me more than I can stand."

Taking her face in his hands, he kissed her softly. "My angel. Don't ever think you're just another destined one. You're more special to me than I can ever explain. I owe you my life. I can't promise our life together will be like other people's because of who I was before you, and you'll never know how sorry I am for that, but I promise I'll never give you any reason to doubt my love, no matter what happens. Of all the gifts I've been given, you're the one I deserve the least and cherish the most."

Thea closed her eyes, and he softly kissed her cheek. He'd

meant what he'd said. Never before had he been blessed so much and deserved it so little. Gently, he lifted her and settled her onto him, his cock pushing into her, filling her. Gentle thrusts gave way to more frenzied movements as he held her by the hips and guided her to ride him. As the water lapped gently against their skin, she moaned the arrival of her orgasm as she dug her nails into the smooth skin of his back, skin she'd healed.

Buried so deeply that her body melded with his, Amon felt his release pump into her and bit her shoulder as she whimpered through the end of her climax. When she finally lifted her head from his neck to look at him, her face wore the sultry, satisfied look he loved to see.

"I like that much better than your humility," she said quietly.

"Me too. Humility never feels anywhere as good," he joked.

But Amon saw the shadow of worry cross her face as she remembered the world outside their watery sanctuary. "Amon, what's going to happen with the Council?"

Amon knew it was likely he'd have to spend the rest of this lifetime and probably the last three of his remaining lifetimes running from the long arm of the Council, never being able to provide Thea with the peace of a stable home. He thought of the life they'd be forced to live, always on the run. What if they'd just conceived minutes earlier? What kind of life would their child have? He couldn't show Thea that any of this concerned him, though. He'd promised her she'd be safe with him, and no matter what it took, he'd ensure that, at least.

Tickling her sides, he made her squirm up against him. "Ready for another round? We're going to have to move to the bed then."

"I'm serious, Amon," she said with a voice to match the look on her face.

"So am I, love. You're starting to prune up."

Thea put her hands on her hips in mock anger and squinted her eyes. "Amon."

"Althea, I don't want you to worry about the Council. I'll take care of that. You just worry about becoming one of the California raisins."

Amon lifted one of her hands to his mouth and kissed her puckered fingertips as he hummed the chorus to "Heard It Through The Grapevine." When Thea saw she wasn't going to get a serious answer about her concerns with the Council, she snatched her hand from his hold and wrinkled her nose in disgust.

Kissing him, she stood to step out of the tub. "You're lucky I love you so much, Amon Kalins."

As he watched her dry off and leave the bathroom, he silently agreed.

I am lucky, and I have no intention of letting the Council or anyone else take me away from that love.

CHAPTER TWENTY-THREE

G ETHEN AND MARKKU SAT DOWNSTAIRS quietly waiting for Amon. His eyes closed, Gethen silently prepared himself for his return to his people. With Thea safely returned and the head of the Council at Nil exposed, he knew the time would soon come for him to leave.

It was with mixed emotions that he decided to leave, but now that Amon was no longer alone in the world, he knew in his heart that it was time to rejoin the world of the Sidhe. With a destined one, Amon would finally have what he'd missed all those lifetimes. At least Gethen hoped he would if his sense of Naomi Cooper was right.

"Why so quiet, old man?"

Markku's intrusion on his thoughts annoyed him, and he shot him a nasty look. "What do you plan to do now that the Soren has lost its leader, Markku?"

The magickian blew the air out of his lungs through puffed cheeks and rolled his eyes. "I don't know, but that's the $64,000 question, isn't it? There aren't many places for someone like me to go in our world."

"Our world?"

"Don't act like you're not one of us, old man. You may not be Aeveren, but after spending lifetimes with the big guy, you're as good as one, even if you're a Sidhe."

Gethen smiled at Markku's attempt at a compliment and for the first time didn't feel revulsion for him. "Thank you, Markku."

"Anytime. Do you mind if I ask you something?"

Cautiously, Gethen answered, "No. Feel free."

"What kind of Sidhe are you?"

"The dark kind."

"You don't say? I know some dark Sidhe—spent last Samhain with them. Now there's some ladies who know how to have a good time, if you know what I mean."

Gethen grimaced in response to the wink Markku made to punctuate his point. Sighing in disgust, he closed his eyes and hoped for once Markku would understand the clues his body language was sending. In no way did he want to hear another of Markku's tales of sexual exploit.

Thankfully, before Markku could misinterpret his silence as his tacit agreement to continue, Amon joined them and took a seat on the couch next to Gethen. Silently, Gethen thanked him for saving him from the torture of another Markku sex story.

Amon smiled his acknowledgement of his message and turned to Markku.

"Did you make sure no one can get into this house?"

"Yeah, just like you said. But that's not a problem

anymore. The councilman's been removed. Nobody's going to be coming after Thea now."

"I don't want to take any chances."

"Amon, you're going to have to deal with the Council, even if Adams has been removed," Gethen said quietly.

"Now isn't the time to think about that. We have to get you back home. It's time I fulfilled the promise I made when I took you from your people."

Gethen nodded solemnly, knowing with a sense of pride that his life since he'd left his people had been enough to help Amon keep his pledge. He had served him faithfully, never harmed another person, and had earned his people's forgiveness.

Markku stood to leave and Amon followed to escort him to the door. An awkward silence hung in the air until Amon said, "If I need you, I'll call."

"No problem, Amon."

As Markku turned to leave, Amon caught him by the sleeve. "I forgot to ask. I wasn't affected by Thea's emotions at Kiril's this time. Any chance the spell Sevine put on me is gone?"

Chuckling, Markku said, "I wouldn't bet on it. Kiril had that place so charmed up, leprechauns couldn't have worked their mojo there. I think you might still have to make her happy. But you never know."

"Thanks, Markku," he said as he slapped his back.

WITH MARKKU GONE, AMON AND Gethen sat reminiscing about the times they'd shared. Neither man wanted to admit how much he was going to miss the other. For Amon, it was seven lifetimes, but for Gethen, it was over two hundred years that would end that day.

Thea joined them as Amon teased Gethen about one of their escapades. "I won't ask about what I just heard about flappers," she joked as she sat down.

Gethen looked at her sheepishly as Amon began to explain one time in France when a young burlesque dancer had taken a fancy to Gethen.

Smiling, she put her hand up to stop the story. "I think it might be better if I pretend I didn't hear this. I'd rather keep my ideas of Gethen."

"As you wish, miss," he said, ever the servant to the end.

When they were finally ready to go, the three began the journey north to the land of the Sidhe. For Gethen, the road home was as fresh in his mind as the day he'd left. Even though much had changed over the years, the realm of his people remained in the hills and forests of Ireland. With each step they took, he felt their presence grow around him.

Feelings of insecurity rose in him as with each step he got closer to the world he'd been absent from for centuries. Would he be accepted back into the world he'd been banished from? He knew he'd paid for his crimes and Amon's word would be proof of that, but he knew memories died hard.

Would he be alone for the rest of his existence, officially forgiven for what he'd done all those years ago but still a pariah?

As he wondered about his future, his thoughts traveled back to his family. Were his parents still living, elderly members of the royal court to the Sidhe king? What had become of his brothers and sisters in the years since he'd left? Had their lives turned out as his parents had hoped— husbands and wives to the royal children?

With his thoughts on the many questions he'd soon have answered, Gethen stepped into the edge of the woods that concealed the realm of the Sidhe. Just a few more minutes and he'd be home.

AMON KEPT AN EYE ON the area around them as they walked, still not convinced Thea was safe. As long as he had his arm around her, he knew he could teleport her out of harm's way, so he made sure to remain close to her.

As he walked, memories of his time with Gethen's people drifted back into his mind, of his friend's exile and his promise to allow him to return when his debt to the Aeveren world had been paid. He'd kept Gethen long after that had been settled, but now he'd finally return him to his rightful place.

After they'd walked in silence for a while, Thea asked, "Can we go all the way to the Sidhe world, or will we have to say goodbye to him before?"

"No. We'll be welcomed by the Sidhe. But I want you to stay close to me there too."

"Why? What's going to happen?"

Smiling, he said, "Nothing bad, but the Sidhe are very seductive creatures."

Thea chuckled and kissed his hand. "Oh, I see. Jealous?"

"And what if I said I was?"

Squeezing his hand at her side, she said, "Well, that would be silly since I only want you. On second thought, maybe I like that. It makes up for how jealous I was with Kiril's women."

Thea stopped walking and dropped her head.

"Oh, Amon! I promised one of the girls I met that I'd get them away from that horrible place when you rescued me. How could I forget them?"

Amon hugged her close to his body and tried to comfort her. "Don't worry. I'll get Markku to find them and as soon as we get back, I'll make sure they get to safety. All of them."

Thea wrapped her arms around him and buried her face in his chest. "Thank you. I can't let them down. I can't believe I forgot them. What kind of healer am I?"

Amon stroked her hair and kissed the top of her head. "Don't ever let me hear you say that again, Althea Forester. I've never met another soul in my forty-seven lifetimes that cared about others as much as you do."

With his forefinger, he lifted her chin up so she faced him. "I mean it, Thea. And don't worry. I won't let you down."

Amon closed his eyes and loved what he heard in Thea's mind. *I have a destined one finally, and he's just what I wished for. A knight in shining armor.* He silently swore he wouldn't disappoint her, no matter what he had to do to find Kiril's former slaves.

THE CANOPY OF TREES SHIELDED the path from sunlight, and Gethen knew he was close. As he realized he'd left Amon and Thea far behind, he turned to wait for them.

"Hello, Sidhe," a man in front of him said as his hand struck out to grab him. Before he could react, he was immobilized, a prisoner of a Council at Nil bounty hunter.

"Where's your master? Seems dangerous to let a servant wander around by himself. But then again, he's got to keep an eye on that girl of his. He can't watch both of you, can he? Oh well. You understand, I'm sure. You liked Aeveren women too, didn't you, Gethen?"

Ryu Jansen held Gethen tightly to him as he spoke, but Gethen didn't fight back. Instead, he focused his thoughts, hoping Amon would hear them.

Amon! The bounty hunter. Get Thea out of here!

Over and over, he repeated the same thoughts, but Amon didn't hear him.

"Looks like your master's forgotten you. No wonder you hate women," Ryu taunted.

"I don't hate women," Gethen said calmly, unable to avoid the bounty hunter's verbal baiting.

"That's not what I hear, Sidhe. Three Aeveren women murdered by you tells me everything I need to know about what you think of the females of my kind."

"I'm not that creature anymore. That was a long time ago."

Gethen hoped if he kept Ryu talking, he could give Amon enough time to get Thea out of danger. Again, he tried to connect with Amon's mind to warn him.

Amon! Turn back around! You're in danger. The bounty hunter!

"I bet you're wondering why he hasn't come to save you yet, Sidhe, aren't you."

Gethen didn't answer, but no, he didn't understand why Amon hadn't sensed his thoughts.

"He can't see either of us thanks to the sorcerers at Nil. See this?" he asked as he raised his left hand to show him a golden brown stone. "Gotta love those sorcerers. When I realized I was going up against one of the Soren's magickians, I asked them for something to give me the upper hand. This is it. This little stone possesses an enchantment that makes us invisible and…and this is the best part, makes it impossible to sense us. That's why your master has no idea he should be helping you instead of playing kissyface with his newest girl."

Gethen's body involuntarily tensed up. Ryu was leading Amon and Thea into the woods where he would suddenly lift the spell and Amon would naturally try to save him. He'd unknowingly put himself and Thea in danger!

Panic raced through him as he watched them walk toward him into a trap. He had to do something to alert him to the danger. Desperate, he began thrashing his arms against the bounty hunter's hold hoping to escape him and the enchantment so he could run back toward Amon and Thea and save them.

"Stop fighting!" Ryu commanded while he threatened Gethen with a knife he placed close to his neck.

"Smell that? One more move to fight me and you're as dead as those women you murdered."

Gethen froze at the knowledge that Ryu had a knife coated in deadly poison pointed at his throat. If he moved to dislodge the charmed stone out of his hand, he risked being stabbed and possibly not alerting Amon to what awaited them. But if he didn't, they'd walk right into Ryu's trap.

One last time he tried to reach Amon's thoughts.

Amon, please. The bounty hunter has me just inside the wooded area. Take yourselves out of here now!

AS HE AND THEA GOT close to the woods, Amon sensed something was wrong. He couldn't see Gethen in front of them, although he knew Gethen understood he wouldn't be allowed back into his world without him. Quickly, he scanned the area around them for anything odd but saw nothing.

"Amon, what is it?"

"Did you see Gethen since we started walking again?"

"I don't think so. I wasn't paying attention. What's wrong?"

"I don't know. He wouldn't try to reenter his world without me. Something's wrong."

At the edge of the woods, he stopped and listened to hear any thoughts, but all he heard were Thea's.

"Amon, if something's wrong, maybe we shouldn't continue. Maybe we should wait for him here."

As his mind raced and he became truly worried about

Gethen, Amon watched in horror as Ryu lifted the spell to show Gethen being held with a knife to his throat. As the odor of Anjer hit his nostrils, Amon saw the bounty hunter's real intentions.

"Let him go. You don't want him. I'm the prize you've come for."

"No, that's where you're wrong, Kalins. You're no longer my assignment. When you and your friend here exposed Adams, it seems you made a friend in the new head of the Council and now I'm out of a job."

Amon saw as the man's eyes flashed wildly that he was a man out of control. Unsure if talking would help, he had to try. Pushing Thea behind him, he hoped to lull the bounty hunter into dropping the knife from Gethen's throat. Then he'd have a chance to overtake him.

"I think you're underestimating how much Adams' friends on the Council would love to see me back in Nil. I've got three lifetimes left after this one."

Ryu laughed a hollow laugh. "You underestimate yourself, Kalins. Nobody on the Council wants to admit any association with Adams. So everything he promised me means shit now."

"Have you ever been to Nil?"

Ryu laughed again. "Yeah, Kalins. I did some time there."

"Then you know what kind of hell it is. Don't tell me they wouldn't want me to pay for my crimes in that hole. Let him go and take me."

Amon felt Thea squeeze his wrist and he quickly touched her mind to reassure her.

If he could only get Ryu to drop his guard.

"You don't want to do this. Think about it."

"Think about it? That's all I've fucking done since that new council head called me in to tell me everything I'd looked forward to had gone to shit! And for what? A fucking murdering tempuster and his murderer Sidhe slave!"

"It doesn't have to be like this. Let him go. Take your anger out on me. He's got nothing to do with this. I'm the one you're supposed to capture."

Amon sensed he was losing this battle. Ryu had nothing to lose, and Amon knew from experience that feeling.

Gethen, this guy wants somebody. I can't let it be you.

Before Amon could continue, Ryu released Gethen's arm and spun him around to face him. In a second, he was gone running into the forest.

"Gethen!"

Amon grabbed him by the shoulders and turned him around, seeing he had nothing but a scratch on his hand. "Thea, wait here with him."

Amon raced to catch Ryu, leaving Gethen staring at the thin red line that crossed his palm.

AMON COULD SEE THE BOUNTY hunter ahead and knew with almost half a foot on him he'd be on top of him in no time. His heart pounded wildly as he pushed his legs to run faster than ever before. Any remnant of his recent injury was overwhelmed by the pure desire to kill the man who'd first taken his destined one and now threatened the one other person he felt closest to in the world. Soon he was within yards of Ryu, and with the intent to send him on to his next life, Amon teleported in front of him, slamming his full weight into him. Rage controlled him, and he lunged at Ryu as he saw him scramble madly to reach the talisman that hung around his neck.

"I'm not fucking chasing you through time," he yelled before grabbing the charm and yanking it from his neck.

Stunned, Ryu seemed unable to react and Amon began to take out his rage on the bounty hunter. Rage at Harold Adams. Rage at the pain of knowing he'd caused the councilman to endanger the lives of those closest to him. With every pound his fists made to Ryu's face, with every bone he broke and every injury he inflicted, he lashed out at the bounty hunter's part in almost taking away the two people he'd die for.

As Ryu lay beaten almost to unconsciousness, Amon heard Thea's voice scream to him at the edge of the woods. His rage not nearly sated enough to save Ryu's life, he grabbed the knife he'd threatened Gethen with from its holder on his belt and with emotion that almost overwhelmed him, he plunged it into the bounty hunter's chest.

He watched as the life and pain in the wide eyes that stared up at him slowly ebbed away as Ryu Jansen's lifetime ended. Exhausted, Amon sat slumped on the ground next to the man's body and felt his emotions begin to return to normal. He tossed the talisman he still held in his hand to the ground next to him and breathed deeply, neither happy nor unhappy about what he'd just done.

Beside him, the bounty hunter's body began to fade as he left that life for his next one. "Godspeed. May your next life be happier than this one," he said quietly as the last of Ryu Jansen disappeared.

Amon felt a sense of relief knowing Thea and Gethen were safe. What the Council would do to him for Ryu's death didn't matter. He'd protected the two of them the way a man protects those he loves.

Thea's voice came across the forest again, its tone full of fear. Still acting on adrenaline, he jumped to his feet and teleported to her side in time to see Gethen fall to the ground.

"Amon, something's wrong."

Dropping to the ground, he knelt next to Gethen, whose pale face turned toward him, his deep green eyes wide with pain. He held his right hand up in front of him to show where he'd been cut by Ryu's knife.

"Amon, I don't have much time. Please make sure I return home."

Confused, Amon shook his head. "Gethen, you're going to be fine. It's just a scratch."

Struggling to speak, Gethen said hoarsely, "Anjer."

CHAPTER TWENTY-FOUR

$\mathbf{A}$MON STARED DUMBFOUNDED AT THE red line on Gethen's palm. Ryu had never intended to try to take Thea again or even take him back to Nil. His target had been Gethen.

How could he have been so mistaken?

He grabbed Thea's hand resting on his shoulder and silently pleaded with her to heal Gethen, his heart full of fear at losing his dearest friend.

Crouching next to Gethen, she softly ran her finger over his injured palm, unable to do anything. The shallow gash remained as she pulled her hand away to caress his face. Looking into his eyes, she whispered, "I'm so sorry, Gethen."

"Thea?"

Turning to Amon, she slowly shook her head. "I'm sorry. I can't help him."

"Gethen, no. We'll get you back to your people and they'll know what to do," Amon said, his voice panicked.

Reaching under his body, he began to lift him from the ground, but Gethen stopped him with his hand on Amon's chest. "No, this is where I die."

"No. No. Not if I can do anything about it," he said, refusing to accept the truth before him.

"Amon, I don't have much time. The poison works fast. I need you to listen to me. I'm so proud of you. You've been like a son to me."

"Stop. Don't do this."

"I've loved you like no other in your world or mine. Don't make the same mistakes of your past. You've been given another chance."

His life fading quickly, Gethen turned to look at Thea. "Take care of him."

With one last look at Amon, Gethen said goodbye. "Amon, it has been the joy of my life to know you."

Amon saw his friend's time had run out. He cried out his name, his voice strangled as the Sidhe exhaled one last time. Dropping his head to rest on his chest, Amon silently said goodbye to his servant of lifetimes and friend like no other in his time on Earth.

Thea wrapped her arms around Amon's shoulders and held him as his body shuddered in sorrow. "I'm so sorry, Amon."

Thankful that at least he'd be able to fulfill Gethen's wish to return home, Amon carefully lifted him in his arms and cradled his friend as he had done when he'd rescued him from Nil. Without a word, he turned and began the sad journey to return Gethen to his people.

WITH THEA AT HIS SIDE, step by step, Amon made his way to the entrance of the Sidhe kingdom, the darkness growing as they walked deeper and deeper into the forest. The sounds of the world around them changed to frightening, ominous noises, and Thea clutched Amon's arm.

"What's happening?"

"The world of the Sidhe is nearby. What you hear are the sounds of those who guard the gateway between our world and the Sidhe's. Don't be afraid. They mean no harm to us. Only to those who would attack the Sidhe."

Amon led her to the darkest part of the woods, where no light shone on their path. Surrounded by eerie sounds that seemed to come from creatures straight from Hell, Thea held onto him tightly as around them changed to as dark as midnight.

Even the trees seemed menacing, their limbs catching on their clothes, as if to prevent them from finally reaching the entrance to Gethen's world. But Amon continued, undeterred by the whip of branches against his face and arms as he held Gethen close to his body to shield him from the trees' attacks. With her face buried in Amon's side, Thea followed his lead, only lifting her head when he stopped walking.

"We're here."

Ahead of them lay an entrance hidden in the hedge. Behind the leafy camouflage appeared stone steps illuminated by a soft light that bathed everything in its pale white rays.

"Watch your step and stay next to me," Amon said turning to her.

THEA COULDN'T IMAGINE WHERE THE stairway led. Were they walking down into the earth? Was the Sidhe realm entered through a cave?

As they walked, she began to see faces peer out from the brush that lined the stairs. As she met their gazes, each possessing the same deep green eyes as Gethen, they quickly disappeared.

"Don't be frightened. They mean no harm. We're strangers here, so they're naturally curious."

"Amon," she whispered as they reached the last stair. "Their eyes… they're all like Gethen's."

"The sign of the Sidhe."

Thea studied with wonder the world they'd entered. Ahead of them was a dazzling castle that seemed to shimmer in the light. To the left and right of them were fields and forests full of lush grass and flowers and dotted with much smaller homes than the castle that dominated the stunning landscape. A stream ran from right to left immediately in front of them, requiring them to cross a small bridge if they intended to make the trip to the castle.

As she watched, the colors of the Sidhe kingdom seemed to become more vivid right before her eyes. The greens of the plants and trees seemed more alive than any she'd ever seen in the world outside. Everything in front of her appeared as if an artist had painted it.

Gasping, she turned to Amon. "It's so beautiful! I don't think I've ever seen a more beautiful place in all my lifetimes."

Sadly, he answered, "I wish you could have seen it through Gethen's eyes. He would've been so happy to finally return home."

Thea saw the sorrow in his eyes when he looked down at the man he held in his arms. And the guilt.

Men, women, and children slowly began to appear from the homes nearby and stood silently looking at them. Their eyes traveled from Amon, to Thea, and finally came to rest on Gethen's peaceful face. Each person's expression registered the same sadness Amon's possessed, as if each one had lost a dear friend.

"Amon, what should we do?" she asked as they watched each Sidhe react to the death of one of their own.

"Nothing," he said as he walked toward the bridge. "We can't understand their sadness."

Thea knew he was mistaken. He wore the same sad face as each of the Sidhe, felt the loss of Gethen as deeply as any of his kind. Each robotic step he took spoke volumes about the grief he was suffering.

They made their way up toward the castle as the Sidhe followed them in an informal funeral procession. Their sadness permeated the air, and Thea noted the contradiction between the almost joyful beauty that surrounded them and the heavy sorrow they expressed in their slow walk behind them. As they got closer to the castle, Amon explained where they were going and why, never taking his eyes from the sight in front of him.

"Gethen was part of the royal court of the Sidhe. For

generations, his family has served the kings and queens that rule over his people. Before he was exiled, he was matched with the king's youngest daughter. Years older than her, he never had the chance at the life he was destined for because he was lured by love into our world."

"What do you mean 'lured by love'?"

"I told you the Sidhe were very seductive creatures, but there is one type of female that can seduce them—Aeveren women. Gethen met an Aeveren woman and fell in love with her. But she was someone's destined one and couldn't give herself to him."

Amon abruptly stopped talking and adjusted his friend in his arms. Thea sensed what he needed to say next troubled him.

"What happened, Amon?"

"He couldn't deal with losing her." After a pause, he continued. "He killed her."

Amon's guilt for his part in Victoria Adams' death filled every word he spoke.

"When it was found that he'd done this twice before, he was banished from his world. The Sidhe king didn't want to bring the wrath of the Aeveren Council to his people, so instead he chose to send Gethen away."

Thea thought about the man who she'd known as Gethen—the man who'd threatened her when she'd first arrived at Amon's house—the loyal friend. But she also thought of the man who'd willingly chosen to leave the only life he'd known for centuries to give Amon a chance at happiness and the man who'd helped him rescue her from the Soren headquarters. The idea that the same man was someone who'd murdered three women seemed almost impossible.

"How did he find you?"

"I found him. The night he killed the last woman, I found him next to her body just as she vanished. He put up no fight and asked me to take him to our people to be punished. Instead, I took him to the king we're going to now and agreed to be responsible for him until he'd earned his way home."

They continued to the castle in silence, and as he stopped to face the king and his court, Thea knew Amon was preparing to say the words to explain Gethen's death. The Sidhe king stepped forward to meet them, his eyes firmly focused on his fallen kinsman. Almost as tall as Amon, he wore his long, jet black hair over his shoulders that seemed to hunch at the recognition of the man in Amon's arms.

"Who brings this long exiled son home?"

Dropping his head in respect, Amon answered, "The one who promised to return him."

"What is your name, Aeveren?"

"I was known as Riordan Blake when I took him, but now I'm called Amon Kalins."

"Welcome, Amon Kalins. We thank you for bringing our son home," the king said lifting his gaze to Amon's.

Amon answered, his voice laced with guilt. "I don't deserve thanks. It's because of my actions that he died, as if I killed him myself, King Nasire."

The Sidhe king studied Amon's face for a long moment

and shook his head. "Do not blame yourself for Gethen's death. I know your thoughts, Aeveren, but you are mistaken. You saved him when he had nowhere to go and no friend in this world. You gave him a life."

The king motioned to men who hurried to attend to him. "Take our fallen son's body to be prepared for his farewell."

The attendants reached for Gethen's body but Amon refused to release him, stonily staring at each to back away. Thea's heart felt heavy at the sight of the man she loved consumed by grief.

"You must let him go now, Aeveren. He must be readied to travel to the Summerlands."

Reluctantly, Amon nodded and carefully placed Gethen's body into the waiting arms of one of the men, who somberly took him away. His arms down at his sides, Amon squeezed Thea's hand as they watched them take his friend.

"Come," the king commanded to them and his court. "We will welcome our visitors."

Thea watched as Amon looked down toward the direction the men had taken with Gethen, his blue eyes full of sorrow. Her heart broke seeing him so utterly devastated.

"Sweetie, let's go," she said quietly as she began to follow the group after the king.

Amon said nothing as he turned to walk with her into the castle. Thea stood in awe of the great hall that welcomed them as they entered. An enormous ceiling towered over their heads, and two massive wood chandeliers hung in the center of the room, each one holding twelve candles flickering light.

A twenty-five foot long table sat underneath them and was hastily being filled with enough food for the king and all the mourners.

"Please sit and join us for the celebration," the king offered as he guided Thea and Amon to each take a seat.

Amon sat quietly looking off in the distance, and Thea explained, "I'm sorry, King Nasire. Amon's not much for celebrating now."

The king took his seat at the end of the table near them as the rest of his court milled about. "Aeveren, there is no reason for mourning. Gethen lived a full life of many years. If you had not taken him all those years ago, he would have faced judgment by your leaders, which would have meant a much harder life. Whatever you believe you did, remember the gift you gave him."

"If I hadn't kept him when I should have let him return… he wouldn't be dead now."

"Do not do this to yourself. Your friend lived many years in your world. I believe they were happy ones, if your grief is any indication of his life."

Amon hung his head. "My grief is only an indication of my regret."

"I am sorry for your loss, but it fills my heart that our son meant so much to you. That itself is the tale of a life well-lived. May we all be missed as much when we are called home."

The king patted Amon's hand before joining his people in the celebration of Gethen's life. Thea watched as they feasted on delicacies and shared memories of their time with him, but

Amon remained quiet, unable to escape his thoughts.

A woman older than most of the others approached them and stood silently looking at Amon, the woman's green eyes kind and sympathetic as they stared down at him.

"Thank you for bringing him home to his people."

Amon made a slight smile and nodded.

"My son never found happiness in our world. Did he find it in yours?" she asked in a voice full of hope.

Thea realized this was Gethen's mother asking if her son had been happy in exile.

"I believe he did," Amon said, his face showing how unsure he was if his answer was honest.

The woman turned to Thea. "Did you know my son?"

Nodding, she smiled. "I did. I only had the pleasure of knowing him for a short time, but I know he loved Amon like a son."

"Did he have any children?" she asked him.

"No," he said slowly shaking his head.

"Then I'm glad he had you."

After Gethen's mother returned to the rest of the court, Amon and Thea sat quietly watching the Sidhe show their respect. As he held her hand, he leaned over to kiss her. "Thank you."

Thea smiled. "He really did see you as a son. I never knew him as anything but your friend, but I think he loved you as a father would a son."

As those around him rejoiced in Gethen's life, Amon thought about what the King and Gethen's mother had said. Gethen had always been more friend than servant, but he'd forced him to do many things that made him complicit in his misdeeds. Had he been happy doing as he commanded? With regret, he admitted to himself that the thought had never crossed his mind.

And what of the other parts of Gethen's life? He'd never spent much time with one woman, never married or settled down, never had any children. His life for hundreds of years had been entirely devoted to Amon.

Guilt overwhelmed Amon as the memory of his time with Gethen paraded through his mind. If he had been a son to him, then Gethen had acted as parents often do, overlooking their children's faults out of love. And what had he given Gethen in return?

When the feast was over, the king and his court, along with Amon and Thea, walked in procession to the outside courtyard where Gethen lay on a funeral pyre. The sight of him lifeless with his hands folded on his stomach made Amon's breath catch in his chest.

As priestesses chanted and called on the gods of the Sidhe to safeguard Gethen on his journey to the Summerlands, the mourners stood silently as his funeral pyre was set aflame. A single drummer beat gently on his drum, rhythmically ushering Gethen's soul to its next home.

Amon stood stiffly watching the flames leap higher, overtaking his friend's body and obscuring it from view. The sight made his chest tighten, and he leaned against Thea as he said his final silent goodbye.

King Nasire returned to once again thank him for taking care of one of his people for so many years. "We owe you a debt of gratitude, Amon Kalins."

Long after the king, his court, and the throng of mourners filed out of the courtyard, Amon stood facing the funeral pyre, staring straight ahead, his eyes staring at the spot where Gethen had laid.

Thea gently touched his arm. "Amon, he's with his people now. He's home."

Amon silently nodded, and as they left the Sidhe king's castle and began their long walk to their world, neither said a word, unable to move past their loss.

Hours later, as Thea lay beside him, her head on his chest as she slept, Amon promised himself that he'd be the man he should've been all along. Whatever he'd thought life was supposed to be, he understood now what Gethen had been trying to tell him.

His past had hurt everyone around him. He had to make sure his present and future were different.

CHAPTER TWENTY-FIVE

A MON WOKE AFTER A MOSTLY sleepless night and silently reached his mind toward Gethen's but sensed only emptiness. The realization he was gone—not like when Amon was in Nil but truly gone from his life—squeezed his heart like a vice.

Next to him, Thea slept facing him with her hands folded under her head. He was struck by how innocent she looked and cringed at the thought of how guilty he was for so many things. As a healer, she was good and kind, someone fellow Aeveren looked to for help to make their lives better. How did he deserve her?

Gethen had been right. Everyone had to deal with their past at some point. He'd been foolish to believe it would stay in the past. Gethen had been right about something else too. He'd been given another chance to fix the past instead of using the opportunity to find more ways to live his life at the expense of others. He owed it to those he loved to use that chance wisely.

As he thought about what life had in store, he

absentmindedly stroked Thea's hair, waking her. She began to stir, and he leaned his head down to meet hers.

"Good morning, angel."

Half asleep, she snuggled close to his body and murmured, "Good morning. You okay?"

Amon inhaled deeply and kissed the top of her head. "I'm okay."

"Good," she cooed kissing the side of his neck.

"I have a lot I want to do today, so it's time to get your sleepy self out of bed."

She rolled onto her back and smoothed the hair from her face to look at him. "Like what?"

He'd spent hours thinking about how he needed to turn his life around and what to do as a first step. It had to be something big. Considering his decision, he announced, "I want to sell two of my homes—this one and the one in Tuscany."

"I understand why you'd want to leave this house, but what's wrong with the Italian house?"

Amon knew she silently questioned what the urgency was to sell the house in Tuscany. "That has nothing to do with Gethen. That house reminds me of a past I need to leave behind."

Sitting up, she tapped his nose with her forefinger. "I don't think I like it when you read my thoughts. It's like when someone finishes your sentences for you. It's irritating."

Amon loved that she was one of the few people he'd ever met who thought to chastise him. And he knew she was right.

Leaning toward her, he touched his forehead to hers and looked up into her eyes. "Point taken, Althea. How about if I promise not to do it again? Will I be forgiven?"

Thea turned her head and kissed him. "Of course. But I expect you'll be breaking that promise if I'm ever in danger?"

Amon leaned back to rest his head on a pillow, folded his arms behind him, and looked up at her. "That goes without saying, angel."

"Just how many houses do you own?"

"We. We own," he corrected.

"Okay. How many houses do we own?"

"A few," he said with a sly smile. "But the one I want you to see the most is in Greece."

"Greece! Just the thought of owning a house in Greece is a dream come true. I've always wanted to visit Greece, and now I have a house there?"

Thea climbed on top of him and straddled his hips. "How did I get so lucky as to have a man like you?"

Amon looked up into her innocent blue eyes and the history of their time together caused guilt to surge in him. "Thea, in the time you've known me, you've been kidnapped twice, held hostage by a sadistic bastard who kept women as slaves, and been in more danger than I prefer to think about. I don't think that's lucky."

Bending down to kiss him, she pressed her lips to his and then whispered, "Thank God your destined one is tougher than she looks."

The body that pressed up against his felt anything but

tough. Running his hands down her sides, he reached her ass and squeezed as he pulled her into his body. He felt her warm breath begin to come in short pants next to his ear, exciting him more. The feel of the softness of her body made him want to possess her at that moment and protect her forever, no matter how strong she claimed to be.

Flipping her over, he pinned her wrists above her head and smiled devilishly down at her as his eyes roamed over her body.

"This is part of that lucky thing I was talking about," she purred before she hooked her legs behind him and around his waist and pulled his body into her warm and waiting body.

Amon felt the emotions of the past few days overwhelm him, and he plunged into her needing the oneness that making love to her could give him. Slowly at first, he thrust into her, desperate for the sensations her body gave him, needing to know at least he could be sure his body could bring her happiness.

Pulling him to her, she cradled his head in her hands. "I love you, Amon."

With her words the tension ebbed from his body, and what he'd been searching for in her body's response he found in her simple declaration of love. As they finished, he whispered, "I love you. I can't imagine life without you."

Stroking his back, she said, "You don't ever have to."

Later, as they dressed, Amon watched her dry her hair and felt happy. Truly happy, like he had all those lifetimes ago in Turkey.

"Marry me."

Thea lifted the towel from over her head and peeked out at him. "What did you say?"

"Marry me. I know you have no real need to since as Aeveren, destined ones don't require marriage to be truly committed, but…"

"Yes."

"Yes?"

"You don't need to explain. I knew the answer to that question the first time you looked at me."

Amon stood up and smiled. "I do like a woman who can make up her mind."

Just as Thea finished explaining that she'd been in love with him since the day they met and wanted to marry him from that moment, they heard a knock at the front door. By the time she joined him downstairs, he had a summons from the Council at Nil in his hand and a bounty hunter on each side of him.

"Amon, what's going on?"

"I have to go for a little while. All the information where the houses are and where my money is located is in the desk drawer there. Don't worry. Everything will be okay."

He wasn't sure how truthful those last words were. If he wanted, he could slip right through the bounty hunters' hands and be lost to them in a million places in time, but he was too far away from Thea to grab her to take her with him, and he wouldn't run without her.

Reading her thoughts and sensing her worry, Amon said,

"Destiny wouldn't bring us together just to separate us. Believe that and believe I'll be back."

"Amon, I remember what you said about your past. They're not going to let you come back to me, no matter what destiny has planned. I'm going with you."

Amon began to protest, as the bounty hunters said, "We only have orders for you."

"I don't care. I'm coming."

The two men shrugged and mumbled about hoping to get bonus pay for bringing in two people.

As they hovered over Amon, Thea marched up and put her arms around him. "I have no intention of letting you go now, Amon Kalins."

BEFORE HE COULD PUT HIS arms around her and again tell her he loved her, they were standing in the chambers of the Council at Nil, his wrists and ankles shackled.

He was a prisoner once again.

Amon watched as Thea looked down between their bodies, stunned at the restraints on his wrists. His black dress shirt remained on his body as it had at the house, but against its darkness was the silver metal that kept his arms immobilized in front of him.

She released her arms from holding him and took a step back. For the first time, she saw him as who he was.

"Thea…" he began, but what could he say? He belonged in this place.

He waited until she lifted her eyes to meet his, desperate to know what she was thinking after his powers had been taken as soon as he'd gotten there. Did she see him like he saw himself—a criminal who deserved the punishment he'd receive?

Quietly, she spoke to him, and her words buoyed his hope that she still loved him. "I know what you are, and I don't care. You're still Amon, my destined one. Have faith. Destiny wouldn't bring us together to separate us."

Somehow, when she said it, he believed it.

Amon lifted his hands to hold hers and bent down to kiss her. He hoped to God she was right but feared this would be the last time he'd ever feel the softness of her lips against his.

"If this doesn't end the way we want it to, remember what I said at the house. I'm sorry that's all I can do," he whispered to her.

The sound of the council members coming in to the chamber made him turn around and look up. Instinctively, Thea stood in front of Amon, her arms slightly out at her sides, to protect him from whatever they planned to do.

"Mr. Kalins, I see you're not alone," Naomi Cooper said with almost an air of respect in her voice. "Have you brought the rest of your entourage with you?" she asked as she scanned the area around them.

"Gethen's dead, councilwoman."

Even over the mumbling noises of the fellow council members, Amon heard Naomi Cooper's sharp intake of breath. As tears threatened her eyes, she composed herself and began to speak to him as if it were only the two of them in the chamber, her voice hitching on the first few words.

"I'm so sorry. How did it happen?"

"Your bounty hunter killed him with Anjer," he said as the sad memory of his friend's last moments flashed through his mind.

"And you then killed the bounty hunter?"

Amon knew she knew the answer to her question but sensed she wanted to hear him say it, not to confirm his guilt but in some way assuage some guilt of her own.

"Yes. I killed him for murdering Gethen."

"Gentlemen, your services are no longer required. You may leave."

The bounty hunters moved from Amon's side and silently left the chamber, leaving Thea standing in front of him.

"Thea, you may stay, but you must move to the side during these proceedings and remain silent," the head councilwoman commanded.

Thea stood defiantly staring up at the council members. "I'm here to plead Amon's case, and I prefer to stay right where I am."

Suddenly, the chamber went silent, and the councilwoman's angry response shot back at her in ancient Etruscan. "Move to the side now or I'll remove you from these proceedings!"

Amon watched in confusion as Thea reluctantly moved off to the side, and he wondered exactly what had been said. But his attention was quickly directed back to the proceedings before him.

"Now, Mr. Kalins, as to you, we've got a lot of ground to cover."

Unlike the first time a year earlier when he stood in this same spot to hear the recitation of his crimes, he dreaded what would be said now because Thea would hear just who he'd been for so many lifetimes. He turned to her and saw her wide eyes looking up at him and knew he couldn't let her find out who he'd been. Not all of it.

"Councilwoman, I request my destined one be removed from the chamber," he said flatly as he stared straight ahead.

Thea grabbed his arm and tried to turn him toward her. "Amon, no! Don't do this!" she pleaded as he struggled to look away.

"It looks like she prefers to stay, Mr. Kalins. I'm inclined to accede to her wishes as she is a respected healer of our people for forty-five lifetimes."

Amon hung his head in resignation. She'd hear everything and refuse to remain his destined one, just as Sevine had. He knew he was going back to Nil, never to see Thea again, but it was killing him that what she'd think of him after he was gone wouldn't be how much he loved her but the details of all his crimes.

"So to begin, Mr. Kalins, could you please provide this Council with details on your powers? All of them, please."

Amon saw where they were going with this. He'd list each of his powers and then they'd have him confess to his crimes once again, categorized by the abuse of each power. They'd use his powers to show how much a monster he was.

"I have the ability to manipulate time—I can travel back in time, return to the current time, stop time. I can teleport within time in addition to through it. I can insert ideas into others' minds, and I can read people's thoughts."

Despite having much of this information in front of them, the Council sat silently, some with their mouths agape, at the laundry list of his powers. For a moment, he enjoyed the feeling of superiority it gave him, but then he remembered what was to come next. Turning to Thea, he saw the shock on her face at hearing the first complete list of what he could do.

"That's quite an impressive list, Mr. Kalins."

For a brief moment, Amon wondered if he was supposed to answer the councilwoman.

Yes, I'm impressive. Now let's get this inquisition over so you can throw me back into that shithole you call Nil.

"Careful, Mr. Kalins. You aren't the only Aeveren with impressive powers."

"Then use them and send me away. But don't force Thea to listen to an entire hearing of what kind of fuck I've been for far too many lifetimes."

Several council members rose from their seats and approached Naomi Cooper's table. As he waited while they surely discussed his lack of respect, he turned to Thea to speak to her for possibly the last time. "I'm sorry, Thea. Why didn't you leave? Now you're going to have to listen to everything I've done."

Thea stepped next to him and took his hands in hers.

"Amon, I don't care what they say you've done. I don't care if you admit to every crime they claim. I love you. You are the only person in forty-five lifetimes to be meant only for me. That's got to count for something."

Standing on her toes, she kissed him sweetly on the lips and then whispered, "I don't think she likes it when people argue with her. Instead of anger, use charm."

"Let's continue, Mr. Kalins. Please inform this council of the reason the former head councilman had to hold a centuries old grudge against you."

Now it begins.

Amon took a deep breath and tried to remember Thea's words from a moment ago. "In my time as Riordan Blake, I committed adultery with his wife."

He knew he had to finish the explanation and that Thea had already heard Adams tell the sordid details of his real crime, but the words seemed stuck in his throat.

"And she committed suicide after I abandoned her."

To his surprise, no one in the chamber, including Thea, made any shocked noises.

"This Council has heard the details of Victoria Adams' death at your first trial, Mr. Kalins, so there is no need to reiterate the information here. And if the Directorate's records are accurate, while you may have never been punished for your crime until this last year, the sons you had as Riordan have been."

"My sons?" Amon asked, unsure why or how they would be punished for his crime.

"Yes. It seems Mrs. Adams was the daughter of a witch who cursed them, and while I'm not at liberty to divulge the information, I can say they've suffered for your actions, Mr. Kalins."

The sick feeling of regret churned inside him. He'd never truly paid for what he'd done to Victoria, but his sons had? He could only imagine what Victoria's mother had done to them, a witch hell bent on vengeance.

"So this council must now deal with your more recent offenses: your escape from Nil and the murders of Kiril Gault and Ryu Jansen."

At least none of those were unknown to Thea, but Amon knew that didn't help him. He was still going back to Nil.

"Mr. Kalins, it may surprise you to know there is no penalty for your escape from Nil. A fortunate bureaucratic oversight due to the simple fact that there have been only a handful of escapes and this council has no official penalty in place for any punishment."

Amon saw the sheepish look on the council members' faces as Naomi Cooper explained that he was going to get off scot-free for escaping from the supposedly impenetrable and inescapable Nil. They hated how their oversight gave him an out, even if it was for just minutes as he stood there.

But Kiril Gault's and the bounty hunter's deaths are a different story.

"Now, as to the deaths of Mr. Gault and Mr. Jansen, there are official penalties for those crimes. However, we will hear any defense you wish to present now, Mr. Kalins."

Amon wasted no time beginning his defense for stabbing Kiril. For this crime, he had no remorse whatsoever. "Kiril and Harold Adams kidnapped Thea. Gault chained her up with his human slaves and when I got to her, had a dagger to her throat. He would've killed her if I didn't kill him first."

"So you killed him to defend your destined one's life?"

Amon looked up defiantly. "I don't regret his death. As her destined one, I have every right to defend the woman I love."

Satisfied by his explanation, Naomi Cooper moved on to Ryu Jansen's murder. "And your defense of your actions that resulted in the death of Mr. Jansen, a bounty hunter for this council?"

He dropped his head slightly at the memory of the man lying on the ground next to him as he faded away from his life. "The bounty hunter murdered my friend, intentionally stabbing him with a knife coated in Anjer, a poison deadly to the Sidhe, that he likely received from this council as a tool to capture me."

Amon knew his tone hadn't been deferent or charming, but he didn't care. If he was to blame for Ryu Jansen's death, then the Council shared part of that blame. And he blamed them for Gethen's death as much as he blamed himself.

"So your killing him was revenge?"

"Yes, I tried to reason with him, but he had nothing to live for, no reason to not blame me once Adams was out of power and all the things promised to him disappeared into thin air. So he killed Gethen because he couldn't get to me."

"This council apologizes for the actions of Mr. Adams and the tragic consequences from them." Naomi Cooper closed the folder in front of her and continued. "I'm ready to pass judgment. Do any of my fellow council members object?"

Amon waited for any objection, but none came.

"Then the chambers will be emptied. This will be a closed verdict," she announced.

CHAPTER TWENTY-SIX

THEA GRABBED AMON'S ARM, INTENDING to resist if they tried to force her from the chamber, but she quickly realized the councilwoman had meant she would deliver the verdict without her fellow council members present.

"What's happening?" she asked Amon as she watched the Council and their assistants leave their places above them.

"I don't know, but I don't think I have much time, Thea. I need you to know that I've never regretted all the things I've done as much as I do right now. I don't know why you were stuck with me as your only destined one, but don't ever forget I love you more than you can ever know."

Tears began to stream down her cheeks as she sobbed. "No."

Behind them appeared Naomi Cooper, and they turned to face her and whatever verdict she had to deliver.

"My heart is heavy because of these proceedings. What my fellow councilman did to endanger your destined one and to contribute to Gethen's death weighs on my conscience. You can be sure his actions will not go unpunished."

Sure this may be her last chance to plead Amon's case, Thea reached out to touch the councilwoman's hand and began to speak in ancient Etruscan.

"Please, for our shared heritage, have mercy. Destiny has finally blessed me with a destined one to love and care for. For the first time in forty-five lifetimes, I have true love. Please don't take that away from me. Is there nothing I can do to change this?"

Naomi Cooper cupped Thea's cheek with her hand. "There are few choices available, child."

"I'll do anything."

"She's not the one on trial. Whatever the verdict is, deal with me."

"Thea, someone must give two lifetimes for your destined one's crimes," the councilwoman said in their ancient language.

"Done. I willingly give two of my lifetimes for his freedom."

Naomi Cooper turned to Amon. "Your destined one has given two of her lifetimes in exchange for your freedom. The final lifetime sentence is commuted due to your part in helping this council see the true nature of Councilman Adams."

He shook his head in disbelief. "No. I won't let her do that. I refuse."

The councilwoman smiled. "I've accepted her gift. It's done."

Before Thea's eyes, his wrist shackles and ankle restraints

disappeared. Amon turned to Thea and in his joy, lifted her into his arms and kissed her.

"How could you do that? How could you give up two lives for me?"

Cradling his face in her hands, she explained, "Amon, I would give up anything—my life—for your freedom. Two lifetimes is a small price to pay for the three lifetimes we'll have together now."

When Amon put Thea back on her feet, Naomi Cooper took her hand. "I need you to know the hardest decision I ever made was to hand you over to the authorities to take you away all those lifetimes ago. Your father and I would've traded everything we had to keep you with us, but your gift made that impossible. We never stopped loving you and prayed every day that you found happiness and could forgive us."

Instantly, Thea was a child again in the hills of Italy all those lifetimes ago watching her mother cry as authorities took her away from her home. Memories she'd thought were buried came flooding back, and she began to cry more out of happiness than sorrow.

As she hugged her first mother, she said, "I never blamed you or papa. I was born with a gift that's meant to help people. You couldn't change that any more than I could."

"Well, I'm happy to know you've finally been given a destined one. I just wish he didn't have such a ….colorful past."

Thea backed away from her and took Amon's hand in hers. "I know you know him as many things, but all I know is that he's the man who's meant for me."

Naomi turned to face Amon. "Please promise you'll be that man and not the man you've been for lifetimes, Amon."

"Councilwoman, I have no interest in being that man anymore. Thea's happiness is my only concern."

"Then this council will have no reason to bother you again. I wish for nothing more than happiness for both of you."

The councilwoman turned to leave and Thea asked, "Will I ever see you again?"

Naomi Cooper shook her head. "Not as your mother. I've already broken the laws by speaking with you like this. But perhaps we'll see each other again."

After she'd gone, Amon tipped Thea's head up toward him. "You're lucky my powers don't work here. If I had known what you were thinking, I wouldn't have let you go through with it."

Thea's formed her lips into a pout. "I told you what I thought of your reading my mind, Amon."

AMON LOOKED OUT AT THE isle of Paxos below and the crystal blue Ionian Sea as Markku fidgeted next to him and complained about the heat.

"Why is it that people always get married in the hottest places?" he asked as he tugged at his tuxedo. "I'm dying in this heat here. Don't you have a house in Germany? Why couldn't you get married there? I bet it's nice there."

"Thea wanted to get married here. Just relax. All you have to do is witness. Nobody cares if you sweat while you do it."

"I thought I was your best man," Markku sulked.

Seeing how unhappy his comment had made Markku, Amon relented. "Technically, you are."

As the smile returned to his face, Markku said, "Oh, okay. That's better."

Amon squeezed the bridge of his nose and smiled as he remembered everything Gethen had said about Markku. He hadn't seen him in six months, but the headache and heartburn he often brought with him had joined him in Paxos.

He'd questioned Thea about inviting Markku to the wedding, but she'd insisted saying he'd been the reason they'd met in the first place. Even though Sevine's spell had worn off, he liked to make her happy, so Markku made it onto the guest list and through his own wheedling, made it into the best man spot.

THEA STARED INTO THE FULL length mirror as Kat and Suzanne fussed over her train and veil. The woman who looked back at her looked like every fantasy she'd ever had about her wedding day to her destined one.

"Oh, Thea," Suzanne cooed as she pressed her head up to Thea's. "You look so beautiful! And I saw Amon. He looks so handsome!"

Kat, who stood behind her fluffing up her train, agreed. "Sweetie, when you finally decide to do it, you sure do it right.

House in Greece, a man who looks like he could be a Greek god, and a wedding that's more beautiful than any I've ever seen."

Thea couldn't argue with that. Her life with Amon was everything she'd ever wished for. She'd even gotten a special dispensation from the Aeveren Council leaders—because of Naomi, she guessed—to relocate to Greece as a healer.

After all those lifetimes alone, destiny had finally smiled on her.

NAOMI TUGGED ON AMON'S COAT sleeve. "It's time."

As he straightened himself and waited to see Thea walk toward him to exchange vows, he thought about how right those who had claimed he was favored by fate were. When Thea appeared in her white wedding gown and veil, she took his breath away. Her long blond hair fell in soft waves toward her waist, just as it had the first time he saw her standing in his bedroom.

"Amon, are you okay?" she whispered as she took her place next to him to begin the ceremony. "You look a million miles away."

"No, just a couple months, angel."

When the reception had ended and all the guests had left, Thea sat on his lap on the balcony of their home and they looked out at the boats coming in at dusk. She played with his blond hair, fully grown in since his release from Nil, and his hand slowly moved back and forth on her thigh.

"Did I tell you how gorgeous you looked in that black tux? I couldn't take my eyes off you as I walked toward the minister."

Smiling, he kissed her softly on the lips. "It's the tux. It makes any man look good. Even Markku."

Thea shook her head. When Amon jokingly tried to defend Markku, she placed her finger on his lips. "I don't want to talk about Markku, Mr. Kalins."

Amon ran his hand along her side and pulled her close to him. "What do you have in mind, Mrs. Kalins?"

Kissing her, he knew exactly what she had in mind. And he loved her way of thinking.

THE END

Read on for an excerpt from

Blood Avenged (Sons of Navarus #1)

I am everything you desire.

I am everything you fear.

I am lust and appetite.

I am vampire.

ONE

THE BEAT OF THE MUSIC slammed into his body like crushing blows from an angry attacker, each note reverberating in his bones. He sat perfectly still and let the beat thrum through him as he picked up the seductive scent wafting across the crowded room, carried by a thick cloud of cigarette smoke. Undetected by all but him, its subtle sweetness teased his nose with a promise of what was to come.

Scanning the room, he watched like a bird tracking its prey. All of humanity seemed to file past him. Desperate, drunk, and powerless, the crowd was a smorgasbord laid out especially for him. With no effort at all, he could have any of them. The brunette dancing between two men, her movements telegraphing that her sex was needy for what they offered. If he chose, in seconds, they'd be gone and she'd be his for the taking. The tanned, muscular male eyeing him from three tables away, who he sensed preferred what hung between his legs to what the brunette offered. The barely legal blonde, whose wide green eyes betrayed just how much of life she hadn't experienced despite the lies her body told.

He could have any of them.

Vasilije watched his victim at the bar. Every bat of an eyelash he felt. Every clank of the ice against the glass he heard as if he were there himself. The distance between them meant nothing.

Through the tightly packed crowd, he saw the woman next to his target lean over, obscuring his view. He watched as she pressed her body next to the man's, a not-so-subtle hint to her interest.

The sweet scent remained, and Vasilije closed his eyes to enjoy it, not interested in the woman or her pathetic attempt to seduce his prey away.

He had no idea the vampire waited patiently for his moment. Vasilije liked the idea that ignorance was bliss. For now. In a few short minutes, another bliss would take them both over, and he'd have what he'd eyed for days.

The man made a move toward the door and every cell in Vasilije's body came alive. Two steps and he was in the thick of the crowd, their bodies pressing up against his as he brushed by them. He weaved through the group like a dark secret whispered from one person to another.

At the exit, he inhaled deeply, his sense of smell filtering out the putrid mixture of exhaust, perfume, and stale alcohol that hovered at the entrance to the street. Only his prey's scent remained, imprinted on him.

He was nearby.

Closing his eyes, Vasilije let his other senses take over. The sound of the man's shoes hitting the pavement echoed in his ears. The feel of his prey's blood pumping through his body throbbed against Vasilije's cool skin, matching his heartbeat.

So healthy. So alive.

He'd tracked him for days, his desire growing with each passing moment. It had taken little time for him to decide he would make him one of his kind. He stirred something inside that hadn't been touched for years.

Such a soul would be a perfect addition to his world.

He moved away from the noise of the club into the streets of London as he gained ground on his target. Now in his view, the man moved much faster. Did he sense the danger that lurked nearby? But it was no use. He would surrender this night.

Vasilije walked calmly, never losing sight of the man. He sensed his fear and took it into himself, relishing the sensation. How long had it been since he'd felt fear—true fear that stole one's breath away and paralyzed the limbs?

A quick left onto a darkened street and his prey broke into a full run, his fear morphing into pure terror that surged through Vasilije's veins. In his ears, he heard the man's heart pound faster and faster, his body reacting to his mind's screams.

Into the night air, he whispered, "Come to me," and

waited for the man to make his way back to him. With each step, Vasilije moved closer, but the man remained out of reach.

Something or someone was helping him escape.

Quickly, Vasilije scanned the area, his eyes darting left and right in the darkness. Was there another of his kind close? He sensed no one, but someone was interrupting his pursuit.

Reluctantly, he accepted the situation and disappeared into thin air, reappearing just mere feet in front of the man. Stunned, he skidded to a stop against Vasilije's chest.

"No more running."

His hand moved to the man's chin and gently held him. Eyes filled with a fear he'd seen a thousand times before stared back at him, pleading for mercy from a being that possessed none.

His voice a deep timbre now, Vasilije began to hypnotize the man. "I've waited long enough for you."

To his surprise, the trick didn't work. The man's eyes grew wide and he opened his mouth to speak, but only weak cries came out. Why was he able to resist?

"Who are you?"

"Alex," he said, his voice almost a whimper.

"Alex, I want you to look into my eyes. Listen to my voice."

"Please don't kill me."

Vasilije stroked the man's cheek and leaned in next to his ear. "I'm going to give you a life you've never dreamed of, Alex."

"Please! Take all my money. Just let me go. I have a girlfriend. Tatiana. I don't want to die!"

Vasilije thought back to the only Tatiana he'd ever known in his over four hundred year existence. Grimacing, he returned his focus to Alex's eyes and pushed his memory of the past out of his mind.

"Well, maybe I'll let you have her."

"Please don't do this!" the man begged, his blue eyes filling with tears.

Cradling his face in his hands, Vasilije concentrated on Alex, and slowly whatever had been protecting him slipped away. His lids became heavy, obscuring his eyes, and the fear left his mind and body.

"Alex." Vasilije let the name rest on his tongue as he hissed out the last syllable. "Mine."

The muscles in Alex's body gave in to his power and all fight evaporated from him. He slumped against the vampire's body as his mind finally succumbed to his persuasion.

Vasilije guided him to a building just a few steps away and leaned him against a stone wall. For a moment, he stilled to look at this human who had so captivated him, more than any other creature in years. His shoulder length blond hair shone like it had been touched each day by the sun. Vasilije gingerly touched the ends with his fingertips, feeling the sun's long forgotten warmth against his fingers.

His eyes moved over Alex's face, past his mouth and cheekbones to eyes hooded by slack lids. Within those slits were blue eyes that stared out passively at him. Eyes that saw what Vasilije commanded as he silently inserted ideas into the man's mind.

Nothing about Alex was unique individually, and despite admiring his beauty, Vasilije couldn't say that was what had drawn him to the human. It was something else, something about him that created the impression of the forbidden.

But now he would be his.

Vasilije's fangs slid seductively into his mouth as he eyed the gentle throbbing in Alex's neck. In just a few moments, they would sink into his skin and sweet blood would fill him. The thought of it made his mouth water.

Unlike the rest of his fellow vampires, he wasn't forced to live under the restrictions of vampire law and obtain permission to turn a human. His sire had been taken from the Earth years ago, and without her, he was free to sire anyone he pleased.

He was truly a being beholden to no one.

Alex would join the hundreds of others scattered across the globe who counted him as their sire. Inside, he knew where each one was at any given moment, like a piece of himself inside another. When he desired to have them around, they were. And when he preferred a life of solitude, the choice of many vampires, he sent them away.

But they were never truly gone.

He would keep Alex with him until he'd completed his initiation period. To do any less would be cruel. A newly turned vampire needed his sire for virtually everything to survive. His blood would nourish him, like no other's could. A human might give him what he needed for a short time, but it could never be what his sire's was. And his knowledge would help Alex learn how to be a vampire and how to grow accustomed to the new life he'd given him.

Vasilije softly pressed his mouth to his neck, feeling the warmth of his skin against his lips. Alex turned his head in response, and Vasilije lifted his head. Staring deeply into his eyes, he silently instructed him to turn his head.

His mouth returned to Alex's neck. As he watched the rhythmic pulse just under his skin, he slid his tongue over his fangs, enjoying the feel of their sharp points.

"Alex, from this moment on, I'm your sire. You belong to me."

Without moving his head, Alex moaned his unneeded agreement. For a long moment, the world around them stood still, as Vasilije pressed his fangs slowly into the tender skin. His canines pierced a vein and blood began to flood over his tongue. Its thickness oozed back toward his throat, the tangy taste sliding over his taste buds, exciting them.

How wonderful he tasted! As Alex's life flowed down Vasilije's throat, he fastened his mouth on his neck and pulled at the vein, careful to take only as much as he should. He'd bring Alex to the point of no return and then, as he lingered between life and death, he'd give him the first of many gifts a sire could provide.

Still human for the moment, Alex struggled against Vasilije's hold, but it was no use. A vampire for centuries, he had the strength of a bull and reflexes of a wild cat. At the first sign of resistance, he tightened his hold on the man's jaw and flung his leg over him, trapping his body between the wall and his own.

"It's futile to struggle," Vasilije whispered low in his ear. "Let it take you."

"Please…" Alex's voice faded to a groan as Vasilije's mouth tugged at his vein with more vigor.

"I want nothing else," Vasilije chuckled as he closed the holes he'd made in Alex's neck.

He carefully laid him on the ground, and as Alex fought to hold on to the last shred of his human life, Vasilije wiped the corners of his mouth. Licking the blood from his fingertips, he savored the taste as he knelt down beside the man who was to be his newest vampire.

Vasilije stroked the blond hair that would never again be touched by the warmth or light of the sun. His fingers glided over the sun kissed skin on Alex's face, which in moments would be reduced to a pallor common to those of the night. Even now, the warmth that had been present in his skin was gone.

Lifting his wrist to his mouth, Vasilije sunk his fangs into his skin to open a vein. Blood ran freely in a stream from his wrist, and he pulled Alex to him to begin the transition from human to vampire. Near death, his head had to be held to Vasilije's wrist, but as if it were his true nature, Alex began drinking seconds after tasting his sire's blood, eagerly sucking the liquid into his mouth.

For Vasilije, this was the part he enjoyed. To feed from the neck of a human could sustain him for a short time, but to take from another like him and give in return was a far more satisfying experience.

Alex's mouth sucked greedily at his wrist, drinking his sire's blood as readily as he'd drunk any liquid as a human. Vasilije watched the sensual scene, enjoying every moment. Blood stained lips pressed against his skin drew from him the most important gift a sire provided. As Alex swallowed every drop that spilled into his mouth, Vasilije watched his Adam's apple bob up and down in his throat. When he neared the end of the first feeding, Alex instinctively looked up to his sire to guide him.

Pulling his arm away, Vasilije let the ache in his wrist touch him inside, loving the sweet pain that accompanied feeding one of his own. Alex wiped his mouth and sat up next to him, unsure as all new vampires were.

"Come, Alex. I want to give you something."

Completely under his spell, his newest vampire followed him back to the club. Vasilije saw the brunette he'd admired earlier, without the two men she'd had before. Remembering how her body had felt against his as he'd pressed through the crowd, he approached her and with little effort, he had her nearly begging to leave with them.

By the time they arrived at his house, she had her hands all over Vasilije, but she wasn't for him.

Turning to Alex, he smiled. "She's yours for the night."

He eagerly took his gift to the couch and began undressing her. Vasilije sat back in his chair and in the dim light of the parlor, he saw his vampire bend her over and ram into her until she screamed out her orgasm. Unsatisfied, Alex pulled her head to his still hard cock and fucked her again as she eagerly swallowed everything he gave her.

Vasilije heard the familiar click of a vampire's teeth dropping as Alex came and in a flash was standing over him.

"No," he said in a deep voice like a growl.

"I'm hungry, and I know it would feel incredible to taste her now. You said she was mine."

"A vampire drinks from his sire whenever possible."

Before he could answer, Vasilije touched his wrist to Alex's mouth and the new vampire began feeding again. The brunette watched with eyes full of fear.

"Don't worry. I won't let him drink from you."

Vasilije watched the fear leave her eyes, replaced with their earlier lustful stare, now fastened on his own cock. Leaving Alex to feed, she crawled up to Vasilije and began rubbing the front of his pants. With little encouragement, she freed his cock and slid the engorged head between her lips. As her hand cupped and squeezed his balls, her mouth sucked his cock while Alex sucked excitedly at his wrist.

Looking down, Vasilije saw this was clearly not the first time this woman had sucked cock. Her tongue expertly slid under the crown, teasing the most sensitive part before she pushed her lips to gently clamp down on the base of his cock as her throat closed in around the head. The effect was incredible. Fighting the urge to come, he yanked her head off him and pulled her to her feet.

He'd said she was Alex's for the night, but now as his young vampire finished feeding for the second time in just a few hours, Alex grew sleepy and his head fell back against the couch. The brunette looked at Alex and then back to Vasilije before she went back to work on his cock, stroking him toward completion as she softly moaned next to his lips.

"Come," he whispered.

Following him to the floor, she pulled at his clothes before he removed them with a mere thought. He ran his hands over her body slowly and then ordered, "Get on your hands and knees."

She willingly did as he commanded, and in seconds she offered him whatever he wanted. Tonight he'd take simply fucking over anything else.

Vasilije placed his hands on her hips and held her tightly in place. His cock found her drenched cunt and he slammed into her, his balls smacking off her skin. She fought against his hold, backing up to meet his hard thrusts.

Fuck, she was eager!

No matter how hard he pounded into her, she met his body's movement equally with one as wanton of her own. Vasilije slid his finger and then a second one into her ass and began fucking her in both places, and she bucked against him like she wanted more.

Roughly, he pulled her up to his chest and continued fucking her cunt. His fangs slammed into his mouth as he ran his lips over her neck.

Alex may not be able to taste her, but there was no reason

he shouldn't.

He bit into her and her moaning grew louder with each pull on her vein. The sounds of their fucking filled the room, and as he drew closer to coming, Vasilije slid his fingers down to her clit and began stroking her. His eyes closed, his mind focused on his cock filling her, his fingers teasing her, and the taste of her blood draining down his throat.

She cried out some words before she came, but he was too focused on the feel of her squeezing his cock to understand or care. Over and over, her body milked him until he filled her with his cum and she filled him with her blood.

When he finally slid out of her, she fell to the floor, her body exhausted from how he'd treated her. Hours later, after he'd fucked her until she begged to become his, a vampire like Alex, he dissolved her memory of everything she'd done and sent her home in a cab.

As dawn approached, Vasilije made sure Alex was safe from daylight in his own bedroom designed to be secure from the sun and crawled into bed for the day. He'd had a productive night, and as he laid his head on the pillow, he smiled at how good it was to be a vampire.

GET YOUR COPY OF BLOOD AVENGED AND START THE SONS OF NAVARUS SERIES TODAY!

ABOUT THE AUTHOR

K.M. Scott writes sexy contemporary romance with characters her readers love. A New York Times and USA Today bestselling author, she's been in love with romance since reading her first romance novel in junior high (she was a very curious girl!). Under her Gabrielle Bisset name, she also writes erotic historical and paranormal romance. She lives in Pennsylvania with her teenage son and a herd of animals and when she's not writing can be found reading or feeding her TV addiction.

Be sure to visit K.M.'s Facebook page at **facebook.com/ kmscottauthor** for all the latest on her books, along with giveaways and other goodies! And to hear all the news on K.M. Scott books first, sign up for her newsletter today and be sure to visit her website at **www.kmscottbooks.com**.

Visit Gabrielle's Facebook page and her website at **www. gabriellebisset.com** to find out about her books too!

BOOKS BY K.M. SCOTT:

Crash Into Me (Heart of Stone #1)

Fall Into Me (Heart of Stone #2)

Give In To Me (Heart of Stone #3)

The Heart of Stone Trilogy Box Set

Ever After (Heart of Stone #4)

A Heart of Stone Christmas (Heart of Stone #5)

Unforgettable (Heart of Stone #6)

Temptation (Club X #1)

Surrender (Club X #2)

Possession (Club X #3)

Satisfaction (Club X #4)

Silk (Volume One)

Silk (Volume Two)

Silk (Volume Three)

Silk (Volume Four)

SILK Box Set

K.M.'S BOOKS ARE IN AUDIOBOOK TOO!

BOOKS BY GABRIELLE BISSET:

Vampire Dreams Revamped (A Sons of Navarus Prequel)

Blood Avenged (Sons of Navarus #1)

Blood Betrayed (Sons of Navarus #2)

Longing (A Sons of Navarus Short Story)

Blood Spirit (Sons of Navarus #3)

The Deepest Cut (A Sons of Navarus Short Story)

Blood Prophecy (Sons of Navarus #4)

The Sons of Navarus Box Set #1

The Sons of Navarus Box Set #2

Blood Craving (Sons of Navarus #5)

Stolen Destiny (Destined Ones Duology #1)

Destiny Redeemed (Destined Ones Duology #2)

Love's Master

Masquerade

The Victorian Erotic Romance Trilogy